D0776760

THE RED BADGE OF COURAGE

An Episode of the American Civil War

Newly Edited from
Crane's Original Manuscript
by Henry Binder

W · W · NORTON & COMPANY · *New York* · *London*

THE RED BADGE OF COURAGE

An Episode of the American Civil War

Stephen Crane

813.4
C 89/ r

Published simultaneously in Canada by George J. McLeod Limited, Toronto.

Printed in the United States of America.

Library of Congress Cataloging in Publication Data
Crane, Stephen, 1871–1900.
    The red badge of courage. An Episode of the American Civil War.
    Newly Edited from Crane's Original Manuscript by Henry Binder.
    Includes bibliographical references.
    1. United States—History—Civil War, 1861–1865—Fiction.
I. Binder, Henry.   II. Title.
PS1449.C85R3   1982   813'.4   81-22419
                                          AACR2

ISBN 0-393-01345-6

W. W. Norton & Company, Inc.
500 Fifth Avenue, New York, N.Y. 10110

W. W. Norton & Company Ltd.
37 Great Russell Street, London WC1B 3NU
    2 3 4 5 6 7 8 9 0

Contents

Introduction   vii

Acknowledgment   ix

The Red Badge of Courage. An Episode of the
American Civil War   1

The *Red Badge of Courage* Nobody Knows   111

Statement of Editorial Policy   159

Textual Notes   167

List of Editorial Emendations   169

v

Introduction

This edition of Stephen Crane's *The Red Badge of Courage* presents, as fully as possible, the novel as it existed in Crane's handwritten manuscript. After Crane had tried to sell the manuscript version for several months in 1894, it was purchased by a New York syndicate and appeared as a newspaper serial in December of that year, reduced from fifty-five thousand to eighteen thousand words. Then in early 1895 it was accepted by D. Appleton & Co. of New York and issued as a book in October. The Appleton text has been the basis for all subsequent editions of the novel, but the text Appleton published differs considerably from the story as it stood in the manuscript. In preparing the story for the Appleton edition, Crane deleted many key words, phrases, sentences, passages, and an entire chapter. The deletions were designed specifically to remove certain pieces of the story—most of which concerned the main character—and they were almost certainly made at the suggestion of Crane's Appleton editor in an attempt to satisfy a broader readership with a simpler and less daring novel than the one Crane had written. Crane was apparently half-hearted about cutting the story, for the deletions were made in a cursory manner, with almost no attempt to compensate for the lapses in continuity and coherence that resulted. In the text printed here the deleted material has been restored and the manuscript followed in other details to offer, for the first time, the story as Crane completed it before the cuts were made.

The text of *The Red Badge of Courage* printed here is not simply an improvement on what Appleton published, but comes close to being a different novel. Although the text Appleton issued in 1895 retained enough of the original power to become a surprising success, it was a version of the original so seriously reduced that it has puzzled students, professional critics, and readers with a more than casual knowledge of the story. It has puzzled them because in the Appleton text the significance of details and their relative importance was often lost, and the narrative was confused and blurred, especially in the final chapter. The most serious effect of the deletions was to obscure or undo the role and function of the various characters in the plot, with the consequence that the Appleton version no longer contained the intricacy of Crane's original conception. The characteristic psychological and moral irony that runs consistently throughout the manuscript of *Red Badge*—and through Crane's other major works—was by turns muddled and diminished.

This volume presents, first and foremost, a new text of *The Red Badge of Courage* based on Stephen Crane's manuscript. In the text printed here, six brief gaps left in the manuscript as a result of the Appleton deletions have been indicated by ellipses. In two places where a gap occurs portions of Crane's early draft of the novel have been substituted for text that is missing. The gaps are explained in the Textual Notes. An essay "The *Red Badge of Courage* Nobody Knows" appears after the text of the novel. This essay discusses the deletions and other events surrounding the publication of the Appleton edition and concludes with an interpretive commentary on the story as printed here. Edited from manuscript, this new text of *The Red Badge of Courage* provides, I believe, the richest and most satisfying version of the story possible—the version Crane himself wrote.

Acknowledgments

The preparation of this edition has involved a number of people. The spirit of their discrimination is especially memorable to me. Their humor has been invaluable. Hershel Parker opened the doors to it all. He and Ron Gottesman and John Benedict provided magnanimity, good counsel, and encouragement along the way. And then, a list of those who were always wonderful and generous in more ways than I can name: Paul Seydor, Jackson Cope, Gerald Graff, Lawrence Green, Peter Bailey, Kay Yonge, Paula Gibson, Debra Brown, Linda Palumbo, Steven Mailloux, Brian Higgins, Sergei Shillabeer, Marshall Van Deusen, Mike Feehan, David Fite, Elizabeth Giffen.

Grateful acknowledgment is also made to the following libraries and collections for permission to reproduce original manuscript pages of *The Red Badge of Courage*. The Stephen Crane Collection in the Clifton Waller Barrett Library at the University of Virginia Library. The Henry W. and Albert A. Berg Collection, The New York Public Library, Astor, Lenox and Tilden Foundations. The Houghton Library, Harvard University. The Butler Library, Columbia University. And to the editors of *Studies in the Novel* for permission to reprint "The *Red Badge of Courage* Nobody Knows."

THE RED
BADGE OF
COURAGE

An Episode of the
American Civil War

The Red Badge of Courage
An Episode of the American Civil War

I

The cold passed reluctantly from the earth and the retiring fogs revealed an army stretched out on the hills, resting. As the landscape changed from brown to green the army awakened and began to tremble with eagerness at the noise of rumors. It cast its eyes upon the roads which were growing from long troughs of liquid mud to proper thoroughfares. A river, amber-tinted in the shadow of its banks, purled at the army's feet and at night when the stream had become of a sorrowful blackness one could see, across, the red eye-like gleam of hostile camp-fires set in the low brows of distant hills.

Once, a certain tall soldier developed virtues and went resolutely to wash a shirt. He came flying back from a brook waving his garment, banner-like. He was swelled with a tale he had heard from a reliable friend who had heard it from a truthful cavalryman who had heard it from his trust-worthy brother, one of the orderlies at division head-quarters. He adopted the important air of a herald in red and gold.

"We're goin' t' move t'morrah—sure," he said pompously to a group in the company street. "We're goin' 'way up th' river, cut across, an' come around in behint'em."

To his attentive audience he drew a loud and elaborate plan of a very brilliant campaign. When he had finished, the blue-clothed men scattered into small arguing groups between the rows of squat brown huts. A negro teamster who had been dancing upon a cracker-box with the hilarious encouragement of two-score soldiers, was deserted. He sat mournfully down. Smoke drifted lazily from a multitude of quaint chimneys.

"It's a lie—that's all it is. A thunderin' lie," said another private loudly. His smooth face was flushed and his hands were thrust sulkily into his trousers' pockets. He took the matter as an affront to him. "I don't believe th' derned ol' army's ever goin' t' move.

We're sot. I've got ready t' move eight times in th' last two weeks an' we aint moved yit."

The tall soldier felt called upon to defend the truth of a rumor he himself had introduced. He and the loud one came near to fighting over it.

A corporal began to swear before the assemblage. He had just put a costly board floor in his house, he said. During the early spring he had refrained from adding extensively to the comfort of his environment because he had felt that the army might start on the march at any moment. Of late, however, he had been impressed that they were in a sort of eternal camp.

Many of the men engaged in a spirited debate. One out-lined in a peculiarly lucid manner all the plans of the commanding general. He was opposed by men who advocated that there were other plans of campaign. They clamored at each other, numbers making futile bids for the popular attention. The while, the soldier who had fetched the rumor bustled about with much importance. He was continually assailed by questions.

"What's up, Jim?"

"Th' army's goin' t' move."

"Ah, what yeh talkin' about? How yeh know it is?"

"Well, yeh kin b'lieve me er not—jest as yeh like. I don't care a hang. I tell yeh what I know an' yeh kin take it er leave it. Suit yerselves. It dont make no difference t' me."

There was much food for thought in the manner in which he replied. He came near to convincing them by disdaining to produce proofs. They grew much excited over it.

There was a youthful private who listened with eager ears to the words of the tall soldier and to the varied comments of his comrades. After receiving a fill of discussions concerning marches and attacks, he went to his hut and crawled through an intricate hole that served it as a door. He wished to be alone with some new thoughts that had lately come to him.

He lay down on a wide bunk that stretched across the end of the room. In the other end, cracker boxes were made to serve as furniture. They were grouped about the fire-place. A picture from an illustrated weekly was upon the log wall and three rifles were paralleled on pegs. Equipments hung on handy projections and some tin dishes lay upon a small pile of fire-wood. A folded tent was serving as a roof. The sun-light, without, beating upon it, made it glow a light yellow shade. A small window shot an oblique square of whiter light upon the cluttered floor. The smoke from the fire at times neglected the clay-chimney and wreathed into the room. And this flimsy chimney of clay and sticks made endless threats to set a-blaze the whole establishment.

The youth was in a little trance of astonishment. So they were at last going to fight. On the morrow perhaps there would be a battle and he would be in it. For a time, he was obliged to labor to make himself believe. He could not accept with assurance an omen that he was about to mingle in one of those great affairs of the earth.

He had of course dreamed of battles all of his life—of vague and bloody conflicts that had thrilled him with their sweep and fire. In visions, he had seen himself in many struggles. He had imagined peoples secure in the shadow of his eagle-eyed prowess. But awake he had regarded battles as crimson blotches on the pages of the past. He had put them as things of the bygone with his thought-images of heavy crowns and high castles. There was a portion of the world's history which he had regarded as the time of wars, but, it, he thought, had been long gone over the horizon and had disappeared forever.

From his home his youthful eyes had looked upon the war in his own country with distrust. It must be some sort of a play affair. He had long despaired of witnessing a Greek-like struggle. Such would be no more, he had said. Men were better, or, more timid. Secular and religious education had effaced the throat-grappling instinct, or, else, firm finance held in check the passions.

He had burned several times to enlist. Tales of great movements shook the land. They might not be distinctly Homeric, but there seemed to be much glory in them. He had read of marches, sieges, conflicts, and he had longed to see it all. His busy mind had drawn for him large pictures, extravagant in color, lurid with breathless deeds.

But his mother had discouraged him. She had affected to look with some contempt upon the quality of his war-ardor and patriotism. She could calmly seat herself and with no apparent difficulty give him many hundreds of reasons why he was of vastly more importance on the farm than on the field of battle. She had had certain ways of expression that told that her statements on the subject came from a deep conviction. Besides, on her side, was his belief that her ethical motive in the argument was impregnable.

At last, however, he had made firm rebellion against this yellow light thrown upon the color of his ambitions. The newspapers, the gossip of the village, his own picturings, had aroused him to an uncheckable degree. They were in truth fighting finely down there. Almost every day, the newspapers printed accounts of a decisive victory.

One night, as he lay in bed, the winds had carried to him the clangoring of the church-bell as some enthusiast jerked the rope frantically to tell the twisted news of a great battle. This voice of the people, rejoicing in the night, had made him shiver in a prolonged ecstasy of excitement. Later, he had gone down to his mother's room and had spoken thus: "Ma, I'm goin' t' enlist."

"Henry, don't you be a fool," his mother had replied. She had then covered her face with the quilt. There was an end to the matter for that night.

Nevertheless, the next morning, he had gone to a considerable town that was near his mother's farm and had enlisted in a company that was forming there. When he had returned home, his mother was milking the brindle cow. Four others stood waiting.

"Ma, I've enlisted," he had said to her diffidently.

There was a short silence. "Th' Lord's will be done, Henry," she had finally replied and had then continued to milk the brindle cow.

When he had stood in the door-way with his soldier's clothes on his back and with the light of excitement and expectancy in his eyes almost defeating the glow of regret for the home bonds, he had seen two tears leaving their hot trails on his mother's scarred cheeks.

Still, she had disappointed him by saying nothing whatever about returning with his shield or on it.[1] He had privately primed himself for a beautiful scene. He had prepared certain sentences which he thought could be used with touching effect. But her words destroyed his plans. She had doggedly peeled potatoes and addressed him as follows: "You watch out, Henry, an' take good keer of yerself in this here fightin' business—you watch out an' take good keer of yerself. Don't go a-thinkin' yeh kin lick th' hull rebel army at th' start, b'cause yeh can't. Yer jest one little feller 'mongst a hull lot 'a others an' yeh've got t' keep quiet an' do what they tell yeh. I know how you are, Henry.

"I've knet yeh eight pair a' socks, Henry, an' I've put in all yer best shirts, b'cause I want my boy t' be jest as warm an' comf'able as anybody in th' army. Whenever they git holes in'em I want yeh t' send'em right-away back t' me, so's I kin dern'em.

"An' allus be keerful an' choose yer comp'ny. There's lots 'a bad men in the army, Henry. Th' army makes'em wild an' they like nothin' better than th' job of leadin' off a young fellah like you—as aint never been away from home much an' has allus had a mother —an' a-learnin' 'im t' drink an' swear. Keep clear 'a them folks, Henry. I don't want yeh t' ever do anythin', Henry, that yeh would be shamed t' let me know about. Jest think as if I was a-watchin' yeh. If yeh keep that in yer mind allus, I guess yeh'll come out about right.

"Young fellers in th' army git awful keerless in their ways, Henry.

---

1. Traditionally, this is the best-known admonishment of a Spartan mother to a son leaving for war. It appears in Plutarch's *Moralia*: "Another as she handed her son his shield, exhorted him saying, 'Either this or upon this.' "

They're away f'm home an' they don't have nobody t' look atter'em. I'm 'feard fer yeh 'bout that. Yeh aint never been used t' doin' fer yerself. So yeh must keep writin' t' me how yer clothes are lastin'.

"Yeh must allus remember yer father, too, child, an' remember he never drunk a drop 'a licker in his life an' seldom swore a cross oath.

"I don't know what else t' tell yeh, Henry, exceptin' that yeh must never do no shirkin', child, on my account. If so be a time comes when yeh have t' be kilt or do a mean thing, why, Henry, don't think of anythin' 'cept what's right, b'cause there's many a woman has to bear up 'ginst sech things these times an' th' Lord'ill take keer of us all. Don't fergit t' send yer socks t' me th' minute they git holes in'em an' here's a little bible I want yeh t' take along with yeh, Henry. I dont presume yeh'll be a-settin' readin' it all day long, child, ner nothin' like that. Many a time, yeh'll fergit yeh got it, I don't doubt. But there'll be many a time, too, Henry, when yeh'll be wantin' advice, boy, an' all like that, an' there'll be nobody round, p'rhaps, t' tell yeh things. Then if yeh take it out, boy, yeh'll find wisdom in it—wisdom in it, Henry—with little or no searchin'. Don't forgit about th' socks an' th' shirts, child, an' I've put a cup of blackberry jam with yer bundle b'cause I know yeh like it above all things. Good-bye, Henry. Watch out an' be a good boy.''

He had of course been impatient under the ordeal of this speech. It had not been quite what he expected and he had borne it with an air of irritation. He departed feeling vague relief.

Still, when he had looked back from the gate, he had seen his mother kneeling among the potato-parings. Her brown face, up-raised, was stained with tears and her spare form was quivering. He bowed his head and went on, feeling suddenly ashamed of his purposes.

From his home, he had gone to the seminary[2] to bid adieu to many schoolmates. They had thronged about him with wonder and admiration. He had felt the gulf now between them and had swelled with calm pride. He and some of his fellows who had donned blue were quite over-whelmed with privileges for all of one afternoon and it had been a very delicious thing. They had strutted.

A certain light-haired girl had made vivacious fun at his martial-spirit but there was another and darker girl whom he had gazed at steadfastly and he thought she grew demure and sad at sight of his blue and brass. As he had walked down the path between the rows of oaks, he had turned his head and detected her at a window watching his departure. As he perceived her, she had immediately

2. An old-fashioned term for any school.

begun to stare up through the high tree branches at the sky. He had seen a good deal of flurry and haste as she changed her attitude. He often thought of it.

On the way to Washington, his spirit had soared. The regiment was fed and caressed at station after station until the youth had believed that he must be a hero. There was a lavish expenditure of bread and cold meats, coffee, and pickles and cheese. As he basked in the smiles of the girls and was patted and complimented by the old men, he had felt growing within him the strength to do mighty deeds of arms.

After complicated journeyings with many pauses, there had come months of monotonous life in a camp. He had had the belief that real war was a series of death-struggles with small time in between for sleep and meals but since his regiment had come to the field, the army had done little but sit still and try to keep warm.

He was brought then gradually back to his old ideas. Greek-like struggles would be no more. Men were better, or more timid. Secular and religious education had effaced the throat-grappling instinct or else firm finance held in check the passions.

He had grown to regard himself merely as a part of a vast blue demonstration. His province was to look out, as far as he could, for his personal comfort. For recreation, he could twiddle his thumbs and speculate on the thoughts which must agitate the minds of the generals. Also, he was drilled and drilled and reviewed, and drilled and drilled and reviewed.

The only foes he had seen were some pickets[3] along the river bank. They were a sun-tanned, philosophical lot who sometimes shot reflectively at the blue pickets. When reproached for this, afterwards, they usually expressed sorrow and swore by their gods that the guns had exploded without permission. The youth on guard duty one night, conversed across the stream with one. He was a slightly ragged man who spat skilfully between his shoes and possessed a great fund of bland and infantile assurance. The youth liked him personally.

"Yank," the other had informed him, "yer a right dum good feller." This sentiment, floating to him upon the still air, had made him temporarily regret war.

Various veterans had told him tales. Some talked of grey, bewhiskered hordes who were advancing, with relentless curses and chewing tobacco with unspeakable valor; tremendous bodies of fierce soldiery who were sweeping along like the Huns. Others spoke of tattered and eternally-hungry men who fired despondent powder.

---

3. Sentinels.

"They'll charge through hell's-fire an' brimstone t' git a holt on a haversack, an' sech stomachs aint a-lastin' long," he was told. From the stories, the youth imagined the red, live bones sticking out through slits in the faded uniforms.

Still he could not put a whole faith in veterans' tales, for recruits were their prey. They talked much of smoke, fire, and blood but he could not tell how much might be lies. They persistently yelled "Fresh fish," at him and were in no wise to be trusted.

However, he perceived now that it did not greatly matter what kind of soldiers he was going to fight, so long as they fought, which fact no one disputed. There was a more serious problem. He lay in his bunk pondering upon it. He tried to mathematically prove to himself that he would not run from a battle.

Previously, he had never felt obliged to wrestle too seriously with this question. In his life, he had taken certain things for granted, never challenging his belief in ultimate success and bothering little about means and roads. But here he was confronted with a thing of moment. It had suddenly appeared to him that perhaps in a battle he might run. He was forced to admit that as far as war was concerned he knew nothing of himself.

A sufficient time before, he would have allowed the problem to kick its heels at the outer portals of his mind but, now, he felt compelled to give serious attention to it.

A little panic-fear grew in his mind. As his imagination went forward to a fight, he saw hideous possibilities. He contemplated the lurking menaces of the future and failed in an effort to see himself standing stoutly in the midst of them. He re-called his visions of broken-bladed glory but in the shadow of the impending tumult, he suspected them to be impossible pictures.

He sprang from the bunk and began to pace nervously to and fro. "Good Lord, what's th' matter with me," he said aloud.

He felt that in this crisis his laws of life were useless. Whatever he had learned of himself was here of no avail. He was an unknown quantity. He saw that he would again be obliged to experiment as he had in early youth. He must accumulate information of himself and, meanwhile, he resolved to remain close upon his guard lest those qualities of which he knew nothing should everlastingly disgrace him. "Good Lord," he repeated in dismay.

After a time, the tall soldier slid dexterously through the hole. The loud private followed. They were wrangling.

"That's all right," said the tall soldier as he entered. He waved his hand expressively. "Yeh kin b'lieve me er not—jest as yeh like. All yeh got t' do is t' sit down an' wait as quiet as yeh kin. Then pretty soon yeh'll find out I was right."

His comrade grunted stubbornly. For a moment he seemed to be searching for a formidable reply. Finally he said: "Well, yeh don't know everythin' in th' world, do yeh?"

"Didn't say I knew everythin' in the world," retorted the other sharply. He began to stow various articles snugly into his knap-sack.

The youth, pausing in his nervous walk, looked down at the busy figure. "Goin' t' be a battle, sure, is there, Jim?" he asked.

"Of course there is," replied the tall soldier. "Of course there is. You jest wait 'til t'morrah an' you'll see one of th' bigges' battles ever was. You jest wait."

"Thunder," said the youth.

"Oh, you'll see fightin' this time, m' boy, what'll be reg'lar out-an'-out fightin'," added the tall soldier with the air of a man who is about to exhibit a battle for the benefit of his friends.

"Huh," said the loud one from a corner.

"Well," remarked the youth, "like as not this here story'll turn out jest like them others did."

"Not much it wont," replied the tall soldier exasperated. "Not much it wont. Didn't th' cavalry all start this mornin'?" He glared about him. No one denied his statement. "Th' cavalry started this mornin'," he continued. "They say there aint hardly any cavalry left in camp. They're goin' t' Richmond or some place while we fight all th' Johnnies. It's some dodge like that. Th' reg'ment's got orders, too. A feller what seen 'em go t' head-quarters told me a little while ago. An' they're raisin' blazes all over camp—anybody kin see that."

"Shucks," said the loud one.

The youth remained silent for a time. At last he spoke to the tall soldier. "Jim!"

"What?"

"How d' yeh think th' reg'ment'll do?"

"Oh, they'll fight all right, I guess, after they onct git inteh it," said the other with cold judgment. He made a fine use of the third person. "There's been heaps 'a fun poked at 'em b'cause they're new, 'a course, an' all that, but they'll fight all right, I guess."

"Think any 'a th' boys'll run?" persisted the youth.

"Oh, there may a few of 'em run but there's them kind in every reg'ment, 'specially when they first goes under fire," said the other in a tolerant way. " 'A course, it might happen that th' hull kit-an'-boodle might start an' run, if some big fightin' come first-off, an' then a'gin, they might stay an' fight like fun. But yeh cant bet on nothin'. A' course they aint never been under fire yit an' it aint likely they'll lick th' hull rebel army all-t'-onct th' first time, but I think they'll fight better than some, if worser than others. That's th' way I figger. They call th' reg'ment 'Fresh fish', an' everythin',

but th' boys come a' good stock an' most 'a 'em'll fight like sin after
—they—onct—git—shootin','" he added with a mighty emphasis
on the four last words.

"Oh, you think you know—" began the loud soldier with scorn.

The other turned savagely upon him. They had a rapid altercation, in which they fastened upon each other various strange epithets.

The youth at last interrupted them. "Did yeh ever think yeh
might run yerself, Jim?" he asked. On concluding the sentence he
laughed as if he had meant to aim a joke. The loud soldier also giggled.

The tall private waved his hand. "Well," said he profoundly,
"I've thought it might git too hot fer Jim Conklin in some 'a them
scrimmages an' if a hull lot a' boys started an' run, why, I s'pose I'd
start an' run. An' if I onct started t' run, I'd run like th' devil an'
no mistake. But if everybody was a-standin' an' a-fightin', why, I'd
stand an' fight. B'jiminy, I would. I'll bet on it."

"Huh," said the loud one.

The youth of this tale felt gratitude for these words of his comrade. He had feared that all of the untried men possessed a great
and correct confidence. He now was, in a measure, re-assured.

II

The next morning, the youth discovered that his tall comrade
had been the fast-flying messenger of a mistake. There was much
scoffing at the latter by those who had yesterday been firm adherents of his views, and there was, even, a little sneering by men who
had never believed the rumor. The tall one fought with a man from
Chatfield Corners and beat him severely.

The youth felt however that his problem was in no wise lifted
from him. There was, on the contrary, an irritating prolongation.
The tale had created in him a great concern for himself. Now, with
the new-born question in his mind he was compelled to sink back
into his old place as part of a blue demonstration.

For days, he made ceaseless calculations, but they were all wondrously unsatisfactory. He found that he could establish nothing.
He finally concluded that the only way to prove himself was to go
into the blaze and then figuratively to watch his legs to discover
their merits and faults. He reluctantly admitted that he could not
sit still and, with a mental slate and pencil, derive an answer. To
gain it, he must have blaze, blood and danger, even as a chemist
requires this, that and the other. So, he fretted for an opportunity.

Meanwhile, he continually tried to measure himself by his comrades. The tall soldier, for one, gave him some assurance. This
man's serene unconcern dealt him a measure of confidence for he

had known him since childhood and from his intimate knowledge he did not see how he could be capable of anything that was beyond him, the youth. Still, he thought that his comrade might be mistaken about himself. Or, on the other hand, he might be a man heretofore doomed to peace and obscurity but, in reality, made to shine in war.

The youth would have liked to have discovered another who suspected himself. A sympathetic comparison of mental notes would have been a joy to him.

He occasionally tried to fathom a comrade with seductive sentences. He looked about to find men in the proper moods. All attempts failed to bring forth any statement which looked, in any way, like a confession to those doubts which he privately acknowledged in himself. He was afraid to make an open declaration of his concern because he dreaded to place some unscrupulous confidant upon the high plane of the unconfessed from which elevation he could be derided.

In regard to his companions, his mind wavered between two opinions, according to his mood. Sometimes, he inclined to believing them all heroes. In fact he usually admitted, in secret, the superior development of the higher qualities in others. He could conceive of men going very insignificantly about the world, bearing a load of courage, unseen, and although he had known many of his comrades through boy-hood, he began to fear that his judgment of them had been blind. Then, in other moments, he flouted these theories and assured himself that his fellows were all privately wondering and quaking.

His emotions made him feel strange in the presence of men who talked excitedly of a prospective battle as of a drama they were about to witness with nothing but eagerness and curiosity apparent in their faces. It was often that he suspected them to be liars.

He did not pass such thoughts without severe condemnation of himself. He dinned reproaches, at times. He was convicted by himself of many shameful crimes against the gods of tradition.

In his great anxiety, his heart was continually clamoring at what he considered to be the intolerable slowness of the generals. They seemed content to perch tranquilly on the river bank and leave him bowed down by the weight of a great problem. He wanted it settled forthwith. He could not long bear such a load, he said. Sometimes, his anger at the commanders reached an acute stage and he grumbled about the camp like a veteran.

One morning, however, he found himself in the ranks of his prepared regiment. The men were whispering speculations and recounting the old rumors. In the gloom before the break of the day, their uniforms glowed a deep purple hue. From across the river the red eyes were still peering. In the eastern sky, there was a yellow patch like a rug laid for the feet of the coming sun. And against it, black and pattern-like, loomed the gigantic figure of the colonel on a gigantic horse.

From off in the darkness, came the trampling of feet. The youth could occasionally see dark shadows that moved like monsters. The regiment stood at rest for what seemed a long time. The youth grew impatient. It was unendurable, the way these affairs were managed. He wondered how long they were to be kept waiting.

As he looked all about him and pondered upon the mystic gloom, he began to believe that at any moment the ominous distance might be a-flare and the rolling crashes of an engagement come to his ears. Staring, once, at the red eyes across the river, he conceived them to be growing larger, as the orbs of a row of dragons, advancing. He turned toward the colonel and saw him lift his gigantic arm and calmly stroke his moustache.

At last, he heard from along the road at the foot of the hill the clatter of a horse's galloping hoofs. It must be the coming of orders. He bended forward scarce breathing. The exciting clickety-click as it grew louder and louder seemed to be beating upon his soul. Presently, a horseman with jangling equipment, drew rein before the colonel of the regiment. The two held a short, sharp-worded conversation. The men in the foremost ranks craned their necks.

As the horseman wheeled his animal and galloped away, he turned to shout over his shoulder. "Don't forget that box of cigars." The colonel mumbled in reply. The youth wondered what a box of cigars had to do with war.

A moment later the regiment went swinging off into the darkness. It was now like one of those moving monsters wending with many feet. The air was heavy and cold with dew. A mass of wet grass, marched upon, rustled like silk.

There was an occasional flash and glimmer of steel from the backs of all these huge crawling reptiles. From the road, came creakings and grumblings as some surly guns were dragged away.

The men stumbled along still muttering speculations. There was a subdued debate. Once, a man fell down and as he reached for his rifle, a comrade, unseeing, trod upon his hand. He of the injured fingers swore bitterly and aloud. A low, tittering laugh went among his fellows.

Presently, they passed into a road-way and marched along with easy strides. A dark regiment moved before them, and, from behind, also, came the tinkle of equipments on the bodies of marching men.

The rushing yellow of the developing day went on behind their backs. When the sun-rays at last struck full and mellowingly upon the earth, the youth saw that the landscape was streaked with two long, thin, black columns which disappeared on the brow of a hill in front and rear-ward vanished in a wood. They were like two serpents crawling from the cavern of the night.

The river was not in view. The tall soldier burst out in praise of what he thought to be his powers of perception. "I told yeh so, didnt I? We're goin' up th' river, cut across, an' come around in behint'em."

"Huh," said the loud soldier.

Some of the tall one's companions cried with emphasis that they too had evolved the same thing and they congratulated themselves upon it. But there were others who said that the tall one's plan was not the true one at all. They persisted with other theories. There was a vigorous discussion.

The youth took no part in them. As he walked along in careless line, he was engaged with his own eternal debate. He could not hinder himself from dwelling upon it. He was despondent and sullen and threw shifting glances about him. He looked ahead often, expecting to hear from the advance the rattle of firing.

But the long serpents crawled slowly from hill to hill without bluster of smoke. A dun-colored cloud of dust floated away to the right. The sky over-head was of a fairy blue.

The youth studied the faces of his companions, ever on the watch to detect kindred emotions. He suffered disappointment. Some ardor of the air which was causing the veteran commands to move with glee, almost with song, had infected the new regiment. The men began to speak of victory as of a thing they knew. Also, the tall soldier received his vindication. They were certainly going to come around in behind the enemy. They expressed commiseration for that part of the army which had been left upon the river-bank felicitating themselves upon being a part of a blasting host.

The youth, considering himself as separated from the others, was saddened by the blithe and merry speeches that went from rank to rank. The company wags all made their best endeavors. The regiment tramped to the tune of laughter.

The loud soldier often convulsed whole files by his biting sarcasms aimed at the tall one.

And it was not long before all the men seemed to forget their mission. Whole brigades grinned in unison and regiments laughed.

A rather fat soldier attempted to pilfer a horse from a door-yard. He planned to load his knapsack upon it. He was escaping with his prize when a young girl rushed from the house and grabbed the animal's mane. There followed, a wrangle.

The observant regiment, standing at rest in the road-way, whooped at once and entered whole-souled upon the side of the maiden. The men became so engrossed in this affair that they

entirely ceased to remember their own large war. They jeered the
piratical private and called attention to various defects in his personal appearance. And they were wildly enthusiastic in support of
the young girl.

"Gin' it to'im, Mary, gin' it to'im."

"Don't let'im steal yer horse."

"Gin' him thunder."

To her from some distance came bold advice. "Hit him with a
stick."

There were crows and cat-calls showered upon him when he
retreated without the horse. The regiment rejoiced at his downfall.
Loud and vociferous congratulations were showered upon the
maiden who stood panting and regarding the troops with defiance.

At night-fall, the column broke into regimental pieces and the
fragments went into the fields to camp. Tents sprang up like
strange plants. Camp-fires, like red, peculiar blossoms, dotted the
night.

The youth kept from intercourse with his companions as much as
circumstances would allow him. In the evening, he wandered a few
paces into the gloom. From this little distance, the many fires with
the black forms of men passing to and fro before the crimson rays
made weird and satanic effects.

He lay down in the grass. The blades pressed tenderly against his
cheek. The moon had been lighted and was hung in a tree-top. The
liquid stillness of the night, enveloping him, made him feel vast
pity for himself. There was a caress in the soft winds. And the
whole mood of the darkness, he thought, was one of sympathy for
him in his distress.

He wished without reserve that he was at home again, making
the endless rounds, from the house to the barn, from the barn to
the fields, from the fields to the barn, from the barn to the house.
He remembered he had often cursed the brindle-cow and her mates,
and had sometimes flung milking-stools. But from his present point
of view, there was a halo of happiness about each of their heads and
he would have sacrificed all the brass buttons on the continent to
have been enabled to return to them. He told himself that he was
not formed for a soldier. And he mused seriously upon the radical
differences between himself and those men who were dodging, imp-
like, around the fires.

As he mused thus, he heard the rustle of grass and, upon turning
his head discovered, the loud soldier. He called out. "Oh, Wilson."

The latter approached and looked down. "Why, hello, Henry, is
it you? What yeh doin' here?"

"Oh—thinkin'," said the youth.

The other sat down and carefully lighted his pipe. "You're gittin' blue, m' boy. You're lookin' thunderin' peek-ed. What th' dickens is wrong with yeh?"

"Oh—nothin'," said the youth.

The loud soldier launched then into the subject of the antici-.pated fight. "Oh, we've got'em now." As he spoke his boyish face was wreathed in a gleeful smile and his voice had an exultant ring. "We've got'em now. At last by th' eternal thunders, we'll lick'em good."

"If th' truth was known," he added more soberly, "*they've* licked *us* about every clip up t' now, but this time—this time, we'll lick'em good."

"I thought yeh was objectin' t' this march a little while ago," said the youth coldly.

"Oh, it wasn't that," explained the other. "I don't mind march-in' if there's goin' t' be fightin' at th' end of it. What I hate is this gittin' moved here an' moved there with no good comin' of it, as far as I kin see, exceptin' sore feet an' damn' short rations."

"Well, Jim Conklin says we'll git a-plenty of fightin' this time."

"He's right fer once, I guess, 'though I can't see how it come. This time we're in for a big battle an' we've got th' best end of it certain-sure. Gee-rod, how we will thump'em."

He arose and began to pace to and fro excitedly. The thrill of his enthusiasm made him walk with an elastic step. He was sprightly, vigorous, fiery in his belief in success. He looked into the future with clear, proud eye. And he swore with the air of an old soldier.

The youth watched him for a moment in silence. When he finally spoke, his voice was as bitter as dregs. "Oh, you're goin' t' do great things, I s'pose."

The loud soldier blew a thoughtful cloud of smoke from his pipe. "Oh, I don't know," he remarked with dignity. "I don't know. I s'pose I'll do as well as th' rest. I'm goin' t' try like thunder." He evidently complimented himself upon the modesty of this state-ment.

"How d' yeh know yeh won't run when th' time comes?" asked the youth.

"Run?" said the loud one. "Run? Of course not." He laughed.

"Well," continued the youth, "lots of good-a-'nough men have thought they was goin' t' do great things before th' fight but when th' time come, they skedaddled."

"Oh, that's all true, I s'pose;" replied the other, "but I'm not goin' t' skedaddle. Th' man that bets on my runnin', will lose his money, that's all." He nodded confidently.

"Oh, shucks," said the youth. "Yeh aint th' bravest man in th' world, are yeh?"

"No, I aint," exclaimed the loud soldier indignantly. "An' I didnt say I was th' bravest man in th' world, neither. I said I was goin' t' do my share of fightin'—that's what I said. An' I am, too. Who are you, anyhow? You talk as if yeh thought yeh was Napolyon Bonypart." He glared at the youth for a moment and then strode away.

The youth called in a savage voice after his comrade. "Well, yeh needn't git mad about it." But the other continued on his way and made no reply.

He felt alone in space when his injured comrade had disappeared. His failure to discover any mite of resemblance in their view-points made him more miserable than before. No one seemed to be wrestling with such a terrific personal problem. He was a mental outcast.

He went slowly to his tent and stretched himself on a blanket by the side of the snoring tall soldier. In the darkness, he saw visions of a thousand-tongued fear that would babble at his back and cause him to flee while others were going coolly about their country's business. He admitted that he would not be able to cope with this monster. He felt that every nerve in his body would be an ear to hear the voices, while other men could remain stolid and deaf.

And as he sweated with the pain of these thoughts he could hear low, serene sentences. "I'll bid five." "Make it six." "Seven." "Seven goes."

He stared at the red, shivering reflection of a fire on the white wall of his tent until exhausted and ill from the monotony of his suffering he fell asleep.

III

When another night came, the columns changed to purple streaks, filed across two pontoon bridges. A glaring fire wine-tinted the waters of the river. Its rays, shining upon the moving masses of troops, brought forth here and there sudden gleams of silver or gold. Upon the other shore, a dark and mysterious range of hills was curved against the sky. The insect-voices of the night sang solemnly.

After this crossing, the youth assured himself that at any moment they might be suddenly and fearfully assaulted from the caves of the lowering woods. He kept his eyes watchfully upon the darkness.

But his regiment went unmolested to a camping-place and its soldiers slept the brave sleep of wearied men. In the morning they were routed out with early energy and hustled along a narrow road that led deep into the forest.

It was during this rapid march that the regiment lost many of the marks of a new command.

The men had begun to count the miles upon their fingers. And they grew tired. "Sore feet an' damned short rations, that's all," said the loud soldier. There was perspiration and grumbling. After a time, they began to shed their knapsacks. Some tossed them unconcernedly down; others hid them carefully, asserting their plans to return for them at some convenient time. Men extricated themselves from thick shirts. Presently, few carried anything but their necessary clothing, blankets, haversacks, canteens, and arms and ammunition. "Yeh kin now eat, drink, sleep an' shoot," said the tall soldier to the youth. "That's all yeh need. What d' yeh wanta do —carry a hotel?" There was sudden change from the ponderous infantry of theory to the light and speedy infantry of practise. The regiment, relieved of a burden, received a new impetus. But there was much loss of valuable knapsacks and, on the whole, very good shirts.

But the regiment was not yet veteran-like in appearance. Veteran regiments in this army were like to be very small aggregations of men. Once, when the command had first come to the field, some perambulating veterans, noting the length of their column, had accosted them thus: "Hay, fellers, what brigade is that?" And when the men had replied that they formed a regiment and not a brigade, the older soldiers had laughed and said: "Oh, Gawd!"[4]

Also, there was too great a similarity in the hats. The hats of a regiment should properly represent the history of head-gear for a period of years.

And, moreover, there were no letters of faded gold speaking from the colors. They were new and beautiful, and the color-bearer habitually oiled the pole.

Presently, the army again sat down to think. The odor of the peaceful pines was in the men's nostrils. The sound of monotonous axe-blows rang through the forest and the insects, nodding upon their perches, crooned like old women. The youth returned to his theory of a blue demonstration.

One grey dawn, however, he was kicked in the leg by the tall soldier and then before he was entirely awake, he found himself running down a wood-road in the midst of men who were panting from the first effects of speed. His canteen banged rhythmically upon his thigh and his haversack bobbed softly. His musket bounced a trifle from his shoulder at each stride and made his cap feel uncertain upon his head.

He could hear the men whisper jerky sentences. "Say—what's all this—about?" "What th' thunder—we—skedaddlin' this way fer?" "Billie—keep off m' feet. Yeh run—like a cow." And the loud soldier's shrill voice could be heard: "What th' devil they in sech a hurry fer?"

---

4. A brigade usually comprises two or more regiments.

The youth thought the damp fog of early morning moved from the rush of a great body of troops. From the distance, came a sudden spatter of firing.

He was bewildered. As he ran with his comrades, he strenuously tried to think but all he knew was that if he fell down, those coming behind would tread upon him. All his faculties seemed to be needed to guide him over and past obstructions. He felt carried along by a mob.

The sun spread disclosing rays and, one by one, regiments burst into view like armed men just born of the earth. The youth perceived that the time had come. He was about to be measured. For a moment he felt in the face of his great trial, like a babe. And the flesh over his heart seemed very thin. He seized time to look about him calculatingly.

But he instantly saw that it would be impossible for him to escape from the regiment. It enclosed him. And there were iron laws of tradition and law on four sides. He was in a moving box.

As he perceived this fact, it occurred to him that he had never wished to come to the war. He had not enlisted of his free will. He had been dragged by the merciless government. And now they were taking him out to be slaughtered!

The regiment slid down a bank and wallowed across a little stream. The mournful current moved slowly on and from the water, shaded black, some white bubble-eyes looked at the men.

As they climbed the hill on the further side artillery began to boom. Here the youth forgot many things as he felt a sudden impulse of curiosity. He scrambled up the bank with a speed that could not be exceeded by a blood-thirsty man.

He expected a battle-scene.

There were some little fields girted and squeezed by a forest. Spread over the grass and in among the tree-trunks, he could see knots and waving lines of skirmishers who were running hither and thither and firing at the landscape. A dark battle-line lay upon a sun-struck clearing that gleamed orange-color. A flag fluttered.

Other regiments floundered up the bank. The brigade was formed in line of battle and, after a pause, started slowly through the woods in the rear of the receding skirmishers who were continually melting into the scene to appear again further on. They were always busy as bees, deeply absorbed in their little combats.

The youth tried to observe everything. He did not use care to avoid trees and branches, and his forgotten feet were constantly knocking against stones or getting entangled in briars. He was aware that these battalions, with their commotions, were woven red and startling into the gentle fabric of softened greens and browns. It looked to be a wrong place for a battle-field.

The skirmishers in advance fascinated him. Their shots into thickets and at distant and prominent trees spoke to him of tragedies, hidden, mysterious, solemn.

Once, the line encountered the body of a dead soldier. He lay upon his back staring at the sky. He was dressed in an awkward suit of yellowish brown. The youth could see that the soles of his shoes had been worn to the thinnest of writing-paper and from a great rent in one, the dead foot projected piteously. And it was as if fate had betrayed the soldier. In death, it exposed to his enemies that poverty which in life he had perhaps concealed from his friends.

The ranks opened covertly to avoid the corpse. The invulnerable dead man forced a way for himself. The youth looked keenly at the ashen face. The wind raised the tawny beard. It moved as if a hand were stroking it. He vaguely desired to walk around and around the body and stare; the impulse of the living to try to read in dead eyes the answer to the Question.

During this march, the ardor which the youth had acquired when out of view of the field rapidly faded to nothing. His curiosity was quite easily satisfied. If an intense scene had caught him with its wild swing as he came to the top of the bank he might have gone roaring on. This advance upon nature was too calm. He had opportunity to reflect. He had time in which to wonder about himself and to attempt to probe his sensations.

Absurd ideas took hold upon him. He thought that he did not relish the landscape. It threatened him. A coldness swept over his back and it is true that his trousers felt to him that they were no fit for his legs at all.

A house, standing placidly in distant fields had to him an ominous look. The shadows of the woods were formidable. He was certain that in this vista there lurked fierce-eyed hosts. The swift thought came to him that the generals did not know what they were about. It was all a trap. Suddenly those close forests would bristle with rifle-barrels. Iron-like brigades would appear in the rear. They were all going to be sacrificed. The generals were stupids. The enemy would presently swallow the whole command. He glared about him, expecting to see the stealthy approach of his death.

He thought that he must break from the ranks and harangue his comrades. They must not all be killed like pigs. And he was sure it would come to pass unless they were informed of these dangers. The generals were idiots to send them marching into a regular pen. There was but one pair of eyes in the corps. He would step forth and make a speech. Shrill and passionate words came to his lips.

The line, broken into moving fragments by the ground went calmly on through fields and woods. The youth looked at the men nearest him and saw, for the most part, expressions of deep interest as if they were investigating something that had fascinated them. One or two stepped with over-valiant airs as if they were already plunged into war. Others walked as upon thin ice. The greater part of the untested men appeared quiet and absorbed. They were going to look at war, the red animal, war, the blood-swollen god. And they were deeply engrossed in this march.

As he looked, the youth gripped his out-cry at his throat. He saw that even if the men were tottering with fear, they would laugh at his warning. They would jeer him and if practicable pelt him with missiles. Admitting that he might be wrong, a frenzied declamation of the kind would turn him into a worm.

He assumed, then, the demeanor of one who knows that he is doomed, alone, to unwritten responsibilities. He lagged, with tragic glances at the sky.

He was surprised, presently, by the lieutenant of his company who began heartily to beat him with a sword, calling out in a loud and insolent voice. "Come, young man, get up into ranks there. No skulking'll do here." He mended his pace with suitable haste. And he hated the lieutenant, who had no appreciation of fine minds. He was a mere brute.

After a time, the brigade was halted in the cathedral-light of a forest. The busy skirmishers were still popping. Through the aisles of the wood could be seen the floating smoke from their rifles. Sometimes it went up in little balls, white and compact.

During this halt, many men in the regiment began erecting tiny hills in front of them. They used stones, sticks, earth and anything they thought might turn a bullet. Some built comparatively large ones while others seemed content with little ones.

This procedure caused a discussion among the men. Some wished to fight like duellists, believing it to be correct to stand erect and be, from their feet to their fore-heads, a mark. They said they scorned the devices of the cautious. But the others scoffed in reply and pointed to the veterans on the flanks who were digging at the ground like terriers. In a short time there was quite a barricade along the regimental front. Directly however they were ordered to withdraw from that place.

This astounded the youth. He forgot his stewing over the advance movement. "Well, then, what did they march us out here fer?" he demanded of the tall soldier. The latter with calm faith began a heavy explanation although he had been compelled to leave a little protection of stones and dirt to which he had devoted much care and skill.

When the regiment was aligned in another position each man's regard for his safety caused another line of small intrenchments. They ate their noon meal behind a third one. They were moved from this one also. They were marched from place to place with apparent aimlessness.

The youth had been taught that a man became another thing in a battle. He saw his salvation in such a change. Hence this waiting was an ordeal to him. He was in a fever of impatience. He considered that there was denoted a lack of purpose on the part of the generals. He began to complain to the tall soldier. "I can't stand this much longer," he cried. "I don't see what good it does t' make us wear out'r legs fer nothin'." He wished to return to camp, knowing that this affair was a blue demonstration; or, else, to go into a battle and discover that he had been a fool in his doubts and was in truth a man of traditional courage. The strain of present circumstances he felt to be intolerable.

The philosophical tall soldier measured a sandwich of cracker and pork and swallowed it in a nonchalant manner. "Oh, I s'pose we must go reconnoiterin' around th' kentry jest t' keep'em from gittin' too clost, or t' develope'm,[5] or something."

"Huh," said the loud soldier.

"Well," cried the youth, still fidgeting, "I'd rather do anythin' 'most than go trampin' 'round th' kentry all day doin' no good t' nobody an' jest tirin' ourselves out."

"So would I," said the loud soldier. "It aint right. I tell yeh if anybody with any sense was a-runnin' this army, it—"

"Oh, shut up," roared the tall private. "Yeh little fool. Yeh little damn'-fool-cuss. Yeh aint had that there coat an' them pants on fer six months yit an' yit yeh talk as if—"

"Well, I wanta do some fightin' anyway," interrupted the other; "I didn't come here t' walk. I could 'a walked t' home, 'round an' 'round th' barn, if I jest wanted t' walk."

The tall one, red-faced, swallowed another sandwich as if taking poison in despair.

But, gradually, as he chewed, his face became again quiet and contented. He could not rage in fierce argument in the presence of such sandwiches. During his meals, he always wore an air of blissful contemplation of the food he had swallowed. His spirit seemed then to be communing with the viands.

He accepted new environment and circumstance with great coolness, eating from his haversack at every opportunity. On the march he went along with the stride of a hunter, objecting to neither gait nor distance. And he had not raised his voice when he had been ordered away from three little protective piles of earth and stone, each of which had been an engineering feat worthy of being made sacred to the name of his grandmother.

---

5. I.e., learn the enemy's strength and position.

In the afternoon, the regiment went out over the same ground it had taken in the morning. The landscape then ceased to threaten the youth. He had been close to it and become familiar with it.

When, however, they began to pass into a new region, his old fears of stupidity and incompetence re-assailed him but this time he doggedly let them babble. He was occupied with his problem and in his desperation he concluded that the stupidity affair did not greatly matter.

Once he thought that he had concluded that it would be better to get killed directly and end his troubles. Regarding death thus out of the corner of his eye, he conceived it to be nothing but rest and he was filled with a momentary astonishment that he should have made an extraordinary commotion over the mere matter of getting killed. He would die; he would go to some place where he would be understood. It was useless to expect appreciation of his profound and fine senses from such men as the lieutenant. He must look to the grave for comprehension.

The unceasing skirmish-fire increased to a long clattering sound. With it was mingled faraway cheering. A battery spoke.

Directly, the youth could see the skirmishers running. They were pursued by the sound of musketry fire. After a time, the hot dangerous flashes of the rifles were visible. Smoke clouds went slowly and insolently across the fields, like observant phantoms. The din became crescendo like the roar of an oncoming train.

A brigade ahead of them and on the right went into action with a rending roar. It was as if it had exploded. And, thereafter, it lay stretched in the distance behind a long grey wall that one was obliged to look twice at to make sure that it was smoke.

The youth, forgetting his neat plan of getting killed, gazed spellbound. His eyes grew wide and busy with the action of the scene. His mouth was a little ways open.

Of a sudden, he felt a heavy and sad hand laid upon his shoulder. Awakening from his trance of observation, he turned and beheld the loud soldier.

"It's m' first an' last battle, ol' boy," said the latter, with intense gloom. He was quite pale and his girlish lip was trembling.

"Eh?" murmured the youth in great astonishment.

"It's m' first an' last battle, ol' boy," continued the loud soldier. "Somethin' tells me—"

"What?"

"—I'm a gone coon this first time an'—an' I w-want yeh t' take these here things—t'—my—folks." He ended in a quavering sob of pity for himself. He handed the youth a little packet done up in a yellow envelope.

"Why, what th' devil—" began the youth again.

But the other gave him a glance as from the depths of a tomb, waved his limp hand in a prophetic manner and turned away.

IV

The brigade was halted in the fringe of a grove. The men crouched among the trees and pointed their restless guns out at the fields. They tried to look beyond the smoke.

Out of this haze they could see running men. Some shouted information, and gestured, as they hurried.

The men of the new regiment watched and listened eagerly, while their tongues ran on in the gossip of the battle. They mouthed rumors that had flown like birds out of the unknown.

"They say Perrey has been driven in with big loss."

"Yes, Carrott went t' th' hospital. He said he was sick. That smart lieutenant is commanding 'G' Company. Th' boys say they won't be under Carrott no more if they all have t' desert. They allus knew he was a—"

"Hannises' bat'try is took."

"It aint either. I saw Hannises' bat'try off on th' left not more'n fifteen minutes ago."

"Well—"

"Th' general, he ses he is goin' t' take th' hull command of th' 304th when we go inteh action an' then he ses we'll do sech fightin' as never another one reg'ment done."

"Th' boys of th' 47th, they took a hull string of rifle-pits."

"It wasn't the 47th a 'tall. It was th' 99th Vermont."

"There haint nobody took no rifle-pits. Th' 47th driv a lot a Johnnies from behint a fence."

"Well—"

"They say we're catchin' it over on th' left. They say th' enemy driv' our line inteh a devil of a swamp an' took Hannises' bat'try."

"No sech thing. Hannises' bat'try was 'long here 'bout a minute ago."

"That young Hasbrouck, he makes a good off'cer. He aint afraid 'a nothin'."

"I met one of th' 148th Maine boys an' he ses his brigade fit th' hull rebel army fer four hours over on th' turnpike-road an' killed about five thousand of'em. He ses one more sech fight as that an' th' war'll be over."

"Bill wasn't scared either. No, sir. It wasn't that. Bill aint a-gittin' scared easy. He was jest mad, that's what he was. When that feller trod on his hand, he up an' sed that he was willin' t' give his hand t' his country but he be dumbed if he was goin' t' have every dumb bushwhacker in th' kentry walkin' 'round on it. So he went t' th' hospital disregardless of th' fight. Three fingers was crunched.

Th' dern doctor wanted t' amputate'm an' Bill, he raised a heluva row, I hear. He's a funny feller."

"Hear that what th' ol' colonel ses, boys. He ses he'll shoot th' first man what'll turn an' run."

"He'd better try it. I'd like t' see him shoot at *me*."

"He wants t' look fer his ownself. *He* don't wanta go 'round talkin' big."

"They say Perrey's division's a-givin'em thunder."

"Ed Williams over in Company A, he ses th' rebs'll all drop their guns an' run an' holler if we onct giv'em one good lickin'."

"Oh, thunder, Ed Williams, what does he know? Ever since he got shot at on picket, he's been runnin' th' war."

"Well, he—"

"Hear th' news, boys? Corkright's crushed th' hull rebel right an' captured two hull divisions. We'll be back in winter quarters by a short cut t'-morrah."

"I tell yeh I've been all over that there kentry where th' rebel right is an' it's th' nastiest part th' rebel line. It's all mussed up with hills an' little damn creeks. I'll bet m'shirt Corkright never harmed'em down there."

"Well he's a fighter an' if they could be licked, he'd lick'em."[6]

· · ·

The din in front swelled to a tremendous chorus. The youth and his fellows were frozen to silence. They could see a flag that tossed in the smoke angrily. Near it were the blurred and agitated forms of troops. There came a turbulent stream of men across the fields. A battery, changing position at a frantic gallop, scattered the stragglers right and left.

A shell, screaming like a storm-banshee, went over the huddled heads of the reserves. It landed in the grove and, exploding redly, flung the brown earth. There was a little shower of pine needles.

Bullets began to whistle among the branches and nip at the trees. Twigs and leaves came sailing down. It was as if a thousand axes, wee and invisible, were being wielded. Many of the men were constantly dodging and ducking their heads.

The lieutenant of the youth's company was shot in the hand. He began to swear so wondrously that a nervous laugh went along the regimental line. The officer's profanity sounded conventional. It relieved the tightened senses of the new men. It was as if he had hit his fingers with a tack-hammer at home.

He held the wounded member carefully away from his side, so that the blood would not drip upon his trousers.

6. The ellipses here and at six subsequent places in Chapters VII, X, XII, and XV indicate a gap where text of the manuscript is missing. Discussion of each gap appears in the Textual Notes.

The captain of the company, tucking his sword under his arm, produced a handkerchief and began to bind with it the lieutenant's wound. And they had a dispute as to how the binding should be done.

The battle-flag in the distance jerked about madly. It seemed to be struggling to free itself from an agony. The billowing smoke was filled with horizontal flashes.

Men running swiftly emerged from it. They grew in numbers until it was seen that the whole command was fleeing. The flag suddenly sank down as if dying. Its motion, as it fell, was a gesture of despair.

Wild yells came from behind the walls of smoke. A sketch in gray and red dissolved into a mob-like body of men who galloped like wild horses.

The veteran regiments on the right and left of the 304th immediately began to jeer. With the passionate song of the bullets and the banshee shrieks of shells were mingled loud cat-calls and bits of facetious advice concerning places of safety.

But the new regiment was breathless with horror.

"Gawd! Saunders's got crushed!" whispered the man at the youth's elbow. They shrank back and crouched, as if compelled to await a flood.

The youth shot a swift glance along the blue ranks of the regiment. The profiles were motionless, carven. And afterward he remembered that the color-serjeant [7] was standing with his legs braced apart, as if he expected to be pushed to the ground.

The bellowing throng went whirling around the flank. Here and there were officers carried along on the stream like exasperated chips. They were striking about them with their swords and, with their left fists, punching every head they could reach. They cursed like highwaymen.

A mounted officer displayed the furious anger of a spoiled child. He raged with his head, his arms and his legs.

Another, the commander of the brigade, was galloping about, bawling. His hat was gone and his clothes were awry. He resembled a man who has come from bed to go to a fire.

The hoofs of his horse often threatened the heads of the running men, but they scampered with singular good fortune. In this rush, they were apparently all deaf and blind. They heeded not the largest and longest of the oaths that were thrown at them from all directions.

Frequently, over this tumult, could be heard the grim jokes of the critical veterans, but the retreating men apparently were not

---

7. I.e., the flag-bearer.

even conscious of the presence of an audience.

The battle-reflection that shone for an instant in the faces on the mad current made the youth feel that forceful hands from Heaven would not have been able to have held him in place if he could have got intelligent control of his legs.

There was an appalling imprint upon these faces. The struggle in the smoke had pictured an exaggeration of itself on the bleached cheeks and in the eyes, wild with one desire.

The sight of this stampede exerted a flood-like force that seemed able to drag sticks and stones and men from the ground. They of the reserves had to hold on. They grew pale and firm, and red and quaking.

The youth achieved one little thought in the midst of this chaos. The composite monster which had caused the other troops to flee had not then appeared. He resolved to get a view of it, and then, he thought, he might, very likely, run better than the best of them.

V

There were moments of waiting. The youth thought of the village street at home before the arrival of the circus-parade on a day in the spring. He remembered how he had stood, a small thrillful boy, prepared to follow the dingy lady upon the white horse or the band in its faded chariot. He saw the yellow road, the lines of expectant people, and the sober houses. He particularly remembered an old fellow who used to sit upon a cracker-box in front of the store and feign to despise such exhibitions. A thousand details of color and form surged in his mind. The old fellow upon the cracker-box appeared in middle prominence.

Some one cried: "Here they come!"

There was rustling and muttering among the men. They displayed a feverish desire to have every possible cartridge ready to their hands. The boxes were pulled around into various positions and adjusted with great care. It was as if seven hundred new bonnets were being tried on.

The tall soldier having prepared his rifle, produced a red handkerchief of some kind. He was engaged in knotting it about his throat, with exquisite attention to its position, when the cry was repeated up and down the line in a muffled roar of sound. "Here they come! Here they come!" Gun-locks clicked.

Across the smoke-infested fields came a brown swarm of running men who were giving shrill yells. They came on stooping and swinging their rifles at all angles. A flag tilted forward sped near the front.

As he caught sight of them, the youth was momentarily startled by a thought that perhaps his gun was not loaded. He stood trying to rally his faltering intellect so that he might recollect the moment when he had loaded. But he could not.

A hatless general pulled his dripping horse to a stand near the colonel of the 304th. He shook his fist in the other's face. "You've got t' hold'em back," he shouted savagely. "You've got t' hold'em back."

In his agitation, the colonel began to stammer. "A-all r-right, general, all right, by Gawd. We-we'll do our—we-we'll d-d-do—do our best, general." The general made a passionate gesture and galloped away. The colonel perchance to relieve his feelings, began to scold like a wet parrot. The youth turning swiftly to make sure that the rear was unmolested, saw the commander regarding his men in a highly resentful manner as if he regretted, above everything, his association with them.

The man at the youth's elbow was mumbling as if to himself: "Oh, we're in for it, now. Oh, we're in for it now."

The captain of the company had been pacing excitedly to and fro in the rear. He coaxed in school-mistress fashion as to a congregation of boys with primers. His talk was an endless repetition. "Reserve your fire, boys—dont shoot 'til I tell you—save your fire— wait 'til they get close up—don't be damned fools—"

Perspiration streamed down the youth's face which was soiled like that of a weeping urchin. He frequently with a nervous movement wiped his eyes with his coat-sleeve. His mouth was still a little ways open.

He got the one glance at the foe-swarming field in front of him and instantly ceased to debate the question of his piece being loaded. Before he was ready to begin, before he had announced to himself that he was about to fight, he threw the obedient, well-balanced rifle into position and fired a first wild shot. Directly, he was working at his weapon like an automatic affair.

He suddenly lost concern for himself and forgot to look at a menacing fate. He became not a man but a member. He felt that something of which he was a part—a regiment, an army, a cause, or a country—was in a crisis. He was welded into a common personality which was dominated by a single desire. For moments, he could not flee no more than a little finger can commit a revolution from a hand.

If he had thought the regiment about to be annihilated perhaps he could have amputated himself from it. But its noise gave him assurance. The regiment was like a fire-work that, once ignited, proceeds superior to circumstances until its blazing vitality fades. It wheezed and banged with a mighty power. He pictured the ground before it as strewn with the discomfited.

There was a consciousness always of the presence of his comrades about him. He felt the subtle battle-brotherhood more potent even than the cause for which they were fighting. It was a mysterious fraternity, born of the smoke and danger of death.

He was at a task. He was like a carpenter who has made many boxes, making still another box, only there was furious haste in his movements. He, in his thoughts, was careering off in other places, even as the carpenter who as he works, whistles and thinks of his friend or his enemy, his home or a saloon. And these jolted dreams were never perfect to him afterward but remained a mass of blurred shapes.

Presently he began to feel the effects of the war-atmosphere—a blistering sweat, a sensation that his eye-balls were about to crack like hot stones. A burning roar filled his ears.

Following this came a red rage. He developed the acute exasperation of a pestered animal, a well-meaning cow worried by dogs. He had a mad feeling against his rifle which could only be used against one life at a time. He wished to rush forward and strangle with his fingers. He craved a power that would enable him to make a world-sweeping gesture and brush all back. His impotency appeared to him and made his rage into that of a driven beast.

Buried in the smoke of many rifles, his anger was directed not so much against the men whom he knew were rushing toward him, as against the swirling battle-phantoms who were choking him, stuffing their smoke-robes down his parched throat. He fought frantically for respite for his senses, for air, as a babe, being smothered, attacks the deadly blankets.

There was a blare of heated rage, mingled with a certain expression of intentness on all faces. Many of the men were making low-toned noises with their mouths and these subdued cheers, snarls, imprecations, prayers, made a wild, barbaric song that went as an under-current of sound, strange and chant-like, with the resounding chords of the war-march. The man at the youth's elbow was babbling. In it there was something soft and tender, like the monologue of a babe. The tall soldier was swearing in a loud voice. From his lips came a black procession of curious oaths. Of a sudden another broke out in a querulous way like a man who has mislaid his hat. "Well, why don't they support us? Why don't they send supports? Do they think—"

The youth in his battle-sleep, heard this as one who dozes, hears.

There was a singular absence of heroic poses. The men bending and surging in their haste and rage were in every impossible attitude. The steel ram-rods clanked and clanged with incessant din as the men pounded them feverishly into the hot rifle-barrels. The flaps of the cartridge-boxes were all unfastened, and flapped and bobbed idiotically with each movement. The rifles, once loaded, were jerked to the shoulder and fired without apparent aim into the smoke or at one of the blurred and shifting forms which upon the field before the regiment had been growing larger and larger like puppets under a magician's hand.

The officers, at their intervals, rearward, neglected to stand in picturesque attitudes. They were bobbing to and fro, roaring directions and encouragements. The dimensions of their howls were extraordinary. They expended their lungs with prodigal wills. And often they near stood upon their heads in their anxiety to observe the enemy on the other side of the tumbling smoke.

The lieutenant of the youth's company had encountered a soldier who had fled, screaming, at the first volley of his comrades. Behind the lines, these two were acting a little isolated scene. The man was blubbering and staring with sheep-like eyes at the lieutenant who had seized him by the collar and was pummeling him. He drove him back into the ranks with many blows. The soldier went mechanically, dully, with his animal-like eyes upon the officer. Perhaps there was to him a divinity expressed in the voice of the other, stern, hard, with no reflection of fear in it. He tried to re-load his gun but his shaking hands prevented. The lieutenant was obliged to assist him.

The men dropped here and there like bundles. The captain of the youth's company had been killed in an early part of the action. His body lay stretched out in the position of a tired man, resting, but upon his face there was an astonished and sorrowful look as if he thought some friend had done him an ill turn. The babbling man was grazed by a shot that made the blood stream widely down his face. He clapped both hands to his head. "Oh," he said and ran. Another grunted suddenly as if he had been struck by a club in the stomach. He sat down and gazed ruefully. In his eyes there was mute, indefinite reproach. Further up the line a man, standing behind a tree, had had his knee-joint splintered by a ball. Immediately, he had dropped his rifle and gripped the tree with both arms. And there he remained, clinging desperately, and crying for assistance that he might withdraw his hold upon the tree.

At last, an exultant yell went along the quivering line. The firing dwindled from an uproar to a last vindictive popping. As the smoke slowly eddied away, the youth saw that the charge had been repulsed. The enemy were scattered into reluctant groups. He saw a man climb to the top of the fence, straddle the rail and fire a parting shot. The waves had receded, leaving bits of dark debris upon the ground.

Some in the regiment began to whoop frenziedly. Many were silent. Apparently, they were trying to contemplate themselves.

After the fever had left his veins, the youth thought that at last he was going to suffocate. He became aware of the foul atmosphere in which he had been struggling. He was grimy and dripping like a laborer in a foundry. He grasped his canteen and took a long swallow of the warmed water.

A sentence with variations went up and down the line. "Well, we've helt'em back. We've helt'em back—derned if we haven't." The men said it blissfully, leering at each other with dirty smiles.

The youth turned to look behind him and off to the right and off to the left. He experienced the joy of a man who at last finds leisure in which to look about him.

Under foot, there were a few ghastly forms, motionless. They lay twisted in fantastic contortions. Arms were bended and heads were turned in incredible ways. It seemed that the dead men must have fallen from some great height to get into such positions. They looked to be dumped out upon the ground from the sky.

From a position in the rear of the grove a battery was throwing shells over it. The flash of the guns startled the youth at first. He thought they were aimed directly at him. Through the trees, he watched the black figures of the gunners as they worked swiftly and intently. Their labor seemed a complicated thing. He wondered how they could remember its formulae in the midst of confusion.

The guns squatted in a row like savage chiefs. They argued with abrupt violence. It was a grim pow-wow. Their busy servants ran hither and thither.

A small procession of wounded men were going drearily toward the rear. It was a flow of blood from the torn body of the brigade.

To the right and to the left were the dark lines of other troops. Far in front, he thought he could see lighter masses protruding in points from the forest. They were suggestive of unnumbered thousands.

Once he saw a tiny battery go dashing along the line of the horizon. The tiny riders were beating the tiny horses.

From a sloping hill came the sound of cheerings and clashes. Smoke welled slowly through the leaves.

Batteries were speaking with thunderous oratorical effort. Here and there were flags, the red in the stripes dominating. They splashed bits of warm color upon the dark lines of troops.

The youth felt the old thrill at the sight of the emblems. They were like beautiful birds strangely undaunted in a storm.

As he listened to the din from the hill side, to a deep, pulsating thunder that came from afar to the left, and to the lesser clamors which came from many directions, it occurred to him that they were fighting too, over there and over there and over there. Heretofore, he had supposed that all the battle was directly under his nose.

As he gazed around him, the youth felt a flash of astonishment at the blue pure sky and the sun-gleamings on the trees and fields. It was surprising that nature had gone tranquilly on with her golden processes in the midst of so much devilment.

VI

The youth awakened slowly. He came gradually back to a position from which he could regard himself. For moments, he had been scrutinizing his person in a dazed way as if he had never before seen himself. Then he picked up his cap from the ground. He wriggled in his jacket to make a more comfortable fit and, kneeling, re-laced his shoe. He thoughtfully mopped his reeking features.

So it was all over at last. The supreme trial had been passed. The red, formidable difficulties of war had been vanquished.

He went into an ecstasy of self-satisfaction. He had the most delightful sensations of his life. Standing as if apart from himself, he viewed the last scene. He perceived that the man who had fought thus was magnificent.

He felt that he was a fine fellow. He saw himself even with those ideals which he had considered as far beyond him. He smiled in deep gratification.

Upon his fellows, he beamed tenderness and good-will. "Gee, aint it hot, hay?" he said affably to a man who was polishing his streaming face with his coat-sleeve.

"You bet," said the other, grinning sociably. "I never seen sech dumb hotness." He sprawled out luxuriously on the ground. "Gee, yes! An' I hope we don't have no more fightin' 'til—'til a week from Monday."

There were some hand-shakings and deep speeches with men whose features only were familiar but with whom the youth now felt the bonds of tied hearts. He helped a cursing comrade to bind up a wound of the shin.

But, of a sudden, cries of amazement broke out along the ranks of the new regiment. "Here they come a'gin! Here they come a'gin!" The man who had sprawled upon the ground, started up and said: "Gosh!"

The youth turned quick eyes upon the field. He discerned forms begin to swell in masses out of a distant wood. He again saw the tilted flag, speeding forward.

The shells, which had ceased to trouble the regiment for a time, came swirling again and exploded in the grass or among the leaves of the trees. They looked to be strange war-flowers bursting into fierce bloom.

The men groaned. The lustre faded from their eyes. Their smudged countenances now expressed a profound dejection. They moved their stiffened bodies slowly and watched in sullen mood the frantic approach of the enemy. The slaves toiling in the temple of this god began to feel rebellion at his harsh tasks.

They fretted and complained each to each. "Oh, say, this is too much of a good thing. Why cant somebody send us supports."

"We aint never goin' t' stand this here second bangin'. I didn't come here t' fight th' hull damn' rebel army."

There was one who raised a doleful cry. "I wish Bill Smithers had trod on my hand insteader me treddin' on his'n."

The sore joints of the regiment creaked as it painfully floundered into position to repulse.

The youth stared. Surely, he thought, this impossible thing was not about to happen. He waited as if he expected the enemy to suddenly stop, apologize and retire, bowing. It was all a mistake.

But the firing began somewhere on the regimental line and ripped along in both directions. The level sheets of flame developed great clouds of smoke that tumbled and tossed in the mild wind near the ground for a moment and then rolled through the ranks as through a grate. The clouds were tinged an earth-like yellow in the sun-rays and, in the shadow were a sorry blue. The flag was sometimes eaten and lost in this mass of vapor but more often it projected, sun-touched, resplendent.

Into the youth's eyes there came a look that one can see in the orbs of a jaded horse. His back was quivering with nervous weakness and the muscles of his arms felt numb and bloodless. His hands, too, seemed large and awkward as if he was wearing invisible mittens. And there was a great uncertainty about his knee-joints.

The words that comrades had uttered previous to the firing began to appear to him. "Oh, say, this is too much of a good thing." "What do they take us fer—why don't they send supports." "I didn't come here to fight th' hull damned rebel army."

He began to exaggerate the endurance, the skill, and the valor of those who were coming. Himself reeling from exhaustion, he was astonished beyond measure at such persistency. They must be machines of steel. It was very gloomy, struggling against such affairs, wound up, perhaps, to fight until sun-down.

He slowly lifted his rifle and catching a glimpse of the thick-spread field he blazed at a cantering cluster. He stopped then and began to peer as best he could through the smoke. He caught changing views of the ground covered with men who were all running like pursued imps, and yelling.

To the youth, it was an onslaught of redoubtable dragons. He became like the man who lost his legs at the approach of the red and green monster. He waited in a sort of a horrified, listening attitude. He seemed to shut his eyes and wait to be gobbled.

A man near him who up to this time had been working feverishly at his rifle, suddenly dropped it and ran with howls. A lad whose face had borne an expression of exalted courage, the majesty of he who dares give his life, was, at an instant smitten abject. He blanched like one who has come to the edge of a cliff at midnight and is suddenly made aware. There was a revelation. He too threw down his gun and fled. There was no shame in his face. He ran like a rabbit.

Others began to scamper away through the smoke. The youth turned his head, shaken from his trance, by this movement as if the regiment was leaving him behind. He saw the few fleeting forms.

He yelled then with fright and swung about. For a moment, in the great clamor, he was like a proverbial chicken. He lost the direction of safety. Destruction threatened him from all points.

Directly he began to speed toward the rear in great leaps. His rifle and cap were gone. His unbuttoned coat bulged in the wind. The flap of his cartridge-box bobbed wildly and his canteen, by its slender cord, swung out behind. On his face was all the horror of those things which he imagined.

The lieutenant sprang forward, bawling. The youth saw his features, wrathfully red, and saw him make a dab with his sword. His one thought of the incident was that the lieutenant was a peculiar creature, to feel interested in such matters upon this occasion.

He ran like a blind man. Two or three times he fell down. Once he knocked his shoulder so heavily against a tree that he went head-long.

Since he had turned his back upon the fight, his fears had been wondrously magnified. Death about to thrust him between the shoulder-blades was far more dreadful than death about to smite him between the eyes. When he thought of it later, he conceived the impression that it is better to view the appalling than to be merely within hearing. The noises of the battle were like stones; he believed himself liable to be crushed.

As he ran on, he mingled with others. He dimly saw men on his right and on his left, and he heard footsteps behind him. He thought that all the regiment was fleeing, pursued by these ominous crashes.

In his flight, the sound of these following footsteps gave him his one meagre relief. He felt vaguely that death must make a first choice of the men who were nearest; the initial morsels for the dragons would be, then, those who were following him. So he displayed the zeal of an insane sprinter in his purpose to keep them in the rear. There was a race.

As he, leading, went across a little field, he found himself in a region of shells. They hurtled over his head with long wild screams. As he heard them, he imagined them to have rows of cruel teeth

that grinned at him. Once, one lit before him and the livid lightning of the explosion effectually barred his way in his chosen direction. He groveled on the ground and then springing up went careering off through some bushes.

He experienced a thrill of amazement when he came within view
of a battery in action. The men there seemed to be in conventional
moods, altogether unaware of the impending annihilation. The battery was disputing with a distant antagonist and the gunners were
wrapped in admiration of their shooting. They were continually
bending in coaxing postures over the guns. They seemed to be pat-
ting them on the back and encouraging them with words. The guns
stolid and undaunted, spoke with dogged valor.

The precise gunners were coolly enthusiastic. They lifted their
eyes every chance to the smoke-wreathed hillock from whence the
hostile battery addressed them. The youth pitied them as he ran.
Methodical idiots! Machine-like fools! The refined joy of planting
shells in the midst of the other battery's formation would appear a
little thing when the infantry came swooping out of the woods.

The face of a youthful rider who was jerking his frantic horse
with an abandon of temper he might display in a placid barn-yard
was impressed deep upon his mind. He knew that he looked upon a
man who would presently be dead.

Too, he felt a pity for the guns, standing, six good comrades, in a
bold row.

He saw a brigade going to the relief of its pestered fellows. He
scrambled upon a wee hill and watched it sweeping finely, keeping
formation in difficult places. The blue of the line was crusted with
steel-color and the brilliant flags projected. Officers were shouting.

This sight, also, filled him with wonder. The brigade was hurrying briskly to be gulped into the infernal mouth of the war-god.
What manner of men were they, anyhow. Ah, it was some wondrous breed. Or else they didnt comprehend—the fools.

A furious order caused commotion in the artillery. An officer on a
bounding horse made maniacal motions with his arms. The teams
went swinging up from the rear, the guns were whirled about, and
the battery scampered away. The cannon with their noses poked
slantingly at the ground grunted and grumbled like stout men,
brave but with objections to hurry.

The youth went on, moderating his pace since he had left the
place of noises.

Later, he came upon a general of division seated upon a horse
that pricked its ears in an interested way at the battle. There was a
great gleaming of yellow and patent-leather about the saddle and
bridle. The quiet man, astride, looked mouse-colored upon such a
splendid charger.

A jingling staff was galloping hither and thither. Sometimes the general was surrounded by horsemen and at other times he was quite alone. He looked to be much harassed. He had the appearance of a business man whose market is swinging up and down.

The youth went slinking around this spot. He went as near as he dared trying to over-hear words. Perhaps the general, unable to comprehend chaos might call upon him for information. And he could tell him. He knew all concerning it. Of a surety the force was in a fix and any fool could see that if they did not retreat while they had opportunity—why—

He felt that he would like to thrash the general, or, at least, approach and tell him in plain words exactly what he thought him to be. It was criminal to stay calmly in one spot and make no effort to stay destruction. He loitered in a fever of eagerness for the division-commander to apply to him.

As he warily moved about, he heard the general call out irritably. "Tompkins, go over an' see Taylor an' tell him not t' be in such all-fired hurry—tell him t' halt his brigade in th' edge of th' woods —tell him t' detach a reg'ment—say I think th' centre'll break if we don't help it out some—tell him t' hurry up."

A slim youth on a fine chestnut horse caught these swift words from the mouth of his superior. He made his horse bound into a gallop almost from a walk in his haste to go upon his mission. There was a cloud of dust.

A moment later, the youth saw the general bounce excitedly in his saddle.

"Yes—by Heavens—they have!" The officer leaned forward. His face was a-flame with excitement. "Yes, by Heavens, they've held'im! They've held'im."

He began to blithely roar at his staff. "We'll wallop'im now. We'll wallop'im now. We've got'em sure." He turned suddenly upon an aide. "Here—you—Jones—quick—ride after Tompkins— see Taylor—tell him t' go in—everlastingly—like blazes—anything."

As another officer sped his horse after the first messenger, the general beamed upon the earth like a sun. In his eyes was a desire to chant a paean.[8] He kept repeating: "They've held'em, by Heavens."

His excitement made his horse plunge and he merrily kicked and swore at it. He held a little carnival of joy on horseback.

---

8. A song of joy, triumph, praise.

VII

The youth cringed as if discovered at a crime. By heavens, they had won after all. The imbecile line had remained and become victors. He could hear cheering.

He lifted himself upon his toes and looked in the direction of the fight. A yellow fog lay wallowing on the tree-tops. From beneath it came the clatter of musketry. Hoarse cries told of an advance.

He turned away, amazed and angry. He felt that he had been wronged.

He had fled, he told himself, because annihilation approached. He had done a good part in saving himself who was a little piece of the army. He had considered the time, he said, to be one in which it was the duty of every little piece to rescue itself if possible. Later, the officers could fit the little pieces together again and make a battle-front. If none of the little pieces were wise enough to save themselves from the flurry of death at such a time, why, then, where would be the army? It was all plain that he had proceeded according to very correct and commendable rules. His actions had been sagacious things. They had been full of strategy. They were the work of a master's legs.

Thoughts of his comrades came to him. The brittle blue line had withstood the blows and won. He grew bitter over it. It seemed that the blind ignorance and stupidity of those little pieces had betrayed him. He had been overturned and crushed by their lack of sense in holding the position, when intelligent deliberation would have convinced them that it was impossible. He, the enlightened man who looks afar in the dark, had fled because of his superior perceptions and knowledge. He felt a great anger against his comrades. He knew it could be proven that they had been fools.

He wondered what they would remark when later he appeared in camp. His mind heard howls of derision. Their density would not enable them to understand his sharper point of view.

He began to pity himself acutely. He was ill-used. He was trodden beneath the feet of an iron injustice. He had proceeded with wisdom and from the most righteous motives under Heaven's blue only to be frustrated by hateful circumstances.

A dull, animal-like rebellion against his fellows, war in the abstract, and fate, grew within him. He shambled along with bowed head, his brain in a tumult of agony and despair. When he looked loweringly up, quivering at each sound, his eyes had the expression of those of a criminal who thinks his guilt little and his punishment great and knows that he can find no words; who, through his suffering, thinks that he peers into the core of things and sees that the judgment of man is thistle-down in wind.

He went from the fields into a thick woods as if resolved to bury himself. He wished to get out of hearing of the crackling shots which were to him like voices.

The ground was cluttered with vines and bushes and the trees grew close and spread out like bouquets. He was obliged to force his way with much noise. The creepers, catching against his legs, cried out harshly as their sprays were torn from the barks of trees. The swishing saplings tried to make known his presence to the world. He could not conciliate the forest. As he made his way, it was always calling out protestations. When he separated embraces of trees and vines, the disturbed foliages waved their arms and turned their face-leaves toward him. He dreaded lest these noisy motions, and cries, should bring men to look at him. So, he went far, seeking dark and intricate places.

After a time, the sound of musketry grew faint and the cannon boomed in the distance. The sun, suddenly apparent, blazed among the trees. The insects were making rhythmical noises. They seemed to be grinding their teeth in unison. A wood-pecker stuck his impudent head around the side of a tree. A bird flew on light-hearted wing.

Off, was the rumble of death. It seemed now that nature had no ears.

This landscape gave him assurance. A fair field, holding life. It was the religion of peace. It would die if its timid eyes were compelled to see blood. He conceived nature to be a woman with a deep aversion to tragedy.

He threw a pine-cone at a jovial squirrel and he ran with chattering fear. High in a tree-top, he stopped and, poking his head cautiously from behind a branch, looked down with an air of trepidation.

The youth felt triumphant at this exhibition. There was the law, he said. Nature had given him a sign. The squirrel immediately upon recognizing a danger, had taken to his legs, without ado. He did not stand stolidly, baring his furry belly to the missile, and die with an upward glance at the sympathetic heavens. On the contrary, he had fled as fast as his legs could carry him. And he was but an ordinary squirrel too; doubtless, no philosopher of his race.

The youth wended, feeling that nature was of his mind. She reinforced his arguments with proofs that lived where the sun shone.

Once he found himself almost into a swamp. He was obliged to walk upon bog-tufts and watch his feet to keep from the oily mire. Pausing at one time to look about him, he saw out at some black water, a small animal pounce in and emerge directly with a silver-gleaming fish.

The youth went again into the deep thickets. The brushed branches made a noise that drowned the sounds of cannon. He walked on, going from obscurity into promises of a greater obscurity.

At length, he reached a place where the high, arching boughs made a chapel. He softly pushed the green doors aside and entered. Pine-needles were a gentle brown carpet. There was a religious half-light.

Near the threshold, he stopped horror-stricken at the sight of a thing.

He was being looked at by a dead man who was seated with his back against a column-like tree. The corpse was dressed in a uniform that once had been blue but was now faded to a melancholy shade of green. The eyes, staring at the youth, had changed to the dull hue to be seen on the side of a dead fish. The mouth was opened. Its red had changed to an appalling yellow. Over the grey skin of the face ran little ants. One was trundling some sort of a bundle along the upper lip.

The youth gave a shriek as he confronted the thing. He was, for moments, turned to stone before it. He remained staring into the liquid-looking eyes. The dead man and the living man exchanged a long look. Then, the youth cautiously put one hand behind him and brought it against a tree. Leaning upon this, he retreated, step by step, with his face still toward the thing. He feared, that if he turned his back, the body might spring up and stealthily pursue him.

The branches, pushing against him, threatened to throw him over upon it. His unguided feet, too, caught aggravatingly in brambles. And, with it all, he received a subtle suggestion to touch the corpse. As he thought of his hand upon it, he shuddered profoundly.

At last, he burst the bonds which had fastened him to the spot and fled, unheeding the underbrush. He was pursued by a sight of the black ants swarming greedily upon the grey face and venturing horribly near to the eyes.

After a time, he paused and, breathless and panting, listened. He imagined some strange voice would come from the dead throat and squawk after him in horrible menaces.

The trees about the portal of the chapel moved sighingly in a soft wind. A sad silence was upon the little, guarding edifice.

Again the youth was in despair. Nature no longer condoled with him. There was nothing, then, after all, in that demonstration she gave—the frightened squirrel fleeing aloft from the missile.

He thought as he remembered the small animal capturing the fish and the greedy ants feeding upon the flesh of the dead soldier, that there was given another law which far-over-topped it—all life existing upon death, eating ravenously, stuffing itself with the hopes of the dead.

And nature's processes were obliged to hurry

. . .

VIII

The trees began softly to sing a hymn of twilight. The burnished sun sank until slanted bronze rays struck the forest. There was a lull in the noises of insects as if they had bowed their beaks and were making a devotional pause. There was silence save for the chanted chorus of the trees.

Then, upon this stillness, there suddenly broke a tremendous clangor of sounds. A crimson roar came from the distance.

The youth stopped. He was transfixed by this terrific medley of all noises. It was as if worlds were being rended. There was the ripping sound of musketry and the breaking crash of the artillery.

His mind flew in all directions. He conceived the two armies to be at each other panther-fashion. He listened for a time. Then he began to run in the direction of the battle. He saw that it was an ironical thing for him to be running thus toward that which he had been at such pains to avoid. But he said, in substance, to himself that if the earth and the moon were about to clash, many persons would doubtless plan to get upon roofs to witness the collision.

As he ran, he became aware that the forest had stopped its music, as if at last becoming capable of hearing the foreign sounds. The trees hushed and stood motionless. Everything seemed to be listening to the crackle and clatter and ear-shaking thunder. The chorus pealed over the still earth.

It suddenly occurred to the youth that the fight in which he had been, was, after all, but perfunctory popping. In the hearing of this present din, he was doubtful if he had seen real battle-scenes. This uproar explained a celestial battle; it was tumbling hordes a-struggle in the air.

Reflecting, he saw a sort of a humor in the point of view of himself and his fellows during the late encounter. They had taken themselves and the enemy very seriously and had imagined that they were deciding the war. Individuals must have supposed that they were cutting the letters of their names deep into everlasting tablets of brass or enshrining their reputations forever in the hearts of their countrymen, while, as to fact, the affair would appear in printed reports under a meek and immaterial title. But he saw that it was good, else, he said, in battle everyone would surely run save forlorn hopes and their ilk.

He went rapidly on. He wished to come to the edge of the forest that he might peer out.

As he hastened, there passed through his mind pictures of stupendous conflicts. His accumulated thought upon such subjects was used to form scenes. The noise was as the voice of an eloquent being, describing.

Sometimes, the brambles formed chains and tried to hold him back. Trees, confronting him, stretched out their arms and forbade him to pass. After its previous hostility, this new resistance of the forest filled him with a fine bitterness. It seemed that nature could not be quite ready to kill him.

But he obstinately took roundabout ways and presently he was where he could see long grey walls of vapor, where lay battle-lines. The voices of cannon shook him. The musketry sounded in long irregular surges that played havoc with his ears. He stood, regardant, for a moment. His eyes had an awe-struck expression. He gawked in the direction of the fight.

Presently, he proceeded again on his forward way. The battle was like the grinding of an immense and terrible machine to him. Its complexities and powers, its grim processes, fascinated him. He must go close and see it produce corpses.

He came to a fence and clambered over it. On the far side, the ground was littered with clothes and guns. A newspaper, folded up, lay in the dirt. A dead soldier was stretched with his face hidden in his arm. Further off, there was a group of four or five corpses, keeping mournful company. A hot sun had blazed upon the spot.

In this place, the youth felt that he was an invader. This forgotten part of the battle-ground was owned by the dead men, and he hurried, in the vague apprehension that one of the swollen and ghastly forms would rise and tell him to begone.

He came finally to a road from which he could see in the distance, dark and agitated bodies of troops, smoke-fringed. In the lane, was a blood-stained crowd streaming to the rear. The wounded men were cursing, groaning and wailing. In the air, always, was a mighty swell of sound that it seemed could sway the earth. With the courageous words of the artillery and the spiteful sentences of the musketry was mingled red cheers. And from this region of noises came the steady current of the maimed.

One of the wounded men had a shoeful of blood. He hopped like a school-boy in a game. He was laughing hysterically.

One was swearing that he had been shot in the arm, through the commanding general's mismanagement of the army.

One was marching with an air imitative of some sublime drum-major. Upon his features was an unholy mixture of merriment and agony. As he marched he sang a bit of doggerel in a high and quavering voice.

> "Sing a song 'a vic'try
> A pocketful 'a bullets
> Five an' twenty dead men
> Baked in a—pie."

Parts of the procession limped and staggered to this tune.

Another had the grey seal of death already upon his face. His lips were curled in hard lines and his teeth were clenched. His hands were bloody from where he had pressed them upon his wound. He seemed to be awaiting the moment when he should pitch headlong. He stalked like the spectre of a soldier, his eyes burning with the power of a stare into the unknown.

There were some who proceeded sullenly, full of anger at their wounds and ready to turn upon anything as an obscure cause.

An officer was carried along by two privates. He was peevish. "Don't joggle so, Johnson, yeh fool," he cried. "Think m'leg is made of iron? If yeh can't carry me decent, put me down an' let some one else do it."

He bellowed at the tottering crowd who blocked the quick march of his bearers. "Say, make way there, can't yeh? Make way, dickens take it all."

They sulkily parted and went to the roadsides. As he was carried past, they made pert remarks to him. When he raged in reply and threatened them, they told him to be damned.

The shoulder of one of the tramping bearers knocked heavily against the spectral soldier who was staring into the unknown.

The youth joined this crowd and marched along with it. The torn bodies expressed the awful machinery in which the men had been entangled.

Orderlies and couriers occasionally broke through the throng in the roadway, scattering wounded men right and left, galloping on, followed by howls. The melancholy march was continually disturbed by the messengers and sometimes by bustling batteries that came swinging and thumping down upon them, the officers shouting orders to clear the way.

There was a tattered man, fouled with dust, blood and powder-stain from hair to shoes who trudged quietly at the youth's side. He was listening with eagerness and much humility to the lurid descriptions of a bearded serjeant. His lean features wore an expression of awe and admiration. He was like a listener in a country-store to wondrous tales told among the sugar-barrels. He eyed the story-teller with unspeakable wonder. His mouth was a-gape in yokel fashion.

The serjeant, taking note of this, gave pause to his elaborate history while he administered a sardonic comment. "Be keerful, honey, you'll be a-ketchin' flies," he said.

The tattered man shrank back, abashed.

After a time, he began to sidle near to the youth and in a diffident way, try to make him a friend. His voice was gentle as a girl's voice and his eyes were pleading. The youth saw with surprise that the soldier had two wounds, one in the head, bound with a blood-soaked rag and the other in the arm, making that member dangle like a broken bough.

After they had walked together for some time, the tattered man mustered sufficient courage to speak. "Was pretty good fight, wa'n't it?" he timidly said. The youth, deep in thought, glanced up at the bloody and grim figure with its lamb-like eyes. "What?"

"Was pretty good fight, wa'n't it?"

"Yes," said the youth shortly. He quickened his pace.

But the other hobbled industriously after him. There was an air of apology in his manner but he evidently thought that he needed only to talk for a time and the youth would perceive that he was a good fellow.

"Was pretty good fight, wa'n't it?" he began in a small voice. And then he achieved the fortitude to continue. "Dern me if I ever see fellers fight so. Laws, how they did fight. I knowed th' boys'd lick when they onct got square at it. Th' boys aint had no fair chanct up t' now, but, this time, they showed what they was. I knowed it'd turn out this way. Yeh can't lick them boys. No sir. They're fighters, they be."

He breathed a deep breath of humble admiration. He had looked at the youth for encouragement several times. He received none, but, gradually he seemed to get absorbed in his subject.

"I was talkin' 'cross pickets with a boy from Georgie, onct, an' that boy, he ses: 'Your fellers'll all run like hell when they onct hearn a gun,' he ses. 'Mebbe they will,' I ses 'but I don't b'lieve none of it,' I ses, 'an' b'jiminy,' I ses back t'um, 'mebbe your fellers'll all run like hell when they onct hearn a gun,' I ses. He larfed.

"Well, they didn't run t'day, did they, hey? No, sir. They fit an' fit an' fit."

His homely face was suffused with a light of love for the army which was to him all things beautiful and powerful.

After a time, he turned to the youth. "Where yeh hit, ol' boy," he asked in a brotherly tone.

The youth felt instant panic at this question although at first its full import was not borne in upon him.

"What?" he asked.

"Where yeh hit?" repeated the tattered man.

"Why," began the youth, "I—I—that is—why—I—"

He turned away suddenly and slid through the crowd. His brow was heavily flushed, and his fingers were picking nervously at one of his buttons. He bended his head and fastened his eyes studiously upon the button as if it were a little problem.

The tattered man looked after him in astonishment.

IX

The youth fell back in the procession until the tattered soldier was not in sight. Then he started to walk on with others.

But he was amid wounds. The mob of men was bleeding. Because of the tattered soldier's question, he now felt that his shame could be viewed. He was continually casting side-long glances to see if the men were contemplating the letters of guilt he felt burned into his brow.

At times, he regarded the wounded soldiers in an envious way. He conceived persons with torn bodies to be peculiarly happy. He wished that he, too, had a wound, a little red badge of courage.

The spectral soldier was at his side like a stalking reproach. The man's eyes were still fixed in a stare into the unknown. His grey, appalling face had attracted attention in the crowd and men, slowing to his dreary pace, were walking with him. They were discussing his plight, questioning him and giving him advice. In a dogged way, he repelled them, signing to them to go on and leave him alone. The shadows of his face were deepening and his tight lips seemed holding in check the moan of great despair. There could be seen a certain stiffness in the movements of his body as if he were taking infinite care not to arouse the passions of his wounds. As he went on, he seemed always looking for a place, like one who goes to choose a grave.

Something in the gesture of the man as he waved the bloody and pitying soldiers away, made the youth start as if bitten. He yelled in horror. Tottering forward, he laid a quivering hand upon the man's arm. As the latter slowly turned his wax-like features toward him, the youth screamed.

"Gawd! Jim Conklin!"

The tall soldier made a little common-place smile. "Hello, Henry," he said.

The youth swayed on his legs and glared strangely. He stuttered and stammered. "Oh, Jim—oh, Jim—oh, Jim—"

The tall soldier held out his gory hand. There was a curious, red and black combination of new blood and old blood upon it. "Where yeh been, Henry?" he asked. He continued in a monotonous voice. "I thought mebbe yeh got keeled over. There's been thunder t' pay t'day. I was worryin' about it a good deal."

The youth still lamented. "Oh, Jim—oh, Jim—oh, Jim—"

"Yeh know," said the tall soldier, "I was out there." He made a careful gesture. "An', Lord, what a circus. An', b'jiminy, I got shot —I got shot. Yes, b'jiminy, I got shot." He reiterated this fact in a bewildered way as if he did not know how it came about.

The youth put forth anxious arms to assist him but the tall soldier went firmly on as if propelled. Since the youth's arrival as a guardian for his friend, the other wounded men had ceased to display much interest. They occupied themselves again in dragging their tragedies toward the rear.

Suddenly, as the two friends marched on, the tall soldier seemed to be over-come by a terror. His face turned to a semblance of grey paste. He clutched the youth's arm and looked all about him, as if dreading to be over-heard. Then he began to speak in a shaking whisper.

"I tell yeh what I'm 'fraid of, Henry—I'll tell yeh what I'm 'fraid of. I'm 'fraid I'll fall down—an' then yeh know—them damned artillery wagons—they like as not'll run over me. That's what I'm 'fraid of—"

The youth cried out to him hysterically. "I'll take keer of yeh, Jim! I'll take keer of yeh! I swear t' Cawd I will."

"Sure—will yeh, Henry?" the tall soldier beseeched.

"Yes—yes—I tell yeh—I'll take keer of yeh, Jim," protested the youth. He could not speak accurately because of the gulpings in his throat.

But the tall soldier continued to beg in a lowly way. He now hung babe-like to the youth's arm. His eyes rolled in the wildness of his terror. "I was allus a good friend t' yeh, wa'n't I, Henry? I've allus been pretty good feller, aint I? An' it aint much t' ask, is it? Jest t' pull me along outer th' road? I'd do it fer you, wouldn't I, Henry?"

He paused in piteous anxiety to await his friend's reply.

The youth had reached an anguish where the sobs scorched him. He strove to express his loyalty but he could only make fantastic gestures.

However, the tall soldier seemed suddenly to forget all those fears. He became again the grim, stalking spectre of a soldier. He went stonily forward. The youth wished his friend to lean upon him but the other always shook his head and strangely protested. "No —no—no—leave me be—leave me be—"

His look was fixed again upon the unknown. He moved with mysterious purpose. And all of the youth's offers he brushed aside. "No —no—leave me be—leave me be—"

The youth had to follow.

Presently the latter heard a voice talking softly near his shoulder. Turning he saw that it belonged to the tattered soldier. "Ye'd better take'im outa th' road, pardner. There's a bat'try comin' helitywhoop down th' road an' he'll git runned over. He's a goner anyhow in about five minutes—yeh kin see that. Ye'd better take 'im outa th' road. Where th' blazes does he git his stren'th from?"

"Lord knows," cried the youth. He was shaking his hands helplessly.

He ran forward, presently, and grasped the tall soldier by the arm. "Jim! Jim!" he coaxed, "come with me."

The tall soldier weakly tried to wrench himself free. "Huh," he said vacantly. He stared at the youth for a moment. At last he spoke as if dimly comprehending.

"Oh! Inteh th' fields? Oh!"

He started blindly through the grass.

The youth turned once to look at the lashing riders and jouncing guns of the battery. He was startled from this view by a shrill outcry from the tattered man.

"Gawd! He's runnin'!"

Turning his head swiftly, the youth saw his friend running in a staggering and stumbling way toward a little clump of bushes. His heart seemed to wrench itself almost free from his body at this sight. He made a noise of pain. He and the tattered man began a pursuit. There was a singular race.

When he over-took the tall soldier, he began to plead with all the words he could find. "Jim—Jim—what are yeh doin'—what makes yeh do this way—yeh'll hurt yerself."

The same purpose was in the tall soldier's face. He protested in a dulled way, keeping his eyes fastened on the mystic place of his intentions. "No—no—don't tech me—leave me be—leave me be—"

The youth, aghast and filled with wonder at the tall soldier, began quaveringly to question him. "Where yeh goin', Jim? What yeh thinkin' about? Where yeh goin'? Tell me, won't yeh, Jim?"

The tall soldier faced about as upon relentless pursuers. In his eyes, there was a great appeal. "Leave me be, can't yeh? Leave me be fer a minnit."

The youth recoiled. "Why, Jim," he said, in a dazed way, "what's th' matter with yeh?"

The tall soldier turned and, lurching dangerously, went on. The youth and the tattered soldier followed, sneaking as if whipped, feeling unable to face the stricken man if he should again confront them. They began to have thoughts of a solemn ceremony. There was something rite-like in these movements of the doomed soldier. And there was a resemblance in him to a devotee of a mad religion, blood-sucking, muscle-wrenching, bone-crushing. They could not understand; they were awed and afraid. They hung back lest he have at command, a dreadful weapon.

At last, they saw him stop and stand motionless. Hastening up, they perceived that his face wore an expression telling that he had at last found the place for which he had struggled. His spare figure was erect; his bloody hands were quietly at his sides. He was waiting with patience for something that he had come to meet. He was at the rendezvous. They paused and stood, expectant.

There was a silence.

Finally, the chest of the doomed soldier began to heave with a strained motion. It increased in violence until it was as if an animal was within and was kicking and tumbling furiously to be free.

This spectacle of gradual strangulation made the youth writhe and once as his friend rolled his eyes, he saw something in them that made him sink wailing to the ground. He raised his voice in a last, supreme call.

"Jim—Jim—Jim—"

The tall soldier opened his lips and spoke. He made a gesture. "Leave me be—don't tech me—leave me be—"

There was another silence, while he waited.

Suddenly, his form stiffened and straightened. Then it was shaken by a prolonged ague. He stared into space. To the two watchers, there was a curious and profound dignity in the firm lines of his awful face.

He was invaded by a creeping strangeness that slowly enveloped him. For a moment, the tremor of his legs caused him to dance a sort of hideous horn-pipe. His arms beat wildly about his head in expression of imp-like enthusiasm.

His tall figure stretched itself to its full height. There was a slight rending sound. Then it began to swing forward, slow and straight, in the manner of a falling tree. A swift muscular contortion made the left shoulder strike the ground first.

The body seemed to bounce a little way from the earth. "Gawd," said the tattered soldier.

The youth had watched, spell-bound, this ceremony at the place of meeting. His face had been twisted into an expression of every agony he had imagined for his friend.

He now sprang to his feet and, going closer, gazed upon the paste-like face. The mouth was open and the teeth showed in a laugh.

As the flap of the blue jacket fell away from the body, he could see that the side looked as if it had been chewed by wolves.

The youth turned, with sudden, livid rage, toward the battle-field. He shook his fist. He seemed about to deliver a philippic.[9]

9. A bitter verbal attack.

"Hell—"

➤ The red sun was pasted in the sky like a fierce wafer.

X

The tattered man stood musing.

"Well, he was reg'lar jim-dandy fer nerve, wa'n't he," said he finally in a little awe-struck voice. "A reg'lar jim-dandy." He thoughtfully poked one of the docile hands with his foot. "I wonner where he got'is stren'th from? I never seen a man do like that before. It was a funny thing. Well, he was a reg'lar jim-dandy."

The youth desired to screech out his grief. He was stabbed. But his tongue lay dead in the tomb of his mouth. He threw himself again upon the ground and began to brood.

The tattered man stood musing.

"Look-a-here, pardner," he said, after a time. He regarded the corpse as he spoke. "He's up an' gone, aint'e, an' we might as well begin t' look out fer ol' number one. This here thing is all over. He's up an' gone, aint'e? An' he's all right here. Nobody won't bother'im. An' I must say I aint enjoyin' any great health m'self these days."

The youth, awakened by the tattered soldier's tone, looked quickly up. He saw that he was swinging uncertainly on his legs and that his face had turned to a shade of blue.

"Good Lord," he cried, in fear, "you aint goin' t'—not you, too."

The tattered man waved his hand. "Nary die," he said. "All I want is some pea-soup an' a good bed. Some pea-soup," he repeated dreamfully.

The youth arose from the ground. "I wonder where he came from. I left him over there." He pointed. "An' now I find'im here. An' he was comin' from over there, too." He indicated a new direction. They both turned toward the body as if to ask of it a question.

"Well," at length spoke the tattered man, "there aint no use in our stayin' here an' tryin' t' ask him anything."

The youth nodded an assent, wearily. They both turned to gaze for a moment at the corpse.

The youth murmured something.

"Well, he was a jim-dandy, wa'n't'e?" said the tattered man as if in response.

They turned their backs upon it and started away. For a time, they stole softly, treading with their toes. It remained laughing there in the grass.

"I'm commencin' t' feel pretty bad," said the tattered man, suddenly breaking one of his little silences. "I'm commencin' t' feel pretty damn' bad."

The youth groaned. "Oh, Lord!" Was he to be the tortured witness of another grim encounter?

But his companion waved his hand re-assuringly. "Oh, I'm not goin' t' die yit. There too much dependin' on me fer me t' die yit. No, sir! Nary die! I *can't*! Ye'd oughta see th' swad a' chil'ren I've got, an' all like that."

The youth glancing at his companion could see by the shadow of a smile that he was making some kind of fun.

As they plodded on, the tattered soldier continued to talk. "Besides, if I died, I wouldn't die th' way that feller did. That was th' funniest thing. I'd jest flop down, I would. I never seen a feller die th' way that feller did.

"Yeh know, Tom Jamison, he lives next door t' me up home. He's a nice feller, he is, an' we was allus good friends. Smart, too. Smart as a steel trap. Well, when we was a-fightin' this atternoon, all-of-a-sudden, he begin t' rip up an' cuss an' beller at me. 'Yer shot, yeh blamed, infernal, tooty-tooty-tooty-too,' (he swear horrible) he ses t' me. I put up m' hand t' m' head an' when I looked at m' fingers, I seen, sure-'nough, I was shot. I give a holler an' begin t' run but b'fore I could git away, another one hit me in th' arm an' whirl' me clean 'round. I got dumb skeared when they was all a-shootin' b'hind me an' I run t' beat all, but I cotch it pretty bad. I've an idee I'd a' been fightin' yit, if t'wa'n't fer Tom Jamison."

Then he made a calm announcement. "There's two of 'em little ones—but they're beginnin' t' have fun with me now. I don't b'lieve I kin walk much furder."

They went slowly on in silence. "Yeh look pretty peek-ed yerself," said the tattered man at last. "I bet yeh've gota worser one than yeh think. Yed better take keer of yer hurt. It don't do t' let sech things go. It might be inside, mostly, an' them plays thunder. Where is it located?" But he continued his harangue without waiting for a reply. "I see a feller git hit plum in th' head when my reg'ment was a-standin' at ease onct. An' everybody yelled out t' 'im: 'Hurt, John? Are yeh hurt much?' 'No,' ses he. He looked kinder surprised an' he went on tellin' 'em how he felt. He sed he didn't feel nothin'. But, by dad, th' first thing that feller knowed he was dead. Yes, he was. Dead—stone dead. So, yeh wanta watch out. Yeh might have some queer kind 'a hurt yerself. Yeh can't never tell. Where is your'n located?"

The youth had been wriggling since the introduction of this topic. He now gave a cry of exasperation and made a furious motion with his hand. "Oh, don't bother me," he said. He was enraged against the tattered man and could have strangled him. Was his companion ever to play such an intolerable part? Was he ever going to up-raise the ghost of shame on the stick of his curiosity? He turned toward him as a man at bay. "Now, don't bother me," he repeated with desperate menace.

"Well, Lord knows I don't wanta bother anybody," said the tattered man. There was a little accent of despair in his voice as he replied. "Lord knows I've gota 'nough m'own t' tend to."

The youth, who had been holding a bitter debate with himself and casting glances of hate and contempt at the tattered man, here spoke in a hard voice. "Good-bye," he said.

The tattered man looked at him in gaping amazement. "Why—why, pardner, where yeh goin'," he asked unsteadily. The youth, looking at him, could see that he, too, like that other one, was beginning to act dumb and animal-like. His thoughts seemed to be floundering about in his head. "Now—now—look-a-here you Tom Jamison—now—I won't have this—this here won't do. Where—where yeh goin'?"

The youth pointed vaguely. "Over there," he replied.

"Well, now, look-a-here—now—" said the tattered man, rambling on in idiot-fashion. His head was hanging forward and his words were slurred. "This thing won't do, now, Tom Jamison. It won't do. I know yeh, yeh pig-headed devil. Yeh wanta go trompin' off with a bad hurt. It aint right—now—Tom Jamison—it aint. Yeh wanta leave me take keer of yeh, Tom Jamison. It aint—right —it aint—fer yeh t' go—trompin' off—with a bad hurt—it aint— aint—aint right—it aint."

In reply, the youth climbed a fence and started away. He could hear the tattered man bleating plaintively.

Once, he faced about angrily. "What?"

"Look-a-here, now, Tom Jamison—now—it aint—"

The youth went on. Turning at a distance he saw the tattered man wandering about helplessly in the fields.

He now thought that he wished he was dead. He believed that he envied those men whose bodies lay strewn over the grass of the fields and on the fallen leaves of the forest.

The simple questions of the tattered man had been knife-thrusts to him. They asserted a society that probes pitilessly at secrets until all is apparent. His late companion's chance persistency made him feel that he could not keep his crime concealed in his bosom. It was sure to be brought plain by one of those arrows which cloud the air and are constantly pricking, discovering, proclaiming those things which are willed to be forever hidden. He admitted that he could not defend himself against this agency. It was not within human vigilance.

Promptly, then, his old rebellious feelings returned. He thought the powers of fate had combined to heap misfortune upon him. He was an innocent victim.

He rebelled against the source of things, according to a law, perchance, that the most powerful shall receive the most blame.

War, he said bitterly to the sky, was a make-shift created because ordinary processes could not furnish deaths enough. Man had been born wary of the grey skeleton and had expended much of his intellect in erecting whatever safe-guards were possible, so that he had long been rather strongly intrenched behind the mass of his inventions. He kept an eye on his bath-tub, his fire-engine, his life-boat, and compelled . . . To seduce her victims, nature had to formulate a beautiful excuse. She made glory. This made the men willing, anxious, in haste, to come and be killed.

And, with heavy humor, he thought of how nature must smile when she saw the men come running. They regarding war-fire and courage as holy things did not see that nature had placed them in hearts because virtuous indignation would not last through a black struggle. Men would grow tired of it. They would go home.

They must be inspired by some sentiment that they could call sacred and enshrine in their heart, something that would cause them to regard slaughter as fine and go at it cheerfully; something that could destroy all the bindings of loves and places that tie men's hearts. She made glory.

From his pinnacle of wisdom, he regarded the armies as large collections of dupes. Nature's dupes, who were killing each other to carry out some great scheme of life. They were under the impression that they were fighting for principles and honor and homes and various things.

Well, to be sure; they were.

Nature was miraculously skilful in concocting excuses, he thought, with a heavy, theatrical contempt. It could deck a hideous creature in enticing apparel.

When he saw how she, as a woman beckons, had cozened him out of his home and hoodwinked him into wielding a rifle, he went into a rage.

He turned in tupenny fury upon the high, tranquil sky. He would have like to have splashed it with a derisive paint.

And he was bitter that among all men, he should be the only one sufficiently wise to understand these things.

XI

He became aware that the furnace-roar of the battle was growing louder. Great brown clouds had floated to the still heights of air before him. The noise, too, was approaching. The woods filtered men and the fields became dotted.

As he rounded a hillock, he perceived that the road-way was now a crying mass of wagons, teams and men. From the heaving tangle issued exhortations, commands, imprecations. Fear was sweeping it all along. The cracking whips bit and horses plunged and tugged. The white-topped wagons strained and stumbled in their exertions like fat sheep.

The youth felt comforted in a measure by this sight. They were all retreating. Perhaps, then, he was not so bad after all. He seated himself and watched the terror-stricken wagons. They fled like soft, ungainly animals. All the roarers and lashers served to help him to magnify the dangers and horrors of the engagement that he might try to prove to himself that the thing with which men could charge him was in truth a symmetrical act. There was an amount of pleasure to him in watching the wild march of this vindication.

Presently, the calm head of a forward-going column of infantry appeared in the road. It came swiftly on. Avoiding the obstructions gave it the sinuous movement of a serpent. The men at the head butted mules with their musket-stocks. They prodded teamsters, indifferent to all howls. The men forced their way through parts of the dense mass by strength. The blunt head of the column pushed. The raving teamsters swore many strange oaths.

The commands to make way had the ring of a great importance in them. The men were going forward to the heart of the din. They were to confront the eager rush of the enemy. They felt the pride of their onward movement when the remainder of the army seemed trying to dribble down this road. They tumbled teams about with a fine feeling that it was no matter so long as their column got to the front in time. This importance made their faces grave and stern. And the backs of the officers were very rigid.

As the youth looked at them, the black weight of his woe returned to him. He felt that he was regarding a procession of chosen beings. The separation was as great to him as if they had marched with weapons of flame and banners of sun-light. He could never be like them. He could have wept in his longings.

He searched about in his mind then for an adequate malediction for the indefinite cause, the thing upon which men turn the words of final blame. It—whatever it was—was responsible for him, he said. There lay the fault.

The haste of the column to reach the battle seemed to the forlorn young man to be something much finer than stout fighting. Heroes, he thought, could find excuses in that long seething lane. They could retire with perfect self-respect and make excuses to the stars.

He wondered what those men had eaten that they could be in such haste to force their way to grim chances of death. As he watched his envy grew until he thought that he wished to change lives with one of them. He would have like to have used a tremendous force, he said, throw off himself and become a better. Swift pictures of himself, apart, yet in himself came to him—a blue desperate figure leading lurid charges with one knee forward and a broken blade high—a blue, determined figure standing before a crimson and steel assault, getting calmly killed on a high place before the eyes of all. He thought of the magnificent pathos of his dead body.

These thoughts up-lifted him. He felt the quiver of war-desire. In his ears, he heard the ring of victory. He knew the frenzy of a rapid successful charge. The music of the trampling feet, the sharp voices, the clanking arms of the column near him made him soar on the red wings of war. For a few moments, he was sublime.

He thought that he was about to start fleetly for the front. Indeed, he saw a picture of himself, dust-stained, haggard, panting, flying to the front at the proper moment to seize and throttle the dark, leering witch of calamity.

Then the difficulties of the thing began to drag at him. He hesitated, balancing awkwardly on one foot.

He had no rifle; he could not fight with his hands, said he, resentfully to his plan. Well, rifles could be had for the picking. They were extraordinarily profuse.

Also, he continued, it would be a miracle if he found his regiment. Well, he could fight with any regiment.

He started forward slowly. He stepped as if he expected to tread upon some explosive thing. Doubts and he were struggling.

He would truly be a worm if any of his comrades should see him returning thus, the marks of his flight upon him. There was a reply that the intent fighters did not care for what happened rear-ward saving that no hostile bayonets appeared there. In the battle-blur his face would, in a way, be hidden like the face of a cowled man.

But then, he said, that his tireless fate would bring forth, when the strife lulled for a moment, a man to ask of him an explanation. In imagination he felt the scrutiny of his companions as he painfully labored through some lies.

Eventually, his courage expended itself upon these objections. The debates drained him of his fire.

He was not cast-down by this defeat of his plan, for, upon studying the affair carefully, he could not but admit that the objections were very formidable.

Furthermore, various ailments had begun to cry out. In their presence, he could not persist in flying high with the red wings of war; they rendered it almost impossible for him to see himself in a heroic light. He tumbled headlong.

He discovered that he had a scorching thirst. His face was so dry and grimy that he thought he could feel his skin crackle. Each bone of his body had an ache in it and seemingly threatened to break with each movement. His feet were like two sores. Also, his body was calling for food. It was more powerful than a direct hunger. There was a dull, weight-like feeling in his stomach and when he tried to walk, his head swayed and he tottered. He could not see with distinctness. Small patches of crimson mist floated before his vision.

While he had been tossed by many emotions, he had not been aware of ailments. Now they beset him and made clamor. As he was at last compelled to pay attention to them, his capacity for self-hate was multiplied. In despair, he declared that he was not like those others. He now conceded it to be impossible that he should ever become a hero. He was a craven loon. Those pictures of glory were piteous things. He groaned from his heart and went staggering off.

A certain moth-like quality within him kept him in the vicinity of the battle. He had a great desire to see, and to get news. He wished to know who was winning.

He told himself that, despite his unprecedented suffering, he had never lost his greed for a victory, yet, he said, in a half-apologetic manner to his conscience, he could not but know that a defeat for the army this time might mean many favorable things for him. The blows of the enemy would splinter regiments into fragments. Thus, many men of courage, he considered, would be obliged to desert the colors and scurry like chickens. He would appear as one of them. They would be sullen brothers in distress and he could then easily believe he had not run any further or faster than they. And if he himself could believe in his virtuous perfection, he conceived that there would be small trouble in convincing all others.

He said, as if in excuse for this hope, that previously the army had encountered great defeats and in a few months had shaken off all blood and tradition of them, emerging as bright and valiant as a new one; thrusting out of sight the memory of disaster and appearing with the valor and confidence of unconquered legions. The shrilling voices of the people at home would pipe dismally for a time but various generals were usually compelled to listen to these sad ditties. He of course felt no compunctions for proposing a general as a sacrifice. He could not tell who the chosen for the barbs might be, so he could centre no direct sympathy upon him. The people were afar and he did not conceive public opinion to be accurate at long range. It was quite probable they would hit the wrong man who after he had recovered from his amazement would perhaps spend the rest of his days in writing replies to the songs of his alleged failure. It would be very unfortunate, no doubt, but in this case, a general was of no consequence to the youth.

In a defeat there would be a roundabout vindication of himself.

He thought it would prove, in a manner, that he had fled early because of his superior powers of perception. A serious prophet, upon predicting a flood, should be the first man to climb a tree. This would demonstrate that he was indeed a seer.

A moral vindication was regarded by the youth as a very important thing. Without salve, he could not, he thought, wear the sore badge of his dishonor through life. With his heart continually assuring him that he was despicable, he could not exist without making it, through his actions, apparent to all men.

If the army had gone gloriously on, he would be lost. If the din meant that now his army's flags were tilted forward he was a condemned wretch. He would be compelled to doom himself to isolation. If the men were advancing, their indifferent feet were trampling upon his chances for a successful life.

As these thoughts went rapidly through his mind, he turned upon them and tried to thrust them away. He denounced himself as a villain. He said that he was the most unutterably selfish man in existence. His mind pictured the soldiers who would place their defiant bodies before the spear of the yelling battle-fiend and as he saw their dripping corpses on an imagined field, he said that he was their murderer.

Again he thought that he wished he was dead. He believed that he envied a corpse. Thinking of the slain, he achieved a great contempt for some of them as if they were guilty for thus becoming lifeless. They might have been killed by lucky chances, he said, before they had had opportunities to flee or before they had been really tested. Yet they would receive laurels from tradition. He cried out bitterly that their crowns were stolen and their robes of glorious memories were shams. However, he still said that it was a great pity he was not as they.

A defeat of the army had suggested itself to him as a means of escape from the consequences of his fall. He considered, now, however, that it was useless to think of such a possibility. His education had been that success for that mighty blue machine was certain; that it would make victories as a contrivance turns out buttons. He presently discarded all his speculations in the other direction. He returned to the creed of soldiers.

When he perceived again that it was not possible for the army to be defeated, he tried to be-think him of a fine tale which he could take back to his regiment and with it turn the expected shafts of derision.

But, as he mortally feared these shafts, it became impossible for him to invent a tale which he felt he could trust. He experimented with many schemes but threw them aside one by one as flimsy. He was quick to see vulnerable places in them all.

Furthermore, he was much afraid that some arrow of scorn might lay him mentally low before he could raise his protecting tale.

He imagined the whole regiment saying: "Where's Henry Fleming? He run, didn't'e? Oh, my!" He recalled various persons who would be quite sure to leave him no peace about it. They would doubtless question him with sneers and laugh at his stammering hesitation. In the next engagement they would try to keep watch of him to discover when he would run.

Wherever he went in camp, he would encounter insolent and lingeringly-cruel stares. As he imagined himself passing near a crowd of comrades, he could hear some one say: "There he goes!"

Then, as if the heads were moved by one muscle, all the faces were turned toward him with wide, derisive grins. He seemed to hear some one make a humorous remark in a low tone. At it, the others all crowed and cackled. He was a slang-phrase.

XII

It was always clear to the youth that he was entirely different from other men; that his mind had been cast in a unique mold. Hence laws that might be just to the ordinary man, were, when applied to him, peculiar and galling outrages. Minds, he said, were not made all with one stamp and colored green. He was of no general pattern. It was not right to measure his acts by a world-wide standard. The laws of the world were wrong because through the vain spectacles of their makers, he appeared, with all men, as of a common size and of a green color. There was no justice on the earth when justice was meant. Men were too puny and prattling to know anything of it. If there was a justice, it must be in the hands of a God.

He regarded his sufferings as unprecedented. No man had ever achieved such misery. There was a melancholy grandeur in the isolation of his experiences. He saw that he was a speck raising his minute arms against all possible forces and fates which were swelling down upon him in black tempests. He could derive some consolation from viewing the sublimity of the odds.

As he went on, he began to feel that nature, for her part, would not blame him for his rebellion. He still distinctly felt that he was arrayed against the universe but he believed now that there was no malice in the vast breasts of his space-filling foes. It was merely law, not merciful to the individual; but just, to a system. Nature had provided the creations with various defenses and ways of escape that they might fight or flee, and she had limited dangers in powers of attack and pursuit that the things might resist or hide with a security proportionate to their strength and wisdom. It was cruel but it was war. Nature fought for her system; individuals fought for liberty to breathe. The animals had the privilege of using their legs and their brains. It was all the same old philosophy. He could not omit a small grunt of satisfaction as he saw with what brilliancy he had reasoned it out.

He now said that, if, as he supposed, his life was being relentlessly pursued, it was not his duty to bow to the approaching death. Nature did not expect submission. On the contrary, it was his business to kick and bite and give blows as a stripling in the hands of a murderer. The law was that he should fight. He would be saved according to the importance of his strength.

His egotism made him feel safe, for a time, from the iron hands.

It being in his mind that he had solved these matters, he eagerly applied his findings to the incident of his flight from the battle. It was not a fault, a shameful thing; it was an act obedient to a law. It was—

But he was aware that when he had erected a vindicating structure of great principles, it was the calm toes of tradition that kicked it all down about his ears. He immediately antagonized then this devotion to the by-gone; this universal adoration of the past. From the bitter pinnacle of his wisdom he saw that mankind not only worshipped the gods of the ashes but that the gods of the ashes were worshipped because they were the gods of the ashes. He perceived with anger the present state of affairs in its bearing upon his case. And he resolved to reform it all.

He had, presently, a feeling that he was the growing prophet of a world-reconstruction. Far down in the untouched depths of his being, among the hidden currents of his soul, he saw born a voice. He conceived a new world modelled by the pain of his life, and in which no old shadows fell blighting upon the temple of thought. And there were many personal advantages in it.

• • •

He thought for a time of piercing orations starting multitudes and of books wrung from his heart. In the gloom of his misery, his eyesight proclaimed that mankind were bowing to wrong and ridiculous idols. He said that if some all-powerful joker should take them away in the night, and leave only manufactured shadows falling upon the bended heads, mankind would go on counting the hollow beads of their progress until the shriveling of the fingers. He was a-blaze with desire to change. He saw himself, a sun-lit figure upon a peak, pointing with true and unchangeable gesture. "There!" And all men could see and no man would falter.

Gradually the idea grew upon him that the cattle which cluttered the earth, would, in their ignorance and calm faith in the next day, blunder stolidly on and he would be beating his fists against the brass of accepted things. A remarkable facility for abuse came to him then and in supreme disgust and rage, he railed. To him there was something terrible and awesome in these words spoken from his heart to his heart. He was very tragic.

. . .

He saw himself chasing a thought-phantom across the sky before the assembled eyes of mankind. He could say to them that it was an angel whose possession was existence perfected; they would declare it to be a greased pig. He had no desire to devote his life to proclaiming the angel, when he could plainly perceive that mankind would hold, from generation to generation, to the theory of the greased pig.

It would be pleasure to reform a docile race. But he saw that there were none and he did not intend to raise his voice against the hooting of continents.

Thus he abandoned the world to its devices. He felt that many men must have so abandoned it, but he saw how they could be reconciled to it and agree to accept the stone idols and the greased pigs, when they contemplated the opportunities for plunder.

For himself, however, he saw no salve, no reconciling opportunities. He was entangled in the errors. He began to rage anew against circumstances which he did not name and against processes of which he knew only the name. He felt that he was being grinded beneath stone feet which he despised. The detached bits of truth which formed the knowledge of the world could not save him. There was a dreadful, unwritten martyrdom in his state.

He made a little search for some thing upon which to concentrate the hate of his despair; he fumbled in his mangled intellect to find the Great Responsibility.

He again hit upon nature. He again saw her grim dogs upon his trail. They were unswerving, merciless and would overtake him at the appointed time. His mind pictured the death of Jim Conklin and in the scene, he saw the shadows of his fate. Dread words had been said from star to star. An event had been penned by the implacable forces.

He was of the unfit, then. He did not come into the scheme of further life. His tiny part had been done and he must go. There was no room for him. On all the vast lands there was not a foot-hold. He must be thrust out to make room for the more important.

Regarding himself as one of the unfit, he believed that nothing could exceed for misery, a perception of this fact. He thought that he measured with his falling heart, tossed in like a pebble by his supreme and awful foe, the most profound depths of pain. It was a barbarous process with affection for the man and the oak, and no sympathy for the rabbit and the weed. He thought of his own capacity for pity and there was an infinite irony in it.

He desired to revenge himself upon the universe. Feeling in his body all spears of pain, he would have capsized, if possible, the world and made chaos. Much cruelty lay in the fact that he was a babe.

Admitting that he was powerless and at the will of law, he yet planned to escape; menaced by fatality he schemed to avoid it. He thought of various places in the world where he imagined that he would be safe. He remembered hiding once in an empty flour-barrel that sat in his mother's pantry. His playmates, hunting the bandit-chief, had thundered on the barrel with their fierce sticks but he had lain snug and undetected. They had searched the house. He now created in thought a secure spot where an all-powerful eye would fail to perceive him; where an all-powerful stick would fail to bruise his life.

There was in him a creed of freedom which no contemplation of inexorable law could destroy. He saw himself living in watchfulness, frustrating the plans of the unchangeable, making of fate a fool. He had ways, he thought, of working out his

* * *

XIII

The column that had butted stoutly at the obstacles in the road-way was barely out of the youth's sight before he saw dark waves of men come sweeping out of the woods and down through the fields. He knew at once that the steel fibres had been washed from their hearts. They were bursting from their coats and their equipments as from entanglements. They charged down upon him like terrified buffaloes.

Behind them, blue smoke curled and clouded above the tree-tops and through the thickets he could sometimes see a distant pink glare. The voices of the cannon were clamoring in interminable chorus.

The youth was horror-stricken. He stared in agony and amazement. He forgot that he was engaged in combating the universe. He threw aside his mental pamphlets on the philosophy of the retreated and rules for the guidance of the doomed. He lost concern for himself.

The fight was lost. The dragons were coming with invincible strides. The army, helpless in the matted thickets, and blinded by the overhanging night, was going to be swallowed. War, the red animal, war, the blood-swollen god, would have bloated fill.

Within him, something bade to cry out. He had the impulse to make a rallying speech, to sing a battle-hymn but he could only get his tongue to call into the air: "Why—why—what—what's th' matter?"

Soon he was in the midst of them. They were leaping and scamp-ering all about him. Their blanched faces shone in the dusk. They seemed, for the most part, to be very burly men. The youth turned from one to another of them as they galloped along. His incoherent questions were lost. They were heedless of his appeals. They did not seem to see him.

They sometimes gabbled insanely. One huge man was asking of the sky: "Say, where de plank-road? Where de plank-road." It was as if he had lost a child. He wept in his pain and dismay.

Presently, men were running hither and thither, in all ways. The artillery booming, forward, rearward, and on the flanks made jumble of ideas of direction. Landmarks had vanished into the gathered gloom. The youth began to imagine that he had gotten into the centre of the tremendous quarrel and he could perceive no way out of it. From the mouths of the fleeing men came a thousand wild questions but no one made answers.

The youth, after rushing about and throwing interrogations at the heedless bands of retreating infantry, finally clutched a man by the arm. They swung around face to face.

"Why—why—" stammered the youth struggling with his balking tongue.

The man screamed. "Letgo me! Letgo me!" His face was livid and his eyes were rolling uncontrolled. He was heaving and panting. He still grasped his rifle, perhaps having forgotten to release his hold upon it. He tugged frantically and the youth being compelled to lean forward was dragged several paces.

"Letgo me! Letgo me!"

"Why—why—" stuttered the youth.

"Well, then—" bawled the man in a lurid rage. He adroitly and fiercely swung his rifle. It crushed upon the youth's head. The man ran on.

The youth's fingers had turned to paste upon the other's arm. The energy was smitten from his muscles. He saw the flaming wings of lightning flash before his vision. There was a deafening rumble of thunder within his head.

Suddenly his legs seemed to die. He sank writhing to the ground. He tried to arise. In his efforts against the numbing pain he was like a man wrestling with a creature of the air.

There was a sinister struggle.

Sometimes, he would achieve a position half-erect, battle with the air for a moment, and then fall again, grabbing at the grass. His face was of a clammy pallor. Deep groans were wrenched from him.

At last, with a twisting movement, he got upon his hands and knees and from thence, like a babe trying to walk, to his feet. Press-ing his hands to his temples, he went lurching over the grass.

He fought an intense battle with his body. His dulled senses wished him to swoon and he opposed them stubbornly, his mind portraying unknown dangers and mutilations if he should fall upon the field. He went, tall soldier-fashion. He imagined secluded spots where he could fall and be unmolested. To reach one, he strove against the tide of his pain.

Once, he put his hand to the top of his head and timidly touched the wound. The scratching pain of the contact made him draw a long breath through his clenched teeth. His fingers were dabbled with blood. He regarded them with a fixed stare.

Around him, he could hear the grumble of jolted cannon as the scurrying horses were lashed toward the front. Once, a young officer on a be-splashed charger nearly ran him down. He turned and watched the mass of guns, men and horses sweeping in a wide curve toward a gap in a fence. The officer was making excited motions with a gauntleted hand. The guns followed the teams with an air of unwillingness of being dragged by the heels.

Some officers of the scattered infantry were cursing and railing like fish-wives. Their scolding voices could be heard above the din. Into the unspeakable jumble in the road-way, rode a squadron of cavalry. The faded yellow of their facings shone bravely. There was a mighty altercation.

The artillery were assembling as if for a conference.

The blue haze of evening was upon the fields. The lines of forest were long purple shadows. One cloud lay along the western sky partly smothering the red.

As the youth left the scene behind him, he heard the guns suddenly roar out. He imagined them shaking in black rage. They belched and roared like brass devils guarding a gate. The soft air was filled with the tremendous remonstrance. With it came the shattering peal of opposing infantry. Turning to look behind him, he could see sheets of orange light illumine the shadowy distance. There were subtle and sudden lightnings in the far air. At times, he thought he could see heaving masses of men.

He hurried on in the dusk. The day had faded until he could barely distinguish place for his feet. The purple darkness was filled with men who lectured and jabbered. Sometimes, he could see them gesticulating against the blue and sombre sky. There seemed to be a great ruck of men and munitions spread about in the forest and in the fields. The little narrow road-way now lay, lifeless. There were over-turned wagons like sun-dried boulders. The bed of the former torrent was choked with the bodies of horses and splintered parts of war-machines.

It had come to pass that his wound pained him but little. He was afraid to move rapidly, however, for a dread of disturbing it. He held his head very still and took many precautions against stumbling. He was filled with anxiety and his face was pinched and drawn in anticipation of the pain of any sudden mistake of his feet in the gloom.

His thoughts, as he walked, fixed intently upon his hurt. There was a cool, liquid feeling about it and he imagined blood moving slowly down under his hair. His head seemed swollen to a size that made him think his neck to be inadequate.

The new silence of his wound made much worriment. The little, blistering voices of pain that had called out from his scalp, were, he thought, definite in their expression of danger. By them, he believed that he could measure his plight. But when they remained ominously silent, he became frightened and imagined terrible fingers that clutched into his brain.

Amidst it, he began to reflect upon various incidents and conditions of the past. He bethought him of certain meals his mother had cooked at home, in which those dishes of which he was particularly fond had occupied prominent positions. He saw the spread table. The pine walls of the kitchen were glowing in the warm light from the stove. Too, he remembered how he and his companions used to go from the school-house to the bank of a shaded pool. He saw his clothes in disorderly array upon the grass of the bank. He felt the swash of the fragrant water upon his body. The leaves of the over-hanging maple rustled with melody in the wind of youthful summer.

He was over-come presently by a dragging weariness. His head hung forward and his shoulders were stooped as if he were bearing a great bundle. His feet shuffled along the ground.

He held continuous arguments as to whether he should lie down and sleep at some near spot, or force himself on until he reached a certain haven. He often tried to dismiss the question but his body persisted in rebellion and his senses nagged at him like pampered babies.

At last, he heard a cheery voice near his shoulder. "Yeh seem t' be in a pretty bad way, boy?"

The youth did not look up but he assented with thick tongue. "Uh."

The owner of the cheery voice took him firmly by the arm. "Well," he said, with a round laugh, "I'm goin' your way. Th' hull gang is goin' your way. An' I guess I kin give yeh a lift." They began to walk like a drunken man and his friend.

As they went along, the man questioned the youth and assisted him with the replies like one manipulating the mind of a child. Sometimes he interjected anecdotes. "What reg'ment do yeh b'long teh? Eh? What's that? Th' 304th N'York? Why, what corps is that

in? Oh, it is? Why, I thought they wasn't engaged t'-day—they're
'way over in th' centre. Oh, they was, eh? Well, pretty nearly everybody got their share 'a fightin' t'-day. By dad, I give myself up fer
dead any number 'a times. There was shootin' here an' shootin'
there, an' hollerin' here an' hollerin' there, in th' damn' darkness,
until I couldn't tell t' save m' soul which side I was on. Sometimes
I thought I was sure-'nough from Ohier an' other times I could 'a
swore I was from th' bitter end of Florida. It was th' most mixed up
dern thing I ever see. An' these here hull woods is a reg'lar mess.
It'll be a miracle if we find our reg'ments t'-night. Pretty soon,
though, we'll meet a-plenty of guards an' provost-guards an' one
thing an' another. Ho, there they go with an off'cer, I guess. Look
at his hand a-draggin'. He's got all th' war he wants, I bet. He
won't be talkin' so big about his reputation an' all, when they go t'
sawin' off his leg. Poor feller. My brother's got whiskers jest that
color. How did yeh git 'way over here anyhow? Your reg'ment is a
long way from here, aint it? Well, I guess we can find it. Yeh know,
there was a boy killed in my comp'ny t'-day that I thought th'
world an' all of. Jack was a nice feller. By ginger, it hurt like thunder t' see ol' Jack jest git knocked flat. We was a-standin' purty
peaceable fer a spell, 'though there was men runnin' ev'ry way all
'round us, an' while we was a-standin' like that, 'long come a big fat
feller. He began t' peck at Jack's elbow an' he ses: 'Say, where's th'
road t' th' river?' An' Jack, he never paid no attention an' th' feller
kept on a-peckin' at his elbow an' sayin': 'Say, where's th' road t'
th' river?' Jack was a-lookin' ahead all th' time tryin' t' see th' Johnnies comin' through th' woods an' he never paid no attention t' this
big fat feller fer a long time but at last he turned 'round an' he ses:
'Ah, go t' hell an' find th' road t' th' river.' An' jest then a shot
slapped him bang on th' side th' head. He was a serjeant, too.
Them was his last words. Thunder, I wish we was sure 'a findin' our
reg'ments t'-night. It's goin' t' be long huntin'. But I guess we kin
do it."

In the search which followed, the man of the cheery voice
seemed, to the youth, to possess a wand of a magic kind. He
threaded the mazes of the tangled forest with a strange fortune. In
encounters with guards and patrols he displayed the keenness of a
detective and the valor of a gamin.[1] Obstacles fell before him and
became of assistance. The youth with his chin still on his breast
stood woodenly by while his companion beat ways and means out
of sullen things.

The forest seemed a vast hive of men buzzing about in frantic
circles but the cheery man conducted the youth without mistakes,

---

1. A neglected street urchin who has acquired an intuitive wisdom for means of survival.

until at last he began to chuckle with glee and self-satisfaction. "Ah, there yeh are! See that fire!"

The youth nodded stupidly.

"Well, there's where your reg'ment is. An', now, good-bye, ol' boy, good luck t' yeh."

A warm and strong hand clasped the youth's languid fingers for an instant, and then he heard a cheerful and audacious whistling, as the man strided away. As he who so be-friended him was thus passing out of his life, it suddenly occurred to the youth that he had not once seen his face.

XIV

The youth went slowly toward the fire indicated by his departed friend. As he reeled, he bethought him of the welcome his comrades would give him. He had a conviction that he would soon feel in his sore heart the barbed missiles of ridicule. He had no strength to invent a tale; he would be a soft target.

He made vague plans to go off into the deeper darkness and hide, but they were all destroyed by the voices of exhaustion and pain from his body. His ailments, clamoring, forced him to seek the place of food and rest, at whatever cost.

He swung unsteadily toward the fire. He could see the forms of men throwing black shadows in the red light and as he went nearer, it became known to him in some way, that the ground was strewn with sleeping men.

Of a sudden, he confronted a black and monstrous figure. A rifle-barrel caught some glinting beams. "Halt—halt." He was dismayed for a moment but he presently thought that he recognized the nervous voice. As he stood tottering before the rifle-barrel, he called out: "Why, hello, Wilson, you—you here?"

The rifle was lowered to a position of caution and the loud soldier came slowly forward. He peered into the youth's face. "That you, Henry?"

"Yes, it's—it's me."

"Well, well, ol' boy," said the other, "by ginger, I'm glad t' see yeh. I give yeh up fer a goner. I thought yeh was dead sure-enough." There was husky emotion in his voice.

The youth found that now he could barely stand upon his feet. There was a sudden sinking of his forces. He thought he must hasten to produce his tale to protect him from the missiles already at the lips of his redoubtable comrade. So staggering before the loud soldier he began. "Yes, yes. I've—I've had an awful time. I've been all over. 'Way over on th' right. Ter'ble fightin' over there. I had an awful time. I got separated from th' reg'ment. Over on th' right, I got shot. In th' head. I never see sech fightin'. Awful time. I don't see how I could 'a got separated from th' reg'ment. I got shot, too."

His friend had stepped forward quickly. "What? Got shot? Why didn't yeh say so first? Poor ol' boy, we must—hol' on a minnit; what am I doin'. I'll call Simpson."

Another figure at that moment loomed in the gloom. They could see that it was the corporal. "Who yeh talkin' to, Wilson?" he demanded. His voice was anger-toned. "Who yeh talkin' to? Yer th' derndest sentinel—why—hello, Henry, you here? Why, I thought you was dead four hours ago. Great Jerusalem, they keep turnin' up every ten minutes or so. We thought we'd lost forty-two men by straight count but if they keep on a-comin' this way, we'll git th' comp'ny all back by mornin' yit—where was yeh?"

"Over on th' right. I got separated—" began the youth with considerable glibness.

But his friend had interrupted hastily. "Yes, an' he got shot in th' head an' he's in a fix an' we must see t' him right away." He rested his rifle in the hollow of his left arm and his right around the youth's shoulder.

"Gee, it must hurt like thunder," he said.

The youth leaned heavily upon his friend. "Yes, it hurts—hurts a good deal," he replied. There was a faltering in his voice.

"Oh," said the corporal. He linked his arm in the youth's and drew him forward. "Come on, Henry. I'll take keer 'a yeh."

As they went on together, the loud private called out after them. "Put'im t' sleep in my blanket, Simpson. An'—hol' on a minnit—here's my canteen. It's full 'a coffee. Look at his head by th' fire an' see how it looks. Maybe it's a pretty bad un. When I git relieved in a couple 'a minnits, I'll be over an' see t' him."

The youth's senses were so deadened that his friend's voice sounded from afar and he could scarcely feel the pressure of the corporal's arm. He submitted passively to the latter's directing strength. His head was in the old manner hanging forward upon his breast. His knees wobbled.

The corporal led him into the glare of the fire. "Now, Henry," he said, "let's have look at yer ol' head."

The youth sat down obediently and the corporal, laying down his rifle began to fumble in the bushy hair of his comrade. He was obliged to turn the other's head so that the full flush of the firelight would beam upon it. He puckered his mouth with a critical air. He drew back his lips and whistled through his teeth when his fingers came in contact with the splashed blood and the rare wound.

"Ah, here we are," he said. He awkwardly made further investigations. "Jest as I thought," he added, presently. "Yeh've been grazed by a ball. It's raised a queer lump jest as if some feller had lammed yeh on th' head with a club. It stopped a-bleedin' long time ago. Th' most about it is that in th' mornin', yeh'll feel that a number-ten hat wouldn't fit yeh. An' your head'll be all het up an' feel as dry as burnt pork. An' yeh may git a lot 'a other sicknesses, too, by mornin'. Yeh can't never tell. Still, I don't much think so. It's jest a damn' good belt on th' head an' nothin' more. Now, you jest sit here an' don't move, while I go rout out th' relief. Then I'll send Wilson t' take keer 'a yeh."

The corporal went away. The youth remained on the ground like a parcel. He stared with a vacant look into the fire.

After a time, he aroused, for some part, and the things about him began to take form. He saw that ground in the deep shadows was cluttered with men, sprawling in every conceivable posture. Glancing narrowly into the more distant darkness, he caught occasional glimpses of visages that loomed pallid and ghostly, lit with a phosphorescent glow. These faces expressed in their lines the deep stupor of the tired soldiers. They made them appear like men drunk with wine. This bit of forest might have appeared to an ethereal wanderer as a scene of the result of some frightful debauch.

On the other side of the fire, the youth observed an officer asleep, seated bolt up-right with his back against a tree. There was something perilous in his position. Badgered by dreams, perhaps, he swayed with little bounces and starts like an old, toddy-stricken grandfather in a chimney corner. Dust and stains were upon his face. His lower jaw hung down as if lacking strength to assume its normal position. He was the picture of an exhausted soldier after a feast of war.

He had evidently gone to sleep with his sword in his arms. These two had slumbered in an embrace. But the weapon had been allowed, in time, to fall unheeded to the ground. The brass-mounted hilt lay in contact with some parts of the fire.

Within the gleam of rose and orange light from the burning sticks were other soldiers, snoring and heaving, or lying death-like in slumber. A few pairs of legs were stuck forth, rigid and straight. The shoes displayed the mud or dust of marches, and bits of rounded trousers, protruding from the blankets, showed rents and tears from hurried pitchings through the dense brambles.

The fire crackled musically. From it swelled light smoke. Overhead, the foliage moved softly. The leaves with their faces turned toward the blaze, were colored shifting hues of silver, often edged with red. Far off to the right, through a window in the forest could be seen a handful of stars laying, like glittering pebbles, on the black level of the night.

Occasionally, in this low-arched hall, a soldier would arouse and turn his body to a new position, the experience of his sleep having taught him of uneven and objectionable places upon the ground under him. Or, perhaps, he would lift himself to a sitting posture, blink at the fire for an unintelligent moment, throw a swift glance at his prostrate companion and then cuddle down again with a grunt of sleepy content.

The youth sat in a forlorn heap until his friend, the loud young soldier, came, swinging two canteens by their light strings. "Well, now, Henry, ol' boy," said the latter, "we'll have yeh fixed up in jest about a minnit."

He had the bustling ways of an amateur nurse. He fussed around the fire and stirred the sticks to brilliant exertions. He made his patient drink largely from the canteen that contained the coffee. It was to the youth a delicious draught. He tilted his head afar back and held the canteen long to his lips. The cool mixture went caressingly down his blistered throat. Having finished, he sighed with comfortable delight.

The loud young soldier watched his comrade with an air of satisfaction. He, later, produced an extensive handkerchief from his pocket. He folded it into a manner of bandage and soused water from the other canteen upon the middle of it. This crude arrangement he bound over the youth's head, tying the ends in a queer knot at the back of the neck.

"There," he said, moving off and surveying his deed, "yeh look like th' devil but I bet yeh feel better."

The youth looked at his friend with grateful eyes. Upon his aching and swelling head, the cold cloth was like a tender woman's hand.

"Yeh don't holler ner say nothin'," remarked his friend, approvingly. "I know I'm a blacksmith at takin' keer 'a sick folks an' yeh never squeaked. Yer a good un, Henry. Most 'a men would 'a been in th' hospital long ago. A shot in th' head aint foolin' business."

The youth made no reply but began to fumble with the buttons of his jacket.

"Well, come, now," continued his friend, "come on. I must put yeh t' bed an' see that yeh git a good night's rest."

The other got carefully erect and the loud young soldier led him among the sleeping forms lying in groups and rows. Presently he stooped and picked up his blankets. He spread the rubber one upon the ground and placed the woolen one about the youth's shoulders.

"There now," he said, "lie down an' git some sleep."

The youth with his manner of dog-like obedience got carefully down like a crone stooping. He stretched out with a murmur of relief and comfort. The ground felt like the softest couch.

But of a sudden, he ejaculated. "Hol' on a minnit. Where you goin' t' sleep?"

His friend waved his hand impatiently. "Right down there by yeh."

"Well, but hol' on a minnit," continued the youth. "What yeh goin' t' sleep in? I've got your—"

The loud young soldier snarled. "Shet up an' go on t' sleep. Don't be makin' a damn' fool 'a yerself," he said, severely.

After this reproof, the youth said no more. An exquisite drowsiness had spread through him. The warm comfort of the blanket enveloped him and made a gentle languor. His head fell forward on his crooked arm and his weighted lids went softly down over his eyes. Hearing a splatter of musketry from the distance, he wondered indifferently if those men sometimes slept. He gave a long sigh, snuggled down into his blanket and in a moment, was like his comrades.

XV

When the youth awoke, it seemed to him that he had been asleep for a thousand years and he felt sure that he opened his eyes upon an unexpected world. Grey mists were slowly shifting before the first efforts of the sun-rays. An impending splendor could be seen in the eastern sky. An icy dew had chilled his face and immediately upon arousing he curled further down into his blanket. He stared, for a while, at the leaves over-head, moving in a heraldic wind of the day.

The distance was splintering and blaring with the noise of fighting. There was in the sound, an expression of a deadly persistency as if it had not began and was not to cease.

About him, were the rows and groups of men that he had dimly seen the previous night. They were getting a last draught of sleep before the awakening. The gaunt, care-worn faces and dusty figures were made plain by this quaint light at the dawning but it dressed the skin of the men in corpse-like hues and made the tangled limbs appear pulseless and dead. The youth started up with a little cry when his eyes first swept over this motionless mass of men, thick-spread upon the ground, pallid and in strange postures. His disordered mind interpreted the hall of the forest as a charnel place. He believed for an instant that he was in the house of the dead and he did not dare to move lest these corpses start up, squalling and squawking. In a second, however, he achieved his proper mind. He swore a complicated oath at himself. He saw that this sombre picture was not a fact of the present, but a mere prophecy.

He heard then the noise of a fire crackling briskly in the cold air and turning his head, he saw his friend pottering busily about a small blaze. A few other figures moved in the fog and he heard the hard cracking of axe-blows.

Suddenly, there was a hollow rumble of drums. A distant bugle sang faintly. Similar sounds, varying in strength, came from near and far over the forest. The bugles called to each other like brazen game-cocks. The near thunder of the regimental drums rolled.

The body of men in the woods rustled. There was a general uplifting of heads. A murmuring of voices broke upon the air. In it there was much bass of grumbling oaths. Strange gods were addressed in condemnation of the early hours necessary to correct war. An officer's peremptory tenor rang out and quickened the stiffened movement of the men. The tangled limbs unravelled. The corpse-hued faces were hidden behind fists that twisted slowly in eye-sockets. It was the soldier's bath.

The youth sat up and gave vent to an enormous yawn. "Thunder," he remarked, petulantly. He rubbed his eyes and then putting up his hand felt carefully of the bandage over his wound. His friend, perceiving him to be awake, came from the fire. "Well, Henry, ol' man, how do yeh feel this mornin'," he demanded.

The youth yawned again. Then he puckered his mouth to a bitter pucker. His head in truth felt precisely like a melon and there was an unpleasant sensation at his stomach.

"Oh, Lord, I feel pretty bad," he said.

"Thunder," exclaimed the other, "I hoped yed feel all right this mornin'. Let's see th' bandage—I guess it's slipped." He began to tinker at the wound in rather a clumsy way until suddenly the youth exploded.

"Gosh-dern it," he said in sharp irritation, "you're th' hangest man I ever see. You wear muffs on yer hands. Why in good-thunderation can't yeh be more easy. I'd rather yed stand off an' throw guns at it. Now, go slow, an' don't act as if yeh was nailin' down carpet."

He glared with insolent command at his friend but the latter answered soothingly. "Well, well, come now, an' git some grub," he said. "Then, maybe, yeh'll feel better."

At the fire-side, the loud young soldier watched over his comrade's wants with tenderness and care. He was very busy, marshalling the little, black vagabonds of tin-cups and pouring into them the steaming, iron-colored mixture from a small and sooty tin-pail. He had some fresh meat which he roasted hurriedly upon a stick. He sat down then and contemplated the youth's appetite with glee.

The youth took note of a remarkable change in his comrade since those days of camp-life upon the river-bank. He seemed no more to be continually regarding the proportions of his personal prowess. He was not furious at small words that pricked his conceits. He was, no more, a loud young soldier. There was about him now a fine reliance. He showed a quiet belief in his purposes and his abilities. And this inward confidence evidently enabled him to be indifferent to little words of other men aimed at him.

The youth reflected. He had been used to regarding his comrade as a blatant child with an audacity grown from his inexperience, thoughtless, head-strong, jealous, and filled with a tinsel courage. A swaggering babe accustomed to strut in his own door-yard. The youth wondered where had been born these new eyes; when his comrade had made the great discovery that there were many men who would refuse to be subjected by him. Apparently, the other had now climbed a peak of wisdom from which he could perceive himself as a very wee thing. And the youth saw that, ever after, it would be easier to live in his friend's neighborhood.

His comrade balanced his ebony coffee-cup on his knee. "Well, Henry," he said, "what d'yeh think th' chances are? D'yeh think we'll wallop'em?"

The youth considered for a moment. "Day-b'fore-yestirday," he finally replied with boldness, "yeh would 'a bet yed lick th' hull kit-an'-boodle all by yerself."

His friend looked a trifle amazed. "Would I?" he asked. He pondered. "Well, perhaps, I would," he decided at last. He stared humbly at the fire.

The youth was quite disconcerted at this surprising reception of his remarks. "Oh, no, yeh wouldn't either," he said, hastily trying to retrace.

But the other made a deprecatory gesture. "Oh, yeh needn't mind, Henry," he said. "I believe I was a pretty big fool in those days." He spoke as after a lapse of years.

There was a little pause.

"All th' off'cers say we've got th' rebs in a pretty tight box," said the friend, clearing his throat in a common-place way. "They all seem t' think we've got'em jest where we want'em."

"I don't know about that," the youth replied. "What I seen over on th' right makes me think it was th' other way about. From where I was, it looked as if we was gittin' a good poundin' yestir-day."

"D'yeh think so?" enquired the friend. "I thought we handled 'em pretty rough yesterday."

"Not a bit," said the youth. "Why, lord, man, yeh didn't see nothin' 'a th' fight. Why—" Then a sudden thought came to him. "Oh! Jim Conklin's dead."

His friend started. "What? Is he? Jim Conklin?"

The youth spoke slowly. "Yep. He's dead. Shot in th' side."

"Yeh don't say so. Jim Conklin? . . . . Poor cuss."

All about them were other small fires surrounded by men with their little black utensils. From one of these, near, came sudden sharp voices in a row. It appeared that two light-footed soldiers had been teasing a huge bearded man, causing him to spill coffee upon his blue knees. The man had gone into a rage and had sworn comprehensively. Stung by his language, his tormentors had immediately bristled at him with a great show of resenting unjust oaths. Possibly there was going to be a fight.

The friend arose and went over to them making pacific motions with his arms. "Oh, here, now, boys, what's th' use?" he said. "We'll be at th' rebs in less'n an hour. What's th' good 'a fightin' 'mong ourselves."

One of the light-footed soldiers turned upon him red faced and violent. "Yeh needn't come around here with yer preachin'. I s'pose yeh don't approve 'a fightin' since Charley Morgan licked yeh but I don't see what business this here is 'a yours or anybody else."

"Well, it aint," said the friend mildly. "Still I hate t' see—"

There was a tangled argument.

"Well, he—" said the two, indicating their opponent with accusative fore-fingers.

The huge soldier was quite purple with rage. He pointed at the two soldiers with his great hand, extended claw-like. "Well, they—"

But during this argumentative time, the desire to deal blows seemed to pass, although they said much to each other. Finally the friend returned to his old seat. In a short while, the three antagonists could be seen together in an amiable bunch.

"Jimmie Rogers ses I'll have t' fight him after th' battle t'-day," announced the friend as he again seated himself. "He ses he don't allow no interferin' in his business. I hate t' see th' boys fightin' 'mong themselves."

The youth laughed. "Yer changed a good bit. Yeh aint at all like yeh was. I remember when you an' that Irish feller—" he stopped and laughed again.

"No, I didn't used t' be that way," said his friend, thoughtfully. "That's true 'nough."

"Well, I didn't mean—" began the youth.

The friend made another deprecatory gesture. "Oh, yeh needn't mind, Henry."

There was another little pause.

"Th' reg'ment lost over half th' men yestirday," remarked the friend, eventually. "I thought 'a course they was all dead but, laws, they kep a-comin' back last night until it seems, after all, we didnt lose but a few. They'd been scattered all over, wanderin' around in th' woods, fightin' with other reg'ments an' everything. Jest like you done."

"So?" said the youth.

He went into a brown mood. He thought with deep contempt of all his grapplings and tuggings with fate and the universe. It now was evident that a large proportion of the men of the regiment had been, if they chose, capable of the same quantity of condemnation of the world and could as righteously have taken arms against everything. He laughed.

He now rejoiced in a view of what he took to be the universal resemblance. He decided that he was not, as he had supposed, a unique man. There were many in his type. And he had believed that he was suffering new agonies and feeling new wrongs. On the contrary, they were old, all of them, they were born perhaps with the first life.

These thoughts took the element of grandeur from his experiences. Since many had had them there could be nothing fine about them. They were now ridiculous.

However, he yet considered himself to be below the standard of traditional man-hood. He felt abashed when confronting memories of some men he had seen.

These thoughts did not appear in his attitude. He now considered the fact of his having fled, as being buried. He was returned to his comrades and unimpeached. So despite the little shadow of his sin upon his mind, he felt his self-respect growing strong within him. His pride had almost recovered its balance and was about

• • •

XVI

The regiment was standing at order-arms at the side of a lane, waiting for the command to march when suddenly the youth remembered the little packet enwrapped in a faded yellow envelope which the loud young soldier with lugubrious words had entrusted to him. It made him start. He uttered an exclamation and turned toward his comrade.

"Wilson!"

"What?"

His friend, at his side in the ranks, was thoughtfully staring down the road. From some cause, his expression was at that moment, very meek. The youth, regarding him with sidelong glances, felt impelled to change his purpose. "Oh, nothin'," he said.

His friend turned his head in some surprise. "Why, what was yeh goin' t' say."

"Oh, nothin'," repeated the youth.

He resolved not to deal the little blow. It was sufficient that the fact made him glad. It was not necessary to knock his friend on the head with the misguided packet.

He had been possessed of much fear of his friend for he saw how easily questionings could make holes in his feelings. Lately, he had assured himself that the altered comrade would not tantalize him with a persistent curiosity but he felt certain that during the first period of leisure his friend would ask him to relate his adventures of the previous day.

He now rejoiced in the possession of a small weapon with which he could prostrate his comrade at the first signs of a cross-examination. He was master. It would now be he who could laugh and shoot the shafts of derision.

The friend had, in a weak hour, spoken with sobs of his own death. He had delivered a melancholy oration previous to his funeral and had, doubtless, in the packet of letters, presented various keep-sakes to relatives. But he had not died, and thus he had delivered himself into the hands of the youth.

The latter felt immensely superior to his friend but he inclined to condescension. He adopted toward him an air of patronizing good-humor.

His self-pride was now entirely restored. In the shade of its flourishing growth, he stood with braced and self-confident legs, and since nothing could now be discovered, he did not shrink from an encounter with the eyes of judges, and allowed no thoughts of his own to keep him from an attitude of manfulness. He had performed his mistakes in the dark, so he was still a man.

Indeed, when he remembered his fortunes of yesterday, and looked at them from a distance he began to see something fine there. He had license to be pompous and veteran-like.

His panting agonies of the past he put out of his sight. The long tirades against nature he now believed to be foolish compositions born of his condition. He did not altogether repudiate them because he did not remember all that he had said. He was inclined to regard his past rebellions with an indulgent smile. They were all right in their hour, perhaps.

In the present, he declared to himself that it was only the doomed and the damned who roared with sincerity at nature. Few, but they, ever did it. A man with a full stomach and the respect of his fellows had no business to scold about anything that he might think to be wrong in the ways of the universe, or, even with the ways of society. Let the unfortunates rail; the others may play marbles.

Since he was comfortable and contented, he had no desire to set things straight. Indeed, he no more contended that they were not straight. How could they be crooked when he was restored to a requisite amount of happiness. There was a slowly developing conviction that in all his red speeches he had been ridiculously mistaken. Nature was a fine thing moving with a magnificent justice. The world was fair and wide and glorious. The sky was kind, and smiled tenderly, full of encouragement, upon him.

Some poets now received his scorn. Yesterday, in his misery, he had thought of certain persons who had written. Their remembered words, broken and detached, had come piece-meal to him. For these people he had then felt a glowing, brotherly regard. They had wandered in paths of pain and they had made pictures of the black landscape that others might enjoy it with them. He had, at that time, been sure that their wise, contemplating spirits had been in sympathy with him, had shed tears from the clouds. He had walked alone, but there had been pity, made before a reason for it.

But he was now, in a measure, a successful man and he could no longer tolerate in himself a spirit of fellowship for poets. He abandoned them. Their songs about black landscapes were of no importance to him since his new eyes said that his landscape was not black. People who called landscapes black were idiots.

He achieved a mighty scorn for such a snivelling race.

He felt that he was the child of the powers. Through the peace of his heart, he saw the earth to be a garden in which grew no weeds of agony. Or, perhaps, if there did grow a few, it was in obscure corners where no one was obliged to encounter them unless a ridiculous search was made. And, at any rate, they were tiny ones.

He returned to his old belief in the ultimate, astonishing success of his life. He, as usual, did not trouble about processes. It was ordained, because he was a fine creation. He saw plainly that he was the chosen of some gods. By fearful and wonderful roads he was to be led to a crown. He was, of course, satisfied that he deserved it.

He did not give a great deal of thought to these battles that lay directly before him. It was not essential that he should plan his ways in regard to them. He had been taught that many obligations of a life were easily avoided. The lessons of yesterday had been that retribution was a laggard and blind. With these facts before him he did not deem it necessary that he should become feverish over the possibilities of the ensuing twenty-four hours. He could leave much to chance. Beside, a faith in himself had secretly blossomed. There was a little flower of confidence growing within him. He was now a man of experience. He had been out among the dragons, he said, and he assured himself that they were not so hideous as he had imagined them. Also, they were inaccurate; they did not sting with precision. A stout heart often defied; and, defying, escaped.

And, furthermore, how could they kill him who was the chosen of gods and doomed to greatness.

He remembered how some of the men had run from the battle. As he re-called their terror-struck faces he felt a scorn for them. They had surely been more fleet and more wild than was absolutely necessary. They were weak mortals. As for himself, he had fled with discretion and dignity.

He was aroused from this reverie by his friend who having hitched about nervously and blinked at the trees for a time, suddenly coughed in an introductory way, and spoke.

"Fleming!"

"What?"

The friend put his hand up to his mouth and coughed again. He fidgeted in his jacket.

"Well," he gulped, at last, "I guess yeh might as well give me back them letters." Dark, prickling blood had flushed into his cheeks and brow.

"All right, Wilson," said the youth. He loosened two buttons of his coat, thrust in his hand and brought forth the packet. As he extended it to his friend, the latter's face was turned from him.

He had been slow in the act of producing the packet because during it he had been trying to invent a remarkable comment upon the affair. He could conjure nothing of sufficient point. He was compelled to allow his friend to escape unmolested with his packet. And for this he took unto himself considerable credit. It was a generous thing.

His friend at his side, seemed suffering great shame. As he contemplated him, the youth felt his heart grow more strong and stout. He had never been compelled to blush in such manner for his acts; he was an individual of extraordinary virtues.

He reflected, with condescending pity: "Too bad! Too bad! Th' poor devil, it makes him feel tough!"

After this incident, and as he reviewed the battle-pictures he had seen, he felt quite competent to return home and make the hearts of the people glow with stories of war. He could see himself in a room of warm tints telling tales to listeners. He could exhibit laurels. They were insignificant; still, in a district where laurels were infrequent, they might shine.

He saw his gaping audience picturing him as the central figure in blazing scenes. And he imagined the consternation and the ejaculations of his mother and the young lady at the seminary as they drank his recitals. Their vague feminine formula for beloved ones doing brave deeds on the field of battle without risk of life, would be destroyed.

XVII

A sputtering of musketry was always to be heard. Later, the cannon had entered the dispute. In the fog-filled air, their voices made a thudding sound. The reverberations were continual. This part of the world led a strange, battleful existence.

The youth's regiment was marched to relieve a command that had lain long in some damp trenches. The men took positions behind a curving line of rifle-pits that had been turned up, like a large furrow, along the line of woods. Before them was a level stretch, peopled with short, deformed stumps. From the woods beyond, came the dull popping of the skirmishers and pickets, firing in the fog. From the right came the noise of a terrific fracas.

The men cuddled behind the small embankment and sat in easy attitudes awaiting their turn. Many had their backs to the firing. The youth's friend lay down, buried his face in his arms, and almost instantly, it seemed, he was in a deep sleep.

The youth leaned his breast against the brown dirt and peered over at the woods and up and down the line. Curtains of trees interfered with his ways of vision. He could see the low line of trenches but for a short distance. A few idle flags were perched on the dirt-hills. Behind them were rows of dark bodies with a few heads sticking curiously over the top.

Always the noise of skirmishers came from the woods on the front and left, and the din on the right had grown to frightful proportions. The guns were roaring without an instant's pause for breath. It seemed that the cannon had come from all parts and were engaged in a stupendous wrangle. It became impossible to make a sentence heard.

The youth wished to launch a joke—a quotation from newspapers. He desired to say: "All quiet on the Rappahannock,"[2] but the guns refused to permit even a comment upon their up-roar. He never successfully concluded the sentence.

But at last, the guns stopped and among the men in the rifle-pits, rumors again flew, like birds, but they were now for the most part, black and croaking creatures who flapped their wings drearily near to the ground and refused to rise on any wings of hope. The men's faces grew doleful from the interpreting of many omens. Tales of hesitation and uncertainty on the part of those high in place and responsibility, came to their ears. Stories of disaster were borne in to

2. An echo of "All quiet along the Potomac," reputed to be a report sent to Washington, D.C., from the headquarters of General George McClellan while he was Commander of the Army of the Potomac in 1861–62. The northern public and newspapers were anxious for McClellan to take action and used the phrase sarcastically in attacking his reticence to launch an offensive.

their minds with many proofs. This din of musketry on the right, growing like a released genie of sound, expressed and emphasized the army's plight.

The men were disheartened and began to mutter. They made gestures expressive of the sentence: "Ah, what more can we do." And it could always be seen that they were bewildered by the alleged news and could not fully comprehend a defeat.

Before the grey mists had been totally obliterated by the sun-rays, the regiment was marching in a spread column that was retiring carefully through the woods. The disordered, hurrying lines of the enemy could sometimes be seen down through the groves and little fields. They were yelling, shrill and exultant.

At this sight, the youth forgot many personal matters and became greatly enraged. He exploded in loud sentence. "B'jiminy, we're generaled by a lot 'a lunkheads."

"More than one feller has said that t'-day," observed a man.

His friend, recently aroused, was still very drowsy. He looked behind him until his mind took in the meaning of the movement. Then he sighed. "Oh, well, I s'pose we got licked," he remarked, sadly.

The youth had a thought that it would not be handsome for him to freely condemn other men. He made an attempt to restrain himself but the words upon his tongue were too bitter. He presently began a long and intricate denunciation of the commander of the forces.

"Mebbe, it wa'n't all his fault—not all together. He did th' best he knowed. It's our luck t' git licked often," said his friend in a weary tone. He was trudging along with stooped shoulders and shifting eyes like a man who has been caned and kicked.

"Well, don't we fight like th' devil? Don't we do all that men kin?" demanded the youth loudly.

He was secretly dumb-founded at this sentiment when it came from his lips. For a moment his face lost its valor and he looked guiltily about him. But no one questioned his right to deal in such words, and, presently, he recovered his air of courage. He went on to repeat a statement he had heard going from group to group at the camp that morning. "Th' brigadier sed he never see a new reg-'ment fight th' way we fit yestirday, didnt he? An' we didn't no better than many another reg'ment, did we? Well, then, yeh can't say it's th' army's fault, kin yeh?"

In his reply, the friend's voice was stern. " 'A course not," he said. "No man dare say we don't fight like th' devil. No man will ever dare say it. Th' boys fight like hell-roosters. But still—still, we don't have no luck."

"Well, then, if we fight like th' devil an' don't ever whip, it must be th' general's fault," said the youth grandly and decisively. "An' I don't see no sense in fightin' an' fightin' an' fightin', yit allus losin' through some derned ol' lunkhead of a general."

A sarcastic man who was tramping at the youth's side, then spoke lazily. "Mebbe yeh think yeh fit th' hull battle yestirday, Flemin'," he remarked.

The speech pierced the youth. Inward, he was reduced to an abject pulp by these chance words. His legs quaked privately. He cast a frightened glance at the sarcastic man.

"Why, no," he hastened to say in a conciliatory voice, "I don't think I fit th' hull battle yestirday."

But the other seemed innocent of any deeper meaning. Apparently, he had no information. It was merely his habit. "Oh," he replied in the same tone of calm derision.

The youth, nevertheless, felt a threat. His mind shrank from going near to the danger and, thereafter, he was silent. The significance of the sarcastic man's words took from him all loud moods that would make him appear prominent. He became suddenly a modest man.

There was low-toned talk among the troops. The officers were impatient and snappy, their countenances clouded with the tales of misfortune. The troops, sifting through the forest, were sullen. In the youth's company once, a man's laugh rang out. A dozen soldiers turned their faces quickly toward him and frowned with vague displeasure.

The noise of firing dogged their foot-steps. Sometimes, it seemed to be driven a little way but it always returned again with increased insolence. The men muttered and cursed, throwing black looks in its direction.

In a clearer space, the troops were at last halted. Regiments and brigades, broken and detached through their encounters with thickets, grew together again and lines were faced toward the pursuing bark of the enemy's infantry.

This noise, following like the yelpings of eager, metallic hounds increased to a loud and joyous burst, and then, as the sun went serenely up the sky, throwing illuminating rays into the gloomy thickets, it broke forth into prolonged pealings. The woods began to crackle as if a-fire.

"Whoop-a-dadee," said a man, "here we are. Everybody fightin'. Blood an' destruction."

"I was willin' t' bet they'd attack as soon as th' sun got fairly up," savagely asserted the lieutenant who commanded the youth's company. He jerked without mercy at his little moustache. He strode to and fro with dark dignity in the rear of his men who were lying down behind whatever protection they had collected.

A battery had trundled into position in the rear and was thoughtfully shelling the distance. The regiment, unmolested as yet, awaited
the moment when the grey shadows of the woods before them
should be slashed by the lines of flame. There was much growling
and swearing.

"Good Gawd," the youth grumbled, "we're allus bein' chased
around like rats. It makes me sick. Nobody seems t' know where we
go ner why we go. We jest git fired around from piller t' post an'
git licked here an' git licked there an' nobody knows what it's done
fer. It make a man feel like a damn' kitten in a bag. Now, I'd like t'
know what th' eternal thunders we was marched inteh these here
woods fer, anyhow, unless it was t' give th' rebs a reg'lar pot-shot at
us. We came in here an' got our legs all tangled up in these here
cussed briars an' then we begin t' fight an' th' rebs had an easy time
of it. Don't tell Me it's jest luck. I know better. It's this derned ol'
—"

The friend seemed jaded but he interrupted his comrade with a
voice of calm confidence. "It'll turn out all right in th' end," he
said.

"Oh, th' devil it will. You allus talk like a dog-hanged parson.
Dont tell Me. I know—"

At this time, there was an interposition by the savage-minded
lieutenant who was obliged to vent some of his inward dissatisfac-
tion upon his men. "You boys shut right up. There no need 'a your
wastin' your breath in long-winded arguments about this an' that
an' th' other. You've been jawin' like a lot 'a old hens. All you've
got t' do is to fight an' you'll get plenty 'a that t' do in about ten
minutes. Less talkin' an' more fightin' is what's best fer you boys. I
never saw sech gabbling jack-asses."

He paused, ready to pounce upon any man who might have the
temerity to reply. No words being said, he resumed his dignified
pacing.

"There's too much chin-music an' too little fightin' in this war,
anyhow," he said to them, turning his head for a final remark.

The day had grown more white until the sun shed his full radi-
ance upon the thronged forest. A sort of a gust of battle came
sweeping toward that part of the line where lay the youth's regiment. The front shifted a trifle to meet it squarely. There was a
wait. In this part of the field there passed slowly the intense
moments that precede the tempest.

A single rifle flashed in a thicket before the regiment. In an
instant, it was joined by many others. There was a mighty song of
clashes and crashes that went sweeping through the woods. The
guns in the rear, aroused and enraged by shells that had been
thrown burr-like at them, suddenly involved themselves in a hideous

altercation with another band of guns. The battle-roar settled to a rolling thunder which was a single, long explosion.

In the regiment, there was a peculiar kind of hesitation denoted in the attitudes of the men. They were worn, exhausted, having slept but little, and labored much. They rolled their eyes toward the advancing battle as they stood awaiting the shock. Some shrank and flinched. They stood as men tied to stakes.

XVIII

This advance of the enemy had seemed to the youth like a ruthless hunting. He began to fume with rage and exasperation. He beat his foot upon the ground and scowled with hate at the swirling smoke that was approaching like a phantom flood. There was a maddening quality in this seeming resolution of the foe to give him no rest, to give him no time to sit down and think. Yesterday, he had fought and had fled rapidly. There had been many adventures. For to-day he felt that he had earned opportunities for contemplative repose. He could have enjoyed portraying to uninitiated listeners various scenes at which he had been a witness, or, ably discussing the processes of war with other proven men. Too, it was important that he should have time for physical recuperation. He was sore and stiff from his experiences. He had received his fill of all exertions and he wished to rest.

But those other men seemed never to grow weary; they were fighting with their old speed. He had a wild hate for the relentless foe. Yesterday, when he had imagined the universe to be against him, he had hated it, little gods and big gods; to-day he hated the army of the foe with the same great hatred. He was not going to be badgered of his life like a kitten chased by boys, he said. It was not well to drive men into final corners; at those moments, they could all develop teeth and claws.

He leaned, and spoke into his friend's ear. He menaced the woods with a gesture. "If they keep on a-chasin' us, by Gawd, they wanta watch out. Can't stand *too* much."

The friend twisted his head and made a calm reply. "If they keep on a-chasin' us, they'll drive us all inteh th' river."

The youth cried out savagely at this statement. He crouched behind a little tree, with his eyes burning balefully and his teeth set in a cur-like snarl. The awkward bandage was still about his head and, upon it, over his wound there was a spot of dry blood. His hair was wondrously towsled and some straggling, moving locks hung over the cloth of the bandage down toward his forehead. His jacket and shirt were open at the neck and exposed his young, bronzed neck. There could be seen spasmodic gulpings at his throat.

His fingers twined nervously about his rifle. He wished that it was an engine of annihilating power. He felt that he and his companions were being taunted and derided from sincere convictions that they were poor and puny. His knowledge of his inability to take vengeance for it made his rage into a dark and stormy spectre that possessed him and made him dream of abominable cruelties. The tormentors were flies sucking insolently at his blood and he thought that he would have given his life for a revenge of seeing their faces in pitiful plights.

The winds of battle had swept all about the regiment until the one rifle, instantly followed by brothers, flashed in its front. A moment later, the regiment roared forth its sudden and valiant retort. A dense wall of smoke settled slowly down. It was furiously slit and slashed by the knife-like fire from the rifles.

To the youth, the fighters were like animals tossed for a death-struggle into a dark pit. There was a sensation that he and his fellows, at bay, were pushing back, always pushing fierce onslaughts of creatures who were slippery. Their beams of crimson seemed to get no purchase upon the bodies of their foes; the latter seemed to evade them with ease and come through, between, around and about, with unopposed skill.

When, in a dream, it occurred to the youth that his rifle was an impotent stick, he lost sense of everything but his hate, his desire to smash into pulp the glittering smile of victory which he could feel upon the faces of his enemies.

The blue, smoke-swallowed line curled and writhed like a snake, stepped upon. It swung its ends to and fro in an agony of fear and rage.

The youth was not conscious that he was erect upon his feet. He did not know the direction of the ground. Indeed, once he even lost the habit of balance and fell heavily. He was up again immediately. One thought went through the chaos of his brain at the time. He wondered if he had fallen because he had been shot. But the suspicion flew away at once. He did not think more of it.

He had taken up a first position behind the little tree with a direct determination to hold it against the world. He had not deemed it possible that his army could that day succeed and, from this, he felt the ability to fight harder. But the throng had surged in all ways until he lost directions and locations, save that he knew where lay the enemy.

The flames bit him and the hot smoke broiled his skin. His rifle-barrel grew so hot that, ordinarily, he could not have borne it upon his palms but he kept on stuffing cartridges into it and pounding them with his clanking, bending ram-rod. If he aimed at some changing form through the smoke, he pulled his trigger with a fierce grunt as if he were dealing a blow of the fist with all his strength.

When the enemy seemed falling back before him and his fellows, he went instantly forward, like a dog who seeing his foes lagging, turns and insists upon being pursued. And when he was compelled to retire again, he did it slowly, sullenly, taking steps of wrathful despair.

Once, he, in his intent hate, was almost alone and was firing when all those near him had ceased. He was so engrossed in his occupation that he was not aware of a lull.

He was re-called by a hoarse laugh and a sentence that came to his ears in a voice of contempt and amazement. "Yeh infernal fool, don't yeh know enough t' quit when there aint anything t' shoot at? Good Gawd!"

He turned then and pausing with his rifle thrown half into position, looked at the blue line of his comrades. During this moment of leisure, they seemed all to be engaged in staring with astonishment at him. They had become spectators. Turning to the front again, he saw, under the lifted smoke, a deserted ground.

He looked, bewildered, for a moment. Then there appeared upon the glazed vacancy of his eyes, a diamond-point of intelligence. "Oh," he said, comprehending.

He returned to his comrades and threw himself upon the ground. He sprawled like a man who has been thrashed. His flesh seemed strangely on fire and the sounds of the battle continued in his ears. He groped blindly for his canteen.

The lieutenant was crowing. He seemed drunk with fighting. He called out to the youth. "By heavens, if I had ten thousand wild-cats like you, I could tear th' stomach outa this war in less'n a week." He puffed out his chest with large dignity as he said it.

Some of the men muttered and looked at the youth in awe-struck ways. It was plain that as he had gone on loading and firing and cursing without the proper intermission, they had found time to regard him. And they now looked upon him as a war-devil.

The friend came staggering to him. There was some fright and dismay in his voice. "Are yeh all right, Fleming? Do yeh feel all right? There aint nothin' th' matter with yeh, Henry, is there?"

"No," said the youth with difficulty. His throat seemed full of knobs and burrs.

These incidents made the youth ponder. It was revealed to him that he had been a barbarian, a beast. He had fought like a pagan who defends his religion. Regarding it, he saw that it was fine, wild and, in some ways, easy. He had been a tremendous figure, no doubt. By this struggle, he had over-come obstacles which he had admitted to be mountains. They had fallen like paper peaks and he was now what he called a hero. And he had not been aware of the process. He had slept and, awakening, found himself a knight.

He lay and basked in the occasional stares of his comrades. Their faces were varied in degree of blackness from the burned powder. Some were utterly smudged. They were reeking with perspiration and their breaths came hard and wheezing. And from these soiled expanses they peered at him.

"Hot work! Hot work!" cried the lieutenant deliriously. He walked up and down restless and eager. Sometimes, his voice could be heard in a wild, incomprehensible laugh.

When he had a particularly profound thought upon the science of war, he always unconsciously addressed himself to the youth.

There was some grim rejoicing by the men. "By thunder, I bet this army'll never see another new reg'ment like us."

"You bet!

'A dog, a woman, an' a walnut tree,
   Th' more yeh beat'em, th' better they be,'

That's like us."

"Lost a piler men, they did. If an ol' woman swep' up th' woods, she'd git a dust-pan full."

"Yes, an' if she'll come around ag'in in 'bout an hour she'll git a pile more."

The forest still bore its burden of clamor. From off under the trees came the rolling clatter of the musketry. Each distant thicket seemed a strange porcupine with quills of flame. A cloud of dark smoke as from smouldering ruins went up toward the sun now bright and gay in the blue, enamelled sky.

XIX

The ragged line had respite for some minutes but during its pause, the struggle in the forest became magnified until the trees seemed to quiver from the firing and the ground to shake from the rushings of the men. The voices of the cannon were mingled in a long and interminable row. It seemed difficult to live in such an atmosphere. The chests of the men strained for a bit of freshness and their throats craved water.

There was one, shot through the body, who raised a cry of bitter lamentation when came this lull. Perhaps, he had been calling out during the fighting also but at that time no one had heard him. But now the men turned at the woful complaints of him upon the ground.

"Who is it? Who is it?"

"It's Jimmie Rogers! Jimmie Rogers."

When their eyes first encountered him there was a sudden halt as if they feared to go near. He was thrashing about in the grass, twisting his shuddering body into many strange postures. He was screaming loudly. This instant's hesitation seemed to fill him with a tremendous, fantastic contempt and he damned them in shrieked sentences.

The youth's friend had a geographical illusion concerning a stream and he obtained permission to go for some water. Immediately, canteens were showered upon him. "Fill mine, will yeh?" "Bring me some, too." "And me, too." He departed, ladened. The youth went with his friend, feeling a desire to throw his heated body into the stream and, soaking there, drink quarts.

They made a hurried search for the supposed stream but did not find it. "No water here," said the youth. They turned without delay and began to retrace their steps.

From their position as they again faced toward the place of the fighting, they could, of course, comprehend a greater amount of the battle than when their visions had been blurred by the hurlying smoke of the line. They could see dark stretches winding along the land and on one cleared space there was a row of guns making grey clouds which were filled with large flashes of orange-colored flame. Over some foliage they could see the roof of a house. One window, glowing a deep, murder-red, shone squarely through the leaves. From the edifice, a tall, leaning tower of smoke went far into the sky.

Looking over their own troops, they saw mixed masses slowly getting into regular form. The sun-light made twinkling points of the bright steel. To the rear, there was a glimpse of a distant road-way as it curved over a slope. It was crowded with retreating infantry. From all the interwoven forest arose the smoke and bluster of the battle. The air was always occupied by a blaring.

Near where they stood, shells were flip-flopping and hooting. Occasional bullets buzzed in the air and spanged into tree-trunks. Wounded men and other stragglers were slinking through the woods.

Looking down an aisle of the grove, the youth and his companion saw a jangling general and his staff almost ride upon a wounded man who was crawling on his hands and knees. The general reined strongly at his charger's opened and foamy mouth and guided it with dexterous horsemanship past the man. The latter scrambled in wild and torturing haste. His strength evidently failed him as he reached a place of safety. One of his arms suddenly weakened, and he fell, sliding over upon his back. He lay stretched out, breathing gently.

A moment later, the small, creaking cavalcade was directly in front of the two soldiers. Another officer, riding with the skilful abandon of a cow-boy, galloped his horse to a position directly before the general. The two unnoticed foot-soldiers made a little show of going on but they lingered near in the desire to over-hear the conversation. Perhaps, they thought, some great, inner historical things would be said.

The general, whom the boys knew as the commander of their division, looked at the other officer and spoke, coolly, as if he were criticising his clothes. "Th' enemy's formin' over there for another charge," he said. "It'll be directed against Whiterside, an' I fear they'll break through there unless we work like thunder t' stop them."

The other swore at his restive horse and then cleared his throat. He made a gesture toward his cap. "It'll be hell t' pay stoppin' them," he said, shortly.

"I presume so," remarked the general. Then he began to talk rapidly and in a lower tone. He frequently illustrated his words with a pointing finger. The two infantrymen could hear nothing until finally he asked: "What troops can you spare?"

The officer who rode like a cow-boy reflected for an instant. "Well," he said, "I had to order in th' 12th to help th' 76th an' I haven't really got any. But there's th' 304th. They fight like a lot 'a mule-drivers. I can spare them best of any."

The youth and his friend exchanged glances of astonishment.

The general spoke sharply. "Get'em ready then. I'll watch developments from here an' send you word when t' start them. It'll happen in five minutes."

As the other officer tossed his fingers toward his cap and, wheeling his horse, started away, the general called out to him in a sober voice: "I don't believe many of your mule-drivers will get back."

The other shouted something in reply. He smiled.

With scared faces, the youth and his companion, hurried back to the line.

These happenings had occupied an incredibly short time yet the youth felt that in them he had been made aged. New eyes were given to him. And the most startling thing was to learn suddenly that he was very insignificant. The officer spoke of the regiment as if he referred to a broom. Some part of the woods needed sweeping, perhaps, and he merely indicated a broom in a tone properly indifferent to its fate. It was war, no doubt, but it appeared strange.

As the two boys approached the line, the lieutenant perceived them and swelled with wrath. "Fleming—Wilson—how long does it take yeh t' git water, anyhow—where yeh been—"

But his oration ceased as he saw their eyes which were large with great tales. "We're goin' t' charge—we're goin' t' charge," cried the youth's friend, hastening with his news.

"Charge?" said the lieutenant. "Charge? Well, b'Gawd! Now, this is real fightin'." Over his soiled countenance there went a boastful smile. "Charge? Well, b'Gawd!"

A little group of soldiers surrounded the two youths. "Are we, sure-'nough? Well, I'll be derned. Charge? What fer? What at? Wilson, you're lyin'."

"I hope t' die," said the youth's friend, pitching his tones to the key of angry remonstrance. "Sure as shootin', I tell yeh."

And the youth spoke in reinforcement. "Not by a blame sight, he aint lyin'. We heard'em talkin'."

They caught sight of two mounted figures a short distance from them. One was the colonel of the regiment and the other was the officer who had received orders from the commander of the division. They were gesticulating at each other. The youth's friend pointing at them, interpreted the scene.

One soldier had a final objection: "How could yeh hear'em talkin'," but the men, for a large part, nodded, admitting that previously the two friends had spoken truth.

They settled back into reposeful attitudes with airs of having accepted the matter. And they mused upon it, with a hundred varieties of expression. It was an engrossing thing to think about. Many tightened their belts carefully and hitched at their trousers.

A moment later, the officers began to bustle among the men, pushing them into a more compact mass and into a better alignment. They chased those that straggled and fumed at a few men who seemed to show by their attitudes, that they had decided to remain at that spot. They were like critical shepherds struggling with sheep.

Presently, the regiment seemed to draw itself up and heave a deep breath. None of the men's faces were mirrors of large thoughts. The soldiers were bended and stooped like sprinters before a signal. Many pairs of glinting eyes peered from the grimy faces toward the curtains of the deeper woods. They seemed to be engaged in deep calculations of time and distance.

They were surrounded by the noises of the monstrous altercation between the two armies. The world was fully interested in other matters. Apparently, the regiment had its small affair to itself.

The youth, turning, shot a quick, enquiring glance at his friend. The latter returned to him the same manner of look. They were the only ones who possessed an inner knowledge. "Mule-drivers—hell t' pay—don't believe many will get back." It was an ironical secret. Still, they saw no hesitation in each other's faces and they nodded a mute and unprotesting assent when a shaggy man near them said in a meek voice: "We'll git swallered."

XX

The youth stared at the land in front of him. Its foliages now seemed to veil powers and horrors. He was unaware of the machinery of orders that started the charge, although from the corners of his eyes, he saw an officer, who looked like a boy a-horseback, come galloping, waving his hat. Suddenly, he felt a straining and heaving among the men. The line fell slowly forward like a toppling wall and with a convulsive gasp that was intended for a cheer, the regiment began its journey. The youth was pushed and jostled for a moment before he understood the movement at all but directly he lunged ahead and began to run.

He fixed his eye upon a distant and prominent clump of trees where he had concluded the enemy were to be met, and he ran toward it as toward a goal. He had believed, throughout that it was mere question of getting over an unpleasant matter as quickly as possible and he ran desperately as if pursued for a murder. His face was drawn hard and tight with the stress of his endeavor. His eyes were fixed in a lurid glare. And with his soiled and disordered dress, his red and inflamed features surmounted by the dingy rag with its spot of blood, his wildly swinging rifle and banging accoutrements, he looked to be an insane soldier.

As the regiment swung from its position out into a cleared space, the woods and thickets before it, awakened. Yellow flames leaped toward it from many directions. The forest made a tremendous objection.

The line lurched straight for a moment. Then the right wing swung forward; it in turn was surpassed by the left. Afterward the centre careered to the front until the regiment was a wedge-shaped mass but an instant later, the opposition of the bushes, trees and uneven places on the ground split the command and scattered it into detached clusters.

The youth, light-footed, was unconsciously in advance. His eyes still kept note of the clump of trees. From all places near it the clannish yell of the enemy could be heard. The little flames of rifles leaped from it. The song of the bullets was in the air and shells snarled among the tree-tops. One tumbled directly into the middle of a hurrying group and exploded in crimson fury. There was an instant's spectacle of a man, almost over it, throwing up his hands to shield his eyes.

Other men, punched by bullets, fell in grotesque agonies. The regiment left a coherent trail of bodies.

They had passed into a clearer atmosphere. There was an effect like a revelation in the new appearance of the landscape. Some men working madly at a battery were plain to them and the opposing infantry's lines were defined by the grey walls and fringes of smoke.

It seemed to the youth that he saw everything. Each blade of the green grass was bold and clear. He thought that he was aware of every change in the thin, transparent vapor that floated idly in sheets. The brown or grey trunks of the trees showed each rough-ness of their surfaces. And the men of the regiment, with their starting eyes and sweating faces, running madly, or falling, as if thrown headlong, to queer, heaped-up corpses, all were compre-hended. His mind took a mechanical but firm impression, so that, afterward, everything was pictured and explained to him, save why he himself was there.

But there was a frenzy made from this furious rush. The men, pitching forward insanely, had burst into cheerings, mob-like and barbaric, but tuned in strange keys that can arouse the dullard and the stoic. It made a mad enthusiasm that, it seemed, would be incapable of checking itself before granite and brass. There was the delirium that encounters despair and death, and is heedless and blind to the odds. It is a temporary but sublime absence of selfish-ness. And because it was of this order was the reason, perhaps, why the youth wondered, afterward, what reasons he could have had for being there.

Presently the straining pace ate up the energies of the men. As if by agreement, the leaders began to slacken their speed. The volleys directed against them had had a seeming wind-like effect. The regi-ment snorted and blew. Among some stolid trees it began to falter and hesitate. The men, staring intently, began to wait for some of the distant walls of smoke to move and disclose to them the scene. Since much of their strength and their breath had vanished, they returned to caution. They were become men again.

The youth had a vague belief that he had run miles and he thought, in a way, that he was now in some new and unknown land.

The moment the regiment ceased its advance, the protesting splutter of musketry became a steadied roar. Long and accurate fringes of smoke spread out. From the top of a small hill, came level belchings of yellow flame that caused an inhuman whistling in the air.

The men, halted, had opportunity to see some of their comrades dropping with moans and shrieks. A few lay under foot, still or wail-ing. And now for an instant the men stood, their rifles slack in their hands, and watched the regiment dwindle. They appeared dazed and stupid. This spectacle seemed to paralyze them, over-come them with a fatal fascination. They stared woodenly at the sights and, lowering their eyes, looked from face to face. It was a strange pause and a strange silence.

Then above the sounds of the outside commotion, arose the roar of the lieutenant. He strode suddenly forth, his infantile features black with rage.

"Come on, yeh fools," he bellowed. "Come on! Yeh can't stay

here. Yeh must come on." He said more, but much of it could not be understood.

He started rapidly forward, with his head turned toward the men. "Come on," he was shouting. The men stared with blank and yokel-like eyes at him. He was obliged to halt and retrace his steps. He stood then with his back to the enemy and delivered gigantic curses into the faces of the men. His body vibrated from the weight and force of his imprecations. And he could string oaths with the facility of a maiden who strings beads.

The friend of the youth aroused. Lurching suddenly forward and dropping to his knees, he fired an angry shot at the persistent woods. This action awakened the men. They huddled no more like sheep. They seemed suddenly to bethink them of their weapons and at once commenced firing. Belabored by their officers they began to move forward. The regiment, involved like a cart involved in mud and muddle, started unevenly with many jolts and jerks. The men stopped, now, every few paces to fire and load, and in this manner moved slowly on from trees to trees.

The flaming opposition in their front grew with their advance until it seemed that all forward ways were barred by the thin leaping tongues and off to the right an ominous demonstration could sometimes be dimly discerned. The smoke, lately generated, was in confusing clouds that made it difficult for the regiment to proceed with intelligence. As he passed through each curling mass, the youth wondered what would confront him on the further side.

The command went painfully forward until an open space interposed between them and the lurid lines. Here, crouching and cowering behind some trees, the men clung with desperation as if threatened by a wave. They looked wild-eyed, and as if amazed, at this furious disturbance they had stirred. In the storm, there was an ironical expression of their importance. The faces of the men, too, showed a lack of a certain feeling of responsibility for being there. It was as if they had been driven. It was the dominant animal failing to remember in the supreme moments, the forceful causes of various superficial qualities. The whole affair seemed incomprehensible to many of them.

As they halted thus, the lieutenant again began to bellow profanely. Regardless of the vindictive threats of the bullets, he went about coaxing, berating and bedamning. His lips, that were habitually in a soft and child-like curve, were now writhed into unholy contortions. He swore by all possible deities.

Once, he grabbed the youth by the arm. "Come on, yeh lunkhead," he roared. "Come on. We'll all git killed if we stay here. We've on'y got t' go across that lot. An' then—" The remainder of his idea disappeared in a blue haze of curses.

The youth stretched forth his arm. "Cross there?" His mouth was puckered in doubt and awe.

"Cer'ly! Jest 'cross th' lot! We can't stay here," screamed the lieutenant. He poked his face close to the youth and waved his bandaged hand. "Come on!" Presently, he grappled with him as if for a wrestling bout. It was as if he planned to drag the youth by the ear on to the assault.

The private felt a sudden unspeakable indignation against his officer. He wrenched fiercely and shook him off.

"Come on yerself, then," he yelled. There was a bitter challenge in his voice.

They galloped together down the regimental front. The friend scrambled after them. In front of the colors, the three men began to bawl. "Come on! Come on!" They danced and gyrated like tortured savages.

The flag, obedient to these appeals, bended its glittering form and swept toward them. The men wavered in indecision for a moment and then with a long, wailful cry, the dilapidated regiment surged forward and began its new journey.

Over the field went the scurrying mass. It was a handful of men splattered into the faces of the enemy. Toward it instantly sprang the yellow tongues. A vast quantity of blue smoke hung before them. A mighty banging made ears valueless.

The youth ran like a madman to reach the woods before a bullet could discover him. He ducked his head low like a foot-ball player. In his haste, his eyes almost closed and the scene was a wild blur. Pulsating saliva stood at the corners of his mouth.

Within him, as he hurled himself forward, was born a love, a despairing fondness for this flag which was near him. It was a creation of beauty and invulnerability. It was a goddess, radiant, that bended its form with an imperious gesture to him. It was a woman, red and white, hating and loving, that called him with the voice of his hopes. Because no harm could come to it, he endowed it with power. He kept near as if it could be a saver of lives and an imploring cry went from his mind.

In the mad scramble, he was aware that the color-serjeant flinched suddenly as if struck by a bludgeon. He faltered and then became motionless, save for his quivering knees.

He made a spring and a clutch at the pole. At the same instant, his friend grabbed it from the other side. They jerked at it, stout and furious, but the color-serjeant was dead and the corpse would not relinquish its trust. For a moment, there was a grim encounter. The dead man, swinging with bended back seemed to be obstinately tugging, in ludicrous and awful ways for the possession of the flag.

It was past in an instant of time. They wrenched the flag furiously from the dead man, and, as they turned again, the corpse swayed forward with bowed head. One arm swung high and the curved hand fell with heavy protest on the friend's unheeding shoulder.

XXI

When the two youths turned with the flag, they saw that much of the regiment had crumbled away and the dejected remnant was coming slowly back. The men having hurled themselves in projectile-fashion, had presently expended their forces. They slowly retreated with their faces still toward the spluttering woods and their hot rifles still replying to the din. Several officers were giving orders, their voices keyed to screams.

"Where in hell yeh goin'?" the lieutenant was asking in a sarcastic howl. And a red-bearded officer, whose voice of triple brass could plainly be heard, was commanding: "Shoot in to'em! Shoot in to'em, Gawd damn their souls." There was a melee of speeches in which the men were ordered to do conflicting and impossible things.

The youth and his friend had a small scuffle over the flag. "Give it t' me." "No—let me keep it." Each felt satisfied with the other's possession of it but each felt bound to declare by an offer to carry the emblem, his willingness to further risk himself. The youth roughly pushed his friend away.

The regiment fell back to the stolid trees. There it halted for a moment to blaze at some dark forms that had begun to steal upon its track. Presently it resumed its march again curving among the tree-trunks. By the time the depleted regiment had again reached the first open space, they were receiving a fast and merciless fire. There seemed to be mobs all about them.

The greater part of the men, discouraged, their spirits worn by the turmoil, acted as if stunned. They accepted the pelting of the bullets with bowed and weary heads. It was of no purpose to strive against walls. It was of no use to batter themselves against granite. And from this consciousness that they had attempted to conquer an unconquerable thing, there seemed to arise a feeling that they had been betrayed. They glowered with bent brows but dangerously upon some of the officers, more particularly upon the red-bearded one with the voice of triple brass.

However, the rear of the regiment was fringed with men who continued to shoot irritably at the advancing foes. They seemed resolved to make every trouble. The lieutenant was perhaps the last man in the disordered mass. His forgotten back was toward the enemy. He had been shot in the arm. It hung straight and rigid. Occasionally he would cease to remember it and be about to emphasize an oath with a sweeping gesture. The multiplied pain caused him to swear with incredible power.

The youth went along with slipping, uncertain feet. He kept watchful eyes rear-ward. A scowl of mortification and rage was upon his face. He had thought of a fine revenge upon the officer who had referred to him and his fellows as mule-drivers. But he saw that it could not come to pass. His dreams had collapsed when the mule-drivers, dwindling rapidly, had wavered and hesitated on the little clearing and then had recoiled. And now the retreat of the mule-drivers was a march of shame to him.

A dagger-pointed gaze from without his blackened face was held toward the enemy but his greater hatred was riveted upon the man, who, not knowing him, had called him a mule-driver. When he knew that he and his comrades had failed to do anything in successful ways that might bring the little pangs of a kind of remorse upon the officer, the youth allowed the rage of the baffled to possess him. This cold officer upon a monument who dropped epithets unconcernedly down, would be finer as a dead man, he thought. So grievous did he think it that he could never possess the secret right to taunt truly in answer. He had pictured red letters of curious revenge. "We *are* mule-drivers, are we?" And now he was compelled to throw them away.

He presently wrapped his heart in the cloak of his pride and kept the flag erect. He harangued his fellows, pushing against their chests with his free hand. To those he knew well, he made frantic appeals, beseeching them by name. Between him and the lieutenant, scolding and near to losing his mind with rage, there was felt a subtle fellowship and equality. They supported each other in all manner of hoarse, howling protests.

But the regiment was a machine run-down. The two men babbled at a forceless thing. The soldiers who had heart to go slowly were continually shaken in their resolves by a knowledge that comrades were slipping with speed back to the lines. It was difficult to think of reputation when others were thinking of skins. Wounded men were left, crying, on this black journey.

The smoke-fringes and flames blustered always. The youth peering once through a sudden rift in a cloud, saw a brown mass of troops interwoven and magnified until they appeared to be thousands. A fierce-hued flag flashed before his vision.

Immediately, as if the up-lifting of the smoke had been pre-arranged, the discovered troops burst into a rasping yell and a hundred flames jetted toward the retreating band. A rolling, grey cloud again interposed as the regiment doggedly replied. The youth had to depend again upon his misused ears which were trembling and buzzing from the melee of musketry and yells.

The way seemed eternal. In the clouded haze, men became panic-stricken with the thought that the regiment had lost its path and was proceeding in a perilous direction. Once, the men who headed the wild procession turned and came pushing back against their comrades screaming that they were being fired upon from points which they had considered to be toward their own lines. At this cry, a hysterical fear and dismay beset the troops. A soldier who heretofore had been ambitious to make the regiment into a wise little band that would proceed calmly amid the huge-appearing difficulties, suddenly sank down and buried his face in his arms with an air of bowing to a doom. From another, a shrill lamentation rang out filled with profane allusions to a general. Men ran hither and thither seeking with their eyes, roads of escape. With serene regularity as if controlled by a schedule, bullets buffed into men.

The youth walked stolidly into the midst of the mob and with his flag in his hands, took a stand as if he expected an attempt to push him to the ground. He unconsciously assumed the attitude of the color-bearer in the fight of the preceding day. He passed over his brow a hand that trembled. His breath did not come freely. He was choking during this small wait for the crisis.

His friend came to him. "Well, Henry, I guess this is good-bye-John."

"Oh, shet up, yeh damn' fool," replied the youth and he would not look at the other.

The officers labored like politicians to beat the mass into a proper circle to face the menaces. The ground was uneven and torn. The men curled into depressions and fitted themselves snugly behind whatever would frustrate a bullet.

The youth noted with vague surprise that the lieutenant was standing mutely with his legs far apart and his sword held in the manner of a cane. The youth wondered what had happened to his vocal organs that he no more cursed.

There was something curious in this little intent pause of the lieutenant. He was like a babe which having wept its fill, raises its eyes and fixes upon a distant toy. He was engrossed in this contemplation, and the soft under-lip quivered from self-whispered words.

Some lazy and ignorant smoke curled slowly. The men, hiding from the bullets, waited anxiously for it to lift and disclose the plight of the regiment.

The silent ranks were suddenly thrilled by the eager voice of the lieutenant bawling out: "Here they come! Right onto us, b'Gawd." His further words were lost in a roar of wicked thunder from the men's rifles.

The youth's eyes had instantly turned in the direction indicated by the awakened and agitated lieutenant and he had seen the haze of treachery disclosing a body of soldiers of the enemy. They were so near that he could see their features. There was a recognition as he looked at the types of faces. He perceived with dim amazement that their uniforms were rather gay in effect, being light grey plentifully accented with a brilliant-hued facing. Too, the clothes seemed new.

These troops had apparently been going forward with caution, their rifles held in readiness, when the lieutenant had discovered them and their movement had been interrupted by the volley from the blue regiment. From the moment's glimpse, it was derived that they had been unaware of the proximity of their dark-suited foes, or, had mistaken the direction. Almost instantly, they were shut utterly from the youth's sight by the smoke from the energetic rifles of his companions. He strained his vision to learn the accomplishment of the volley but the smoke hung before him.

The two bodies of troops exchanged blows in the manner of a pair of boxers. The fast, angry firings went back and forth. The men in blue were intent with the despair of their circumstances and they seized upon the revenge to be had at close range. Their thunder swelled loud and valiant. Their curving front bristled with flashes and the place resounded with the clangor of their ram-rods. The youth ducked and dodged for a time and achieved a few unsatisfactory views of the enemy. There appeared to be many of them and they were replying swiftly. They seemed moving toward the blue regiment, step by step. He seated himself gloomily on the ground with his flag between his knees.

As he noted the vicious, wolf-like temper of his comrades, he had a sweet thought that if the enemy was about to swallow the regimental broom as a large prisoner, it could at least have the consolation of going down with bristles forward.

But the blows of the antagonist began to grow more weak. Fewer bullets ripped the air and finally when the men slackened to learn of the fight, they could see only dark, floating smoke. The regiment lay still and gazed. Presently, some chance whim came to the pestering blur and it began to coil heavily away. The men saw a ground vacant of fighters. It would have been an empty stage if it were not for a few corpses that lay thrown and twisted into fantastic shapes upon the sward.

At sight of this tableau, many of the men in blue sprang from behind their covers and made an ungainly dance of joy. Their eyes burned and a hoarse cheer of elation broke from their dry lips.

It had begun to seem to them that events were trying to prove that they were impotent. These little battles had evidently endeavored to demonstrate that the men could not fight well. When on the verge of submission to these opinions, the small duel had showed them that the proportions were not impossible, and by it they had revenged themselves upon their misgivings and upon the foe.

The impetus of enthusiasm was theirs again. They gazed about them with looks of uplifted pride, feeling new trust in the grim, always-confident weapons in their hands. And they were men.

XXII

Presently they knew that no firing threatened them. All ways seemed once more opened to them. The dusty blue lines of their friends were disclosed a short distance away. In the distance there were many colossal noises but in all this part of the field there was a sudden stillness.

They perceived that they were free. The depleted band drew a long breath of relief and gathered itself into a bunch to complete its trip.

In this last length of journey, the men began to show strange emotions. They hurried with nervous fear. Some who had been dark and unfaltering in the grimmest moments now could not conceal an anxiety that made them frantic. It was perhaps that they dreaded to be killed in insignificant ways after the times for proper military deaths had passed. Or, perhaps, they thought it would be too ironical to get killed at the portals of safety. With backward looks of perturbation, they hastened.

As they approached their own lines, there was some sarcasm exhibited on the part of a gaunt and bronzed regiment that lay resting in the shade of trees. Questions were wafted to them.

"Where th' hell yeh been?"

"What yeh comin' back fer?"

"Why didn't yeh stay there?"

"Was it warm out there, sonny?"

"Goin' home now, boys?"

One shouted in taunting mimicry. "Oh, mother, come quick an' look at th' sojers."

There was no reply from the bruised and battered regiment save that one man made broad-cast challenges to fist-fights and the red-bearded officer walked rather near and glared in great swashbuckler style at a tall captain in the other regiment. But the lieutenant suppressed the man who wished to fist-fight, and the tall captain, flushing at the little fanfare of the red-bearded one, was obliged to look intently at some trees.

The youth's tender flesh was deeply stung by these remarks. From under his creased brows, he glowered with hate at the mockers. He meditated upon a few revenges. Still, many in the regiment hung their heads in criminal fashion so that it came to pass that the men trudged with sudden heaviness as if they bore upon their bended shoulders the coffin of their honor. And the lieutenant recollecting himself began to mutter softly in black curses.

They turned, when they arrived at their old position, to regard the ground over which they had charged.

The youth, in this contemplation, was smitten with a large astonishment. He discovered that the distances, as compared with the brilliant measurings of his mind, were trivial and ridiculous. The stolid trees, where much had taken place, seemed incredibly near. The time, too, now that he reflected, he saw to have been short. He wondered at the number of emotions and events that had been crowded into such little spaces. Elfin thoughts must have exaggerated and enlarged everything, he said.

It seemed, then, that there was bitter justice in the speeches of the gaunt and bronzed veterans. He veiled a glance of disdain at his fellows who strewed the ground, choking with dust, red from perspiration, misty-eyed, dishevelled.

They were gulping at their canteens, fierce to wring every mite of water from them. And they polished at their swollen and watery features with coat-sleeves and bunches of grass.

However, to the youth there was a considerable joy in musing upon his performances during the charge. He had had very little time, previously, in which to appreciate himself, so that there was now much satisfaction in quietly thinking of his actions. He recalled bits of color that in the flurry, had stamped themselves unawares upon his engaged senses.

As the regiment lay heaving from its hot exertions, the officer who had named them as mule drivers came galloping along the line. He had lost his cap. His towsled hair streamed wildly and his face was dark with vexation and wrath. His temper was displayed with more clearness by the way in which he managed his horse. He jerked and wrenched savagely at his bridle, stopping the hard-breathing animal with a furious pull near the colonel of the regiment. He immediately exploded in reproaches which came unbidden to the ears of the men. They were suddenly alert, being always curious about black words between officers.

"Oh, thunder, MacChesnay, what an awful bull you made of this thing," began the officer. He attempted low tones but his indignation caused certain of the men to learn the sense of his words. "What an awful mess you made. Good Lord, man, you stopped about a hundred feet this side of a very pretty success. If your men had gone a hundred feet further you would have made a great charge, but as it is—what a lot of mud-diggers you've got anyway."

The men, listening with bated breath, now turned their curious eyes upon the colonel. They had a ragamuffin interest in this affair. The colonel was seen to straighten his form and put one hand forth in oratorical fashion. He wore an injured air; it was as if a deacon had been accused of stealing. The men were wiggling in an ecstasy of excitement.

But, of a sudden, the colonel's manner changed from that of a deacon to that of a Frenchman. He shrugged his shoulders. "Oh, well, general, we went as far as we could," he said calmly.

" 'As far as you could'? Did you, b'Gawd?" snorted the other. "Well, that wasn't very far, was it?" he added with a glance of cold contempt into the other's eyes. "Not very far, I think. You were intended to make a diversion in favor of Whiterside. How well you succeeded, your own ears can now tell you." He wheeled his horse and rode stiffly away.

The colonel, bidden to hear the jarring noises of an engagement in the woods to the left, broke out in vague damnations.

The lieutenant who had listened with an air of impotent rage to the interview spoke suddenly in firm and undaunted tones. "I don't care what a man is—whether he is a general, or what—if he says th' boys didn't put up a good fight out there, he's a damned fool."

"Lieutenant," began the colonel, severely, "this is my own affair and I'll trouble you—"

The lieutenant made an obedient gesture. "All right, colonel, all right," he said. He sat down with an air of being content with himself.

The news that the regiment had been reproached went along the line. For a time, the men were bewildered by it. "Good thunder," they ejaculated staring at the vanishing form of the general. They conceived it to be a huge mistake.

Presently, however, they began to believe that in truth their efforts had been called light. The youth could see this conviction weigh upon the entire regiment until the men were like cuffed and cursed animals but, withal, rebellious.

The friend, with a grievance in his eye, went to the youth. "I wonder what he does want," he said. "He must think we went out there an' played marbles. I never see sech a man."

The youth developed a tranquil philosophy for these moments of irritation. "Oh, well," he rejoined, "he probably didnt see nothin' of it at all an' got mad as blazes an' concluded we were a lot 'a sheep, jest b'cause we didnt do what he wanted done. It's a pity ol' Grandpa Henderson got killed yestirday—he'd a knowed we done our best an' fit good. It's jest our awful luck, that's what."

"I should say so," replied the friend. He seemed to be deeply wounded at an injustice. "I should say we did have awful luck.

There's no fun in fightin' fer people when everything yeh do—no matter what—aint done right. I have a notion t' stay behind next time an' let'em take their ol' charge an' go t' th' devil with it."

The youth spoke soothingly to his comrade. "Well, we both done good. I'd like t' see th' fool what'd say we both didnt do as good as we could."

"'A course, we did," declared the friend stoutly, "An' I'd break th' feller's neck if he was as big as a church. But we're all right, anyhow, fer I heared one feller say that we two fit th' best in th' reg'ment an' they had a great argyment 'bout it. Another feller, 'a course, he had t' up an' say it was a lie—he seen all what was goin' on an' he never seen us from th' beginnin' t' th' end. An' a lot more struck in an' ses it wasn't a lie—we did fight like thunder, an' they give us quite a send-off. But this is what I can't stand—these everlastin' ol' soldiers, titterin' an' laughin', an' then that general, he's crazy."

The youth exclaimed with sudden exasperation. "He's a lunkhead. He makes me mad. I wish he'd come along next time. We'd show'im what—"

He ceased because several men had come hurrying up. Their faces expressed a bringing of great news.

"Oh, Flem, yeh jest oughta heard," cried one, eagerly.

"Heard what?" said the youth.

"Yeh jest oughta heard," repeated the other and he arranged himself to tell his tidings. The others made an excited circle. "Well, sir, th' colonel met your lieutenant right by us—it was damndest thing I ever heard—an' he ses, 'Ahem, ahem,' he ses, 'Mr. Hasbrouck,' he ses, 'by th' way, who was that lad what carried th' flag?' he ses. There, Flemin', what d' yeh think 'a that? 'Who was th' lad what carried th' flag?' he ses, an' th' lieutenant, he speaks up right away: 'That's Flemin', an' he's a jim-hickey,' he ses, right away. What? I say he did. 'A jim-hickey,' he ses—thos'r his words. He did, too. I say, he did. If you kin tell this story better than I kin, go ahead an' tell it. Well, then, keep yer mouth shet. Th' lieutenant, he ses: 'He's a jim-hickey,' an' th' colonel, he ses: 'Ahem, ahem, he is indeed a very good man t' have, ahem. He kep th' flag 'way t' th' front. I saw'im. He's a good un,' ses th' colonel. 'You bet,' ses th' lieutenant, 'he an' a feller named Wilson was at th' head 'a th' charge, an' howlin' like Indians, all th' time,' he ses. 'Head 'a th' charge all th' time,' he ses. 'A feller named Wilson,' he ses. There, Wilson, m'boy, put that in a letter an' send it hum t' yer mother, hay? 'A feller named Wilson,' he ses. An' th' colonel, he ses: 'Were they, indeed? Ahem, ahem. My sakes,' he ses. 'At th' head 'a th' reg-'ment?' he ses. 'They were,' ses th' lieutenant. 'My sakes,' ses th' colonel. He ses: 'Well, well, well,' he ses, 'those two babies?' 'They

were!' ses th' lieutenant. 'Well, well,' ses th' colonel, 'they deserve
t' be major-generals,' he ses. 'They deserve t' be major-generals.' "
The youth and his friend had said: "Huh!" "Yer lyin', Thomp-
son." "Oh, go t' blazes." "He never sed it." "Oh, what a lie."
"Huh." But despite these youthful scoffings and embarrassments,
they knew that their faces were deeply flushing from thrills of pleasure. They exchanged a secret glance of joy and congratulation.
They speedily forgot many things. The past held no pictures of
error and disappointment. They were very happy and their hearts
swelled with grateful affection for the colonel and the lieutenant.

XXIII

When the woods again began to pour forth the dark-hued masses
of the enemy, the youth felt serene self-confidence. He smiled
briefly when he saw men dodge and duck at the long screechings of
shells that were thrown in giant handfuls over them. He stood,
erect and tranquil, watching the attack begin against a part of the
line that made a blue curve along the side of an adjacent hill. His
vision being unmolested by smoke from the rifles of his companions, he had opportunities to see parts of the hard fight. It was a
relief to perceive at last from whence came some of these noises
which had been roared into his ears.

Off a short way, he saw two regiments fighting a little separate
battle with two other regiments. It was in a cleared space, wearing a
set-apart look. They were blazing as if upon a wager, giving and
taking tremendous blows. The firings were incredibly fierce and
rapid. These intent regiments apparently were oblivious of all larger
purposes of war and were slugging each other as if at a matched
game.

In another direction, he saw a magnificent brigade going with the
evident intention of driving the enemy from a wood. They passed
in out of sight and presently there was a most awe-inspiring racket
in the wood. The noise was unspeakable. Having stirred this prodigious up-roar and, apparently, finding it too prodigious, the brigade,
after a little time, came marching airily out again with its fine formation in no wise disturbed. There were no traces of speed in its
movements. The brigade was jaunty and seemed to point a proud
thumb at the yelling wood.

On a slope to the left, there was a long row of guns, gruff and
maddened, denouncing the enemy who down through the woods
were forming for another attack in the pitiless monotony of conflicts. The round, red discharges from the guns made a crimson flare
and a high, thick smoke. Occasional glimpses could be caught of
groups of the toiling artillerymen. In the rear of this row of guns
stood a house, calm and white, amid bursting shells. A congregation

of horses, tied to a long railing, were tugging frenziedly at their bridles. Men were running hither and thither.

The detached battle between the four regiments lasted for some time. There chanced to be no interference and they settled their dispute by themselves. They struck savagely and powerfully at each other for a period of minutes and then the lighter-hued regiments faltered and drew back, leaving the dark, blue lines, shouting. The youth could see the two flags shaking and laughing amid the smoke-remnants.

Presently, there was a stillness, pregnant with meaning. The blue lines shifted and changed a trifle and stared expectantly at the silent woods and fields before them. The hush was solemn and church-like, save for a distant battery that, evidently unable to remain quiet sent a faint rolling thunder over the ground. It irritated, like the noises of unimpressed boys. The men imagined that it would prevent their perched ears from hearing the first words of the new battle.

Of a sudden, the guns on the slope roared out a message of warning. A spluttering sound had begun in the woods. It swelled with amazing speed to a profound clamor that involved the earth in noises. The splitting crashes swept along the lines until an interminable roar was developed. To those in the midst of it, it became a din fitted to the universe. It was the whirring and thumping of gigantic machinery, complications among the smaller stars. The youth's ears were filled cups. They were incapable of hearing more.

On an incline over which a road wound, he saw wild and desperate rushes of men. It was perpetually backward and forward in riotous surges. These parts of the opposing armies were two long waves that pitched upon each other madly at dictated points. To and fro, they swelled. Sometimes, one side by its yells and cheers would proclaim decisive blows but, a moment later, the other side would be all yells and cheers. Once, the youth saw a spray of light forms go in hound-like leaps toward the waving blue lines. There was much howling and presently it went away with a vast mouthful of prisoners. Again, he saw a blue wave dash with such thunderous force against a grey obstruction that it seemed to clear the earth of it and leave nothing but trampled sod. And, always, in these swift and deadly rushes to and fro, the men screamed and yelled like maniacs.

Particular pieces of fence or secure positions behind collections of trees were wrangled over, as gold thrones or pearl bedsteads. There were desperate lunges at these chosen spots seemingly every instant and most of them were bandied like light toys between the contending forces. The youth could not tell from the battle-flags, flying like crimson foam in many directions, which color of cloth was winning.

His emaciated regiment bustled forth with undiminished fierceness when its time came. When assaulted again by bullets, the men burst out in a barbaric cry of rage and pain. They bended their heads in aims of intent hatred behind the projected hammers of their guns. Their ram-rods clanged loud with fury as their eager arms pounded the cartridges into the rifle-barrels. The front of the regiment was a smoke-wall penetrated by the flashing points of yellow and red.

Wallowing in the fight, they were in an astonishingly short time, re-smudged. They surpassed in stain and dirt all their previous appearances. Moving to and fro with strained exertion, jabbering the while, they were, with their swaying bodies, black faces and glowing eyes, like strange and ugly fiends jigging heavily in the smoke.

The lieutenant, returning from a tour after a bandage, produced from a hidden receptacle of his mind, new and portentous oaths suited to the emergency. Strings of expletives he swung lash-like over the backs of his men. And it was evident that his previous efforts had in no wise impaired his resources.

The youth, still the bearer of the colors, did not feel his idleness. He was deeply absorbed as a spectator. The crash and swing of the great drama made him lean forward, intent-eyed, his face working in small contortions. Sometimes, he prattled, words coming unconsciously from in him in grotesque exclamations. He did not know that he breathed; that the flag hung silently over him, so absorbed was he.

A formidable line of the enemy came within dangerous range. They could be seen plainly, tall, gaunt men with excited faces running with long strides toward a wandering fence.

At sight of this danger, the men suddenly ceased their cursing monotone. There was an instant of strained silence before they threw up their rifles and fired a plumping volley at the foes. There had been no order given; the men upon recognizing the menace, had immediately let drive their flock of bullets without waiting for word of command.

But the enemy were quick to gain the protection of the wandering line of fence. They slid down behind it with remarkable celerity and from this position, they began briskly to slice up the blue men.

These latter braced their energies for a great struggle. Often, white clenched teeth shone from the dusky faces. Many heads surged to and fro, floating upon a pale sea of smoke. Those behind the fence frequently shouted and yelped in taunts and gibe-like cries but the regiment maintained a stressed silence. Perhaps, at this new assault, the men re-called the fact that they had been named mud-diggers and it made their situation thrice bitter. They were breath-lessly intent upon keeping the ground and thrusting away the rejoic-ing body of the enemy. They fought swiftly and with a despairing savageness denoted in their expressions.

The youth had resolved not to budge whatever should happen. Some arrows of scorn that had buried themselves in his heart, had generated strange and unspeakable hatreds. It was clear to him that his final and absolute revenge was to be achieved by his dead body lying, torn and gluttering, upon the field. This was to be a poignant retaliation upon the officer who had said "mule-driver," and, later, "mud-digger." For, in all the wild graspings of his mind for a unit responsible for his sufferings and commotions, he always seized upon the man who had dubbed him wrongly. And it was his idea, vaguely formulated, that his corpse would be for those eyes a great and salt reproach.

The regiment bled extravagantly. Grunting bundles of blue began to drop. The orderly-serjeant of the youth's company was shot through the cheeks. Its supports being injured, his jaw hung afar down, disclosing in the wide cavern of his mouth, a pulsing mass of blood and teeth. And, with it all, he made attempts to cry out. In his endeavor there was a dreadful earnestness as if he conceived that one great shriek would make him well.

The youth saw him presently go rearward. His strength seemed in no wise impaired. He ran swiftly casting wild glances for succor.

Others fell down about the feet of their companions. Some of the wounded crawled out and away, but many lay still, their bodies twisted into impossible shapes.

The youth looked once for his friend. He saw a vehement young man, powder-smeared and frowsled, whom he knew to be him. The lieutenant, also, was unscathed in his position at the rear. He had continued to curse but it was now with the air of a man who was using his last box of oaths.

For the fire of the regiment had begun to wane and drip. The robust voice that had come strangely from the thin ranks, was grow-ing rapidly weak.

XXIV

The colonel came running along back of the line. There were other officers following him. "We must charge'm," they shouted. "We must charge'm." They cried with resentful voices, as if antici-pating a rebellion against this plan by the men.

The youth, upon hearing the shouts, began to study the distance between him and the enemy. He made vague calculations. He saw that to be firm soldiers, they must go forward. It would be death to stay in the present place and, with all the circumstances, to go backward would exalt too many others. Their hope was to push the galling foes away from the fence.

He expected that his companions, weary and stiffened, would have to be driven to this assault but as he turned toward them, he perceived with a certain surprise that they were giving quick and unqualified expressions of assent. There was an ominous, clanging overture to the charge when the shafts of the bayonets rattled upon the rifle-barrels. At the yelled words of command, the soldiers sprang forward in eager leaps. There was new and unexpected force in the movement of the regiment. A knowledge of its faded and jaded condition made the charge appear like a paroxysm, a display of the strength that comes before a final feebleness. The men scampered in insane fever of haste, racing as if to achieve a sudden success before an exhilarating fluid should leave them. It was a blind and despairing rush by the collection of men in dusty and tattered blue, over a green sward and under a sapphire sky, toward a fence, dimly out-lined in smoke, from behind which spluttered the fierce rifles of enemies.

The youth kept the bright colors to the front. He was waving his free arm in furious circles, the while shrieking mad calls and appeals, urging on those that did not need to be urged. For, it seemed that the mob of blue men hurling themselves on the dangerous group of rifles were again grown suddenly wild with an enthusiasm of unselfishness. From the many firings starting toward them, it looked as if they would merely succeed in making a great sprinkling of corpses on the grass between their former position and the fence. But they were in a state of frenzy, perhaps because of forgotten vanities, and it made an exhibition of sublime recklessness. There was no obvious questionings, nor figurings, nor diagrams. There was, apparently, no considered loop-holes. It appeared that the swift wings of their desires would have shattered against the iron gates of the impossible.

He himself felt the daring spirit of a savage, religion-mad. He was capable of profound sacrifices, a tremendous death. He had no time for dissections but he knew that he thought of the bullets only as things that could prevent him from reaching the place of his endeavor. There were subtle flashings of joy within him, that thus should be his mind.

He strained all his strength. His eye-sight was shaken and dazzled by the tension of thought and muscle. He did not see anything excepting the mist of smoke gashed by the little knives of fire but he knew that in it lay the aged fence of a vanished farmer protecting the snuggled bodies of the grey men.

As he ran, a thought of the shock of contact gleamed in his mind. He expected a great concussion when the two bodies of troops crashed together. This became a part of his wild battle-madness. He could feel the onward swing of the regiment about him and he conceived of a thunderous, crushing blow that would prostrate the resistance and spread consternation and amazement for miles. The flying regiment was going to have a catapultian effect. This dream made him run faster among his comrades who were giving vent to hoarse and frantic cheers.

But presently he could see that many of the men in grey did not intend to abide the blow. The smoke, rolling, disclosed men who ran, their faces still turned. These grew to a crowd who retired stubbornly. Individuals wheeled frequently to send a bullet at the blue wave.

But at one part of the line there was a grim and obdurate group that made no movement to go. They were settled firmly down behind posts and rails. A flag, ruffled and fierce, waved over them and their rifles dinned fiercely.

The blue whirl of men got very near until it seemed that in truth there would be a close and frightful scuffle. There was an expressed disdain in the opposition of the little group, that changed the meaning of the cheers of the men in blue. They became yells of wrath, directed, personal. The cries of the two parties were now in sound an interchange of scathing insults.

They in blue showed their teeth; their eyes shone all white. They launched themselves as at the throats of those who stood resisting. The space between dwindled to an insignificant distance.

The youth had centred the gaze of his soul upon that other flag. Its possession would be high pride. It would express bloody minglings, near blows. He had a gigantic hatred for those who made great difficulties and complications. They caused it to be as a craved treasure of mythology, hung amid tasks and contrivances of danger.

He plunged like a mad horse at it. He was resolved it should not escape if wild blows and darings of blows could seize it. His own emblem, quivering and a-flare was winging toward the other. It seemed there would shortly be an encounter of strange beaks and claws, as of eagles.

The swirling body of blue men came to a sudden halt at close and disastrous range and roared a swift volley. The group in grey was split and broken by this fire but its riddled body still fought. The men in blue yelled again and rushed in upon it.

The youth, in his leapings, saw as through a mist, a picture of four or five men stretched upon the ground or writhing upon their knees with bowed heads as if they had been stricken by bolts from the sky. Tottering among them was the rival color-bearer whom the youth saw had been bitten vitally by the bullets of the last formidable volley. He perceived this man fighting a last struggle, the struggle of one whose legs are grasped by demons. It was a ghastly battle. Over his face was the bleach of death but set upon it was the dark and hard lines of determined purpose. With this grin of resolution, he hugged his precious flag to him and was stumbling and staggering in his design to go the way that led to safety for it.

But his wounds always made it seem that his feet were retarded, held, and he fought a grim fight as with invisible ghouls, fastened greedily upon his limbs.

Those in advance of the scampering blue men, howling cheers, leaped at the fence. The despair of the lost was in his eyes, as he glanced back at them.

The youth's friend went over the obstruction in a tumbling heap and sprang at the flag as a panther at prey. He pulled at it, and wrenching it free, swung up its red brilliancy with a mad cry of exultation even as the color-bearer, gasping, lurched over in a final throe and stiffening convulsively turned his dead face to the ground. There was much blood upon the grass-blades.

At the place of success there began more wild clamorings of cheers. The men gesticulated and bellowed in an ecstasy. When they spoke it was as if they considered their listener to be a mile away. What hats and caps were left to them, they often slung high in the air.

At one part of the line, four men had been swooped upon and they now sat as prisoners. Some blue men were about them in an eager and curious circle. The soldiers had trapped strange birds and there was an examination. A flurry of fast questions was in the air.

One of the prisoners was nursing a superficial wound in the foot. He cuddled it, baby-wise, but he looked up from it often to curse with an astonishing utter abandon straight at the noses of his captors. He consigned them to red regions; he called upon the pestilential wrath of strange gods. And with it all he was singularly free from recognition of the finer points of the conduct of prisoners-of-war. It was as if a clumsy clod had trod upon his tender toe and he conceived it to be his privilege, his duty, to use deep, resentful oaths.

Another, who was a boy in years, took his plight with great calmness and apparent good-nature. He conversed with the men in blue, studying their faces with his bright and keen eyes. They spoke of battles and conditions. There was an acute interest in all their faces during this exchange of view-points. It seemed a great satisfaction to hear voices from where all had been darkness and speculation.

The third captive sat with a morose countenance. He preserved a stoical and cold attitude. To all advances, he made one reply, without variation. "Ah, go t' hell."

The last of the four was always silent and, for the most part, kept his face turned in unmolested directions. From the views the youth received, he seemed to be in a state of absolute dejection. Shame was upon him and with it profound regret that he was perhaps no more to be counted in the ranks of his fellows. The youth could detect no expression that would allow him to believe that the other was giving a thought to his narrowed future, the pictured dungeons, perhaps, and starvations and brutalities, liable to the imagination. All to be seen was shame for captivity and regret for the right to antagonize.

After the men had celebrated sufficiently, they settled down behind the old rail fence, on the opposite side to the one from which their foes had been driven. A few shot perfunctorily at distant marks.

There was some long grass. The youth nestled in it and rested, making a convenient rail support the flag. His friend, jubilant and glorified, holding his treasure with vanity, came to him there. They sat side by side and congratulated each other.

XXV

The roarings that had stretched in a long line of sound across the face of the forest began to grow intermittent and weaker. The stentorian speeches of the artillery continued in some distant encounter but the crashes of the musketry had almost ceased. The youth and his friend, of a sudden looked up, feeling a deadened form of distress at the waning of these noises which had become a part of life. They could see changes going on among the troops. There were marchings this way and that way. A battery wheeled leisurely. On the crest of a small hill was the thick gleam of many departing muskets.

The youth arose. "Well, what now, I wonder," he said. By his tone, he seemed to be preparing to resent some new monstrosity in the way of dins and smashes. He shaded his eyes with his grimy hand and gazed over the field.

His friend also arose and stared. "I bet we're goin' t' git along outa this an' back over th' river," said he.

"Well, I swan," said the youth.

They waited, watching. Within a little while, the regiment received orders to retrace its way. The men got up grunting from the grass, regretting the soft reposes behind the rails. They jerked their stiffened legs and stretched their arms over their heads. One man swore as he rubbed his eyes. They all groaned. "Oh, Lord." They had as many objections to this change as they would have had to a proposal for a new battle.

They tramped slowly back over the field across which they had run in a mad scamper. The fence, deserted, resumed with its careening posts and disjointed bars, an air of quiet rural depravity. Beyond it, there lay spread a few corpses. Conspicuous, was the contorted body of the color-bearer in grey whose flag the youth's friend was now bearing away.

The regiment marched until it had joined its fellows. The re-formed brigade, in column, aimed through a wood at the road. Directly they were in a mass of dust-covered troops and were trudging along in a way parallel to the enemy's lines, as these had been defined by the previous turmoil.

They passed within view of the stolid white house and saw in front of it, groups of their comrades lying in wait behind a neat breastwork. A row of guns were booming at a distant enemy. Shells thrown in reply were raising clouds of dust and splinters. Horsemen dashed along the line of entrenchments.

As they passed near other commands, men of the dilapidated regiment procured the captured flag from the youth's friend and, tossing it high into the air cheered tumultuously as it turned, with apparent reluctance, slowly over and over.

At this point of its march, the division curved away from the field and went winding off in the direction of the river. When the significance of this movement had impressed itself upon the youth, he turned his head and looked over his shoulder toward the trampled and debris-strewed ground. He breathed a breath of new satisfaction. He finally nudged his friend. "Well, it's all over," he said to him.

His friend gazed backward. "B'Gawd, it is," he assented.

They mused.

For a time, the youth was obliged to reflect in a puzzled and uncertain way. His mind was under-going a subtle change. It took moments for his mind to cast off its battleful ways and resume its accustomed course of thought. Gradually his brain emerged from the clogged clouds and at last he was enabled to more closely comprehend himself and circumstance.

He understood then that the existence of shot and counter-shot was in the past. He had dwelt in a land of strange, squalling upheavals and had come forth. He had been where there was red of blood and black of passion, and he was escaped. His first thoughts were given to rejoicings at this fact.

Later, he began to study his deeds—his failures and his achievements. Thus fresh from scenes where many of his usual machines of reflection had been idle, from where he had proceeded sheep-like, he struggled to marshall all his acts.

At last, they marched before him clearly. From this present viewpoint, he was enabled to look upon them in spectator fashion and to criticise them with some correctness, for his new condition had already defeated certain sympathies.

His friend, too, seemed engaged with some retrospection for he suddenly gestured and said: "Good Lord!"

"What?" asked the youth.

"Good Lord!" repeated his friend. "Yeh know Jimmie Rogers? Well, he—gosh, when he was hurt I started t' git some water fer'im an', thunder, I aint seen'im from that time 'til this. I clean forgot what I—say, has anybody seen Jimmie Rogers?"

"Seen'im? No! He's dead," they told him.

His friend swore.

But the youth, regarding his procession of memory, felt gleeful and unregretting, for, in it, his public deeds were paraded in great and shining prominence. Those performances which had been witnessed by his fellows marched now in wide purple and gold, hiding various deflections. They went gaily, with music. It was pleasure to watch these things. He spent delightful minutes viewing the gilded images of memory.

He saw that he was good. He re-called with a thrill of joy the respectful comments of his fellows upon his conduct. He said to himself again the sentence of the insane lieutenant: "If I had ten thousand wild-cats like you, I could tear th' stomach outa this war in less'n a week." It was a little coronation.

Nevertheless, the ghost of his flight from the first engagement appeared to him and danced. Echoes of his terrible combat with the arrayed forces of the universe came to his ears. There were small shoutings in his brain about these matters. For a moment, he blushed, and the light of his soul flickered with shame.

However, he presently procured an explanation and an apology. He said that those tempestuous moments were of the wild mistakes and ravings of a novice who did not comprehend. He had been a mere man railing at a condition but now he was out of it and could see that it had been very proper and just. It had been necessary for him to swallow swords that he might have a better throat for grapes.[3] Fate had in truth, been kind to him; she had stabbed him with benign purpose and diligently cudgeled him for his own sake. In his rebellion, he had been very portentous, no doubt, and sin-

---

3. This is one of the most striking of those passages where Crane introduces vestiges of Biblical imagery and ideas into Henry's thoughts. The relevant passage is: "And out of his mouth goeth a sharp sword, that with it he should smite the nations: and he shall rule them with a rod of iron: and he treadeth the winepress of the fierceness and wrath of Almighty God" (Revelation 19.15).

cere, and anxious for humanity, but now that he stood safe, with no lack of blood, it was suddenly clear to him that he had been wrong not to kiss the knife and bow to the cudgel. He had foolishly squirmed.

But the sky would forget. It was true, he admitted, that in the world it was the habit to cry devil at persons who refused to trust what they could not trust, but he thought that perhaps the stars dealt differently. The imperturbable sun shines on insult and worship.

As the youth was thus fraternizing again with nature, a spectre of reproach came to him. There loomed the dogging memory of the tattered soldier, he, who gored by bullets and faint for blood, had fretted concerning an imagined wound in another, he, who had loaned his last of strength and intellect for the tall soldier, he who blind with weariness and pain had been deserted in the field.

For an instant, a wretched chill of sweat was upon him at the thought that he might be detected in the thing. As it stood persistently before his vision, he gave vent to a cry of sharp irritation and agony.

His friend turned. "What's th' matter, Henry?" he demanded.

The youth's reply was an outburst of crimson oaths.

As he marched along the little branch-hung road-way among his prattling companions, this vision of cruelty brooded over him. It clung near him always and darkened his view of the deeds in purple and gold. Whichever way his thoughts turned, they were followed by the sombre phantom of the desertion in the fields. He looked stealthily at his companions feeling sure that they must discern in his face evidences of this pursuit. But they were plodding in ragged array, discussing with quick tongues, the accomplishment of the late battle.

"Oh, if a man should come up an' ask me, I'd say we got a dum good lickin'."

"Lickin'—in yer eye. We aint licked, sonny. We're goin' down here aways, swing aroun', an' come in behint'em."

"Oh, hush, with yer comin' in behint'em. I've seen all 'a that I wanta. Don't tell me about comin' in behint—"

"Bill Smithers, he ses he'd rather been in ten hunderd battles than been in that heluva hospital. He ses they got shootin' in th' night-time an' shells dropped plum among'em in th' hospital. He ses sech hollerin' he never see."

"Hasbrouck? He's th' best off'cer in this here reg'ment. He's a Whale."

"Didn't I tell yeh we'd come aroun' in behint'em? Didn't I tell yeh so? We—"

"Oh, shet yer mouth."

"You make me sick."

"G' home, yeh fool."

For a time, this pursuing recollection of the tattered man took all elation from the youth's veins. He saw his vivid error and he was afraid that it would stand before him all of his life. He took no share in the chatter of his comrades, nor did he look at them or know them, save when he felt sudden suspicion that they were seeing his thoughts and scrutinizing each detail of the scene with the tattered soldier.

Yet gradually he mustered force to put the sin at a distance. And then he regarded it with what he thought to be great calmness. At last, he concluded that he saw in it quaint uses. He exclaimed that its importance in the aftertime would be great to him if it even succeeded in hindering the workings of his egotism. It would make a sobering balance. It would become a good part of him. He would have upon him often the consciousness of a great mistake. And he would be taught to deal gently and with care. He would be a man.

This plan for the utilization of a sin did not give him complete joy but it was the best sentiment he could formulate under the circumstances and when it was combined with his successes, or public deeds, he knew that he was quite contented.

His eyes seemed to be opened to some new ways. He found that he could look back upon the brass and bombast of his earlier gospels and see them truly. He was gleeful when he discovered that he now despised them.

He was emerged from his struggles, with a large sympathy for the machinery of the universe. With his new eyes, he could see that the secret and open blows which were being dealt about the world with such heavenly lavishness were in truth blessings. It was a deity laying about him with the bludgeon of correction.

His loud mouth against these things had been lost as the storm ceased. He would no more stand upon places high and false, and denounce the distant planets. He beheld that he was tiny but not inconsequent to the sun. In the space-wide whirl of events no grain like him would be lost.

With this conviction came a store of assurance. He felt a quiet manhood, non-assertive but of sturdy and strong blood. He knew that he would no more quail before his guides wherever they should point. He had been to touch the great death and found that, after all, it was but the great death and was for others. He was a man.

So it came to pass that as he trudged from the place of blood and wrath, his soul changed. He came from hot-ploughshares to prospects of clover tranquilly and it was as if hot-ploughshares were not. Scars faded as flowers.

It rained. The procession of weary soldiers became a bedraggled train, despondent and muttering, marching with churning effort, in a trough of liquid brown mud under a low, wretched sky. Yet the youth smiled, for he saw that the world was a world for him though many discovered it to be made of oaths and walking-sticks. He had rid himself of the red sickness of battle. The sultry night-mare was in the past. He had been an animal blistered and sweating in the heat and pain of war. He turned now with a lover's thirst, to images of tranquil skies, fresh meadows, cool brooks; an existence of soft and eternal peace.

The Red Badge of Courage
Nobody Knows

This essay concerns a novel by Stephen Crane entitled *The Red Badge of Courage*, a novel that existed only in Crane's manuscript, not in any published version of the story.[1] In the manuscript the novel is longer and much different from the *Red Badge* that was first issued as a book by D. Appleton & Co. of New York in October 1895. The Appleton edition pleased the contemporary audience and has become a classic of American literature, but it is not what Crane conceived the story to be. Most contemporary readers found the Appleton *Red Badge* to be an account of a young man's growth from confused youth to resolute manhood; but ever since the first close readings appeared in the 1940s, modern critics have argued inconclusively as to whether or not this growth takes place, and still others have said that *Red Badge* is a flawed work that cannot be satisfactorily explicated.[2] What happened is that Crane wrote an ironic story in the manuscript, a story in which the central character does not undergo any positive growth; and then apparently in response to editorial suggestions at Appleton, he made or allowed two series of deletions in the novel just prior to publication. These deletions confused the original irony; reduced the psychological complexity of Henry Fleming, the main character; obscured or obviated the function of Wilson, the tattered soldier, the cheery man, and Jimmie Rogers; and left the text incoherent at several places, in particular the final chapter. The interpretive disagreements about *Red Badge* arise mainly because of the problematic state of the text Appleton published, a text which, owing to the cuts, no longer embodied Crane's intentions.

Crane's dealings with his Appleton editor Ripley Hitchcock began in late 1892 or early 1893 when Crane offered and had the editor reject his first novel, *Maggie, A Girl of the Streets*, which Crane later had privately printed.[3] Approximately two years afterward, following a successful newspaper serialization of *Red Badge*, Hitchcock accepted the war story for Appleton. Then, on the strength of the surprising success of *Red Badge* as a book, Hitchcock set Crane to work revising *Maggie* for Appleton publication. With Crane an instant celebrity *Maggie* could be redeemed; but in the months between Hitchcock's acceptance of *Red Badge* and its publication, Crane had no celebrity and no power. He was anxious for publication and had reason to be cynical about the literary climate of his time; and he was apparently willing to abide by extensive suggestions for revision from Hitchcock before *Red Badge* was published. Editorial requests, with Crane taking only a limited interest in carrying them out, are the only explanation for the kinds of cuts that were made in the story. In arguing that the manuscript, not the Appleton, version is the *Red Badge* that Crane wrote, it is necessary to distinguish between revisions brought about by an author's wish to improve his work and revisions that are the consequence of an editor's stipulations, in this case revisions performed largely by Crane himself though required by the publisher.

The intention of this essay is to reopen the case of *The Red Badge of Courage* by presenting all of the pertinent evidence, that argues in various ways, for reading the story as Crane had it in manuscript. The first section describes the material cut from the novel and discusses apparent reasons for the different deletions. The next section relates the story of the Appleton publication, analyzing the historical and biographical evidence that indicates the deletions were made in response to editorial suggestions. The third section shows why the final chapter of the Appleton text is problematic and then offers a contrasting critical analysis of that chapter as it stands in the manuscript. The last section is a new reading of the novel based on the text that appears in the present edition.

I

The Nature of the Cuts

The Red Badge of Courage has an intricate textual history. The most important extant document is the bound manuscript which survives in the Stephen Crane Collection in the Clifton Waller Barrett Library at the University of Virginia Library. Four of six leaves removed from this manuscript when the original chapter twelve was deleted are scattered among the Butler Library at Columbia, the Houghton Library at Harvard, and the Berg Collec-

tion in the New York Public Library.[4] On the versos of many
manuscript leaves appear portions of an early draft of the story
(Crane was conserving paper as he copied and revised from the
draft to the final manuscript). Before the novel was issued in book
form by Appleton, a much-shortened version (reduced from fifty-
five thousand to eighteen thousand words) was issued by the
Bacheller & Johnson syndicate and appeared in several newspapers
in December 1894 and belatedly in July 1895.[5] In August 1895 a
prepublication excerpt from chapter four was printed in a New
York journal *Current Literature.*[6] The Appleton edition appeared
in early October. There were at least two typescripts made of the
novel, but neither survives: one was used by the syndicate for
typesetting; the other by Appleton. The first section of this essay
describes the extensive cuts made in *Red Badge* prior to publication by Appleton, and shows that the deleted material comprised,
for the most part, thoughts by Henry Fleming which were intended
to expose him as a uniquely problematical character. These cuts
were performed in two separate stages, partially in the manuscript
and partially in the Appleton typescript or proofs.

The first stage of excisions was made in Crane's manuscript by
pencil deletions on pages that were retained and by the removal
of whole pages. These first-stage cuts comprised the deletion of an
entire chapter (the original chapter twelve) and the endings of
chapters seven, ten, and fifteen (this last in Crane's original numbering before chapter twelve was removed). Since chapter twelve
was deleted in toto, all six of its pages were removed from the
manuscript. Crane shortened chapters seven, ten, and fifteen by de-
leting the lower portions of pages 65, 85, and 125 in pencil and
then removing subsequent pages to the end of each chapter.
He then indicated the gaps left by the missing pages with a
"bridge" notation (e.g., "66-67") at the top of the first page
following each of these cuts.

Because these first-stage cuts involved several contiguous paragraphs or pages, they were the boldest of the cuts made before
Appleton publication. A similarity existed between all of these
passages: the material in chapter twelve and in the excised endings
of chapters seven and ten comprised interior monologues by Henry
Fleming, and the ending to chapter fifteen consisted, in part, of
his evaluation of these monologues. In the monologues (rendered
in third-person paraphrase with none of the more modern strategy
of dispensing with conventional syntax or punctuation) Henry
rebels against or bitterly accepts a variously named cosmic agency
—"nature," "the powers of fate," "the source of things," "a God,"
"the Great Responsibility"—as the ultimate cause of his own actions. Each of the monologues in chapters seven, ten, and twelve

occurs after Henry has run from battle; each is an escape into self-justification, self-pity, or philosophical scheming that begins when he comes to a point of despair and frustration over his failure to meet traditional standards of manhood.

In the deleted conclusion to chapter seven, seeing that nature's laws will not justify his flight, Henry decides that nature is universally malevolent. Repeating this thought in an angrier mood at the close of chapter ten, he concludes that nature must have created glory in order to entice men to war "because ordinary processes could not furnish deaths enough" (p. 49). The original chapter twelve presents a climax in this philosophizing, with Henry envisioning himself the "growing prophet of a world-reconstruction," the spiritual founder of a "new world modelled by the pain of his life," prepared to show men the folly of their tradition-founded illusions (p. 55). All of these monologues are empty rationalizations that Henry later refers to as his "rebellions." His strategy in rebelling is to envision his behavior as determined by a universal causality and then assume a vain stance of contempt for the race of human beings who, unlike him, are unable to recognize the deterministic state of affairs he sees. At the close of the original chapter fifteen Henry has returned to his regiment and feels relatively secure that his flight from battle will not be discovered, but when he learns from Wilson that other men were separated from the regiment he is angered that the previous day's "experiences" which occasioned his rebellions are no proof of his uniqueness among the soldiers; he retrospectively feels a contempt for "all his grapplings and tuggings with fate and the universe" (p. 70).

These first-deleted passages in which Henry questions cosmic justice may have struck the Appleton editor, Ripley Hitchcock, as the most patently questionable material in the original story, and Crane's consent to these large deletions may have been crucial to Appleton publication. After the author made the cuts, Hitchcock apparently negotiated further revisions. The typescript was made by midsummer 1895, for Crane had the manuscript to do with as he pleased in August. Since neither this typescript nor the Appleton proofs survive, there is no visual evidence for the process of the later, second-stage deletions which removed material that is still intact in the manuscript but does not appear in the first edition.[7] A conspicuous distinction between the longer, first-stage cuts and the second-stage deletions is that the latter involved a more specific excision of short paragraphs, sentences, brief passages, and single words, not extended passages. The second-stage cuts, then, would have required a closer scrutiny of the text in order to isolate the material to be excised and seem clearly to be a finalization of the process begun with the cuts made in the manuscript.

Most of the second-stage deletions were made in chapter sixteen and in chapter twenty-five (the final chapter in the original numbering before chapter twelve was removed). In Crane's plotting of the original *Red Badge* these two chapters contained markedly parallel material that provided an ironic frame for Henry Fleming's combat successes in the intervening chapters, seventeen through twenty-four. The cuts made in chapters sixteen and twenty-five can be seen as of a piece with the first-stage excisions, in that references to Henry's earlier and already deleted rebellions against nature were removed, and, again, interior monologues in which he explained his behavior and his "fate" as cosmically decided were cut. Also deleted was material that specifically laid bare Henry's enduring egocentrism.

In the manuscript text of both chapters sixteen and twenty-five Henry finds peace of mind by fantastical and selfish rationalizations; in both chapters he scorns his earlier rebellions against an indifferent or malevolent nature and decides that he is, after all, of special consequence to a benign cosmic order: "He saw plainly that he was the chosen of some gods" (ch. 16, p. 72); "He beheld that he was tiny but not inconsequent to the sun" (ch. 25, p. 108). In both chapters he thinks of himself as a "man," but in each case this appears as a spurious notion in the light of a thought that precedes it: "He had performed his mistakes in the dark, so he was still a man" (ch. 16, p. 71); "death . . . was for others. He was a man" (ch. 25, p. 108). And in both chapters he thinks that he has avoided death because of his uniqueness: "how could they kill him who was the chosen of gods and doomed to greatness" (ch. 16, p. 73); "He had been to touch the great death and found that, after all, it was but the great death and was for others" (ch. 25, p. 108). In chapter sixteen he predicts that "by fearful and wonderful roads" he will "be led to a crown" (p. 72); then in the final chapter he deems this prediction fulfilled: "He saw that he was good. He re-called with a thrill of joy the respectful comments of his fellows upon his conduct. He said to himself again the sentence of the insane lieutenant: 'If I had ten thousand wild-cats like you, I could tear th' stomach outa this war in less'n a week.' It was a little coronation" (p. 106). Finally, in both chapters, Henry is contrasted with Wilson in poignant and dramatic scenes that are designed to reveal him as hopelessly self-concerned. In chapter sixteen Wilson asks Henry to return some letters he gave him before the first battle, but Henry is reluctant, wanting to keep them as insurance against Wilson's possible questioning his whereabouts at the battle the previous day; in the final chapter the indictment is much more subtle when Wilson's concern over the death of a fellow soldier, Jimmie Rogers, appears side by side with Henry's blithe self-absorption.

Much of the parallel material was removed from these two chapters with the result that the reader could progress through the final chapter without ever being reminded of chapter sixteen. But chapter twenty-five provided the final evidence about Henry that was more crucial to the story, and it was more heavily cut.

In chapter sixteen Henry's thought that he is "the chosen of some gods" was deleted with the removal of a long passage, although a subsequent echo of this idea in the same chapter was allowed to stand, perhaps inadvertently, as part of his notion that fate has prevented his death in battle. In chapter twenty-five his corresponding thought that he is "tiny but not inconsequent to the sun" was cut as well as his notion that death is "for others." In both chapters his conclusion that he is a "man" was allowed to stand, with the preceding ironic thought remaining in chapter sixteen but not in chapter twenty-five. The image of the crown in chapter sixteen and the mention of Henry's "coronation" in the final chapter, originally intended as an important symbol in his mental posturing, were both cut (Henry thinks of heroism in terms of a "crown" beginning in the first chapter when his romantic concept of war is linked "with this thought-images of heavy crowns and high castles"). Also in chapter sixteen Henry's repudiation of "some poets" and "their songs about black landscapes" (p. 72) was removed.[8] And in the final chapter his "plan for the utilization of a sin" (p. 108) to justify his desertion of the tattered soldier was cut.[9] The scene in which Wilson asks Henry to return his letters in chapter sixteen was left intact for the Appleton edition, but the parallel scene, the much more damning report of Jimmie Rogers's death and Wilson's response, was deleted entirely from the final chapter.

A distinction between the first-stage and the second-stage deletions is necessary to describe the chronological order of the excisions. But the second-stage deletions made in chapters sixteen and twenty-five were apparently an extension of the first-stage cuts: the cumulative effect of both stages of excision being to change Henry Fleming from a youth who rebels against the "powers of fate" and chronically employs specious rationalizing to justify himself to a youth who undergoes a change of character in battle. The first-stage cuts removed the most blatant of Henry's offbeat, near-blasphemous tergiversations concerning cosmic determinism. The second-stage cuts weeded out references to passages already excised, removed minor instances of Henry's "fraternizing with nature," and deleted specific clues that indicated his moral intransigence. Since the consultations between Hitchcock and Crane regarding *Red Badge* apparently took place in the Appleton offices, and since neither the Appleton typescript nor the Appleton proofs (which would provide the best evidence about the second-stage cuts) survive, we will probably never know the exact nature or extent of the editor's suggestions. But we do know their outcome. If these revisions were intended to offer the public a conventional war-story protagonist, one who ends as a hero and a man as in the successful newspaper serialization, then the excisions were the quickest way to obtain this. The editor would have known that a psychologically complex character, whose thought revealed a vain cynicism concerning God, country, and all humanity, might needlessly unsettle or confuse a wide range of the often finicky readership of the 1890s.

In addition to the material deleted from chapters sixteen and twenty-five, a motley array of other cuts, some that were related to Henry Fleming's characterization and others that were not, were made at various points in the story. In chapter one the farewell speech by Henry's mother was reduced by the omission of her repetitious admonishment that Henry avoid bad company and send his clothing home for repair as well as the mention of a Bible she gives him to take to war. It is difficult to say why her speech was shortened; the dialogue may have seemed artlessly repetitive and sentimental, especially since she appears later only in Henry's passing thoughts. In chapter four a sizable portion of the soldiers' rumors that originally comprised the opening half of the chapter was not used by Appleton. Again, it is difficult to say for certain why this cut was made. The excision begins at the point where a soldier reports the colonel as saying, "he'll shoot th' first man what'll turn an' run" (p. 23). Various comments by the men follow. The rumor is unpleasantly realistic; however, it serves, along with Henry's early interrogation of Conklin and Wilson in regard to running from battle and the description of the soldier whose flight is arrested by Lieutenant Hasbrouck in chapter five, as a preparation for Henry's own flight. In chapter seven perhaps the most curious of all these cuts was made in a sentence that fused Henry's guilt and vanity: "When he looked loweringly up, quivering at each sound, his eyes had the expression of those of a criminal who thinks his guilt little and his punishment great and knows that he can find no words; who, through his suffering, thinks that he peers into the core of things and sees that the judgment of man is thistle-down in wind" (pp. 35–36). In the Appleton edition the part of this sentence after "he can find no words" was not printed. The deleted clause contains one of the most remarkable metaphors that Crane wrote in *Red Badge*. Because it is a mention of insight by virtue of suffering, it seems the image was intended to be linked with Henry's dream of "a new world modelled by the pain of his life" (p. 55) in the deleted chapter twelve, and with his passing feeling of kinship for poets who "had wandered in paths of pain" (p. 72) that was also deleted.

In the ninth chapter two important instances occur where single words were excised. At the outset of the chapter in the manuscript, Henry wishes for "a little red badge of courage"; but in the Appleton edition "little" did not appear. The concluding sentence to this chapter appears in the manuscript as "The red sun was pasted in the sky like a fierce wafer"; but Appleton did not print "fierce." The obtrusive irony of a "little" red badge was removed, no doubt, because of the changed tenor of the story after the large-scale Appleton excisions were made. Concerning the excision of "fierce," any number of scruples might have required the excision of an adjective intended to characterize the powers of fate at one of the most extreme moments of Henry's rebellious anger.

In chapters ten, fifteen, and twenty-five some conspicuous details were deleted. In chapter ten the tattered soldier recalls his friend, Tom Jamison, as telling him, " 'Yer shot, yeh blamed, infernal, tooty-tooty-tooty-too,' (he swear horrible)" which appeared, somewhat illogically, in the Appleton text with the adjective "infernal" but without "tooty-tooty-tooty-too" (p. 47).[10] In the original chapter fifteen a description of the awakening troops reads, "The corpse-hued faces were hidden behind fists that twisted slowly in eye-sockets. It was the soldier's bath" (p. 67); but Appleton did not print the second of these sentences. (This sentence was also cut from the newspaper version: we can guess that to any responsible editor of the time, this comment would have seemed unnecessarily coarse.) Then in the final chapter a description was cut of "the contorted body of the color-bearer in grey whose flag the youth's friend was now bearing away"; and a few sentences later, a related one-sentence paragraph was removed: "As they passed near other commands, men of the dilapidated regiment procured the captured flag from the youth's friend and, tossing it high into the air cheered tumultuously as it turned, with apparent reluctance, slowly over and over" (p. 105). Whatever the reason for this cut, with the loss of the paragraph there remained no moment in which the men of Henry's regiment parade their battle victory before the eyes of other commands, no resolution to the mockery and degradation they incur first from the catcalls of the veterans and then from the dressing-down the general's staff officer gives their colonel. In sum, these scattered cuts mostly consisted of what, for the time, would have been considered "realistic" details that could be classified as vulgar or shocking, the cuts being made without any apparent concern for damage to the story.

Two small additions to *Red Badge* also appeared for the first time in the Appleton edition. One was appended to a humorous incident in chapter two: "A rather fat soldier attempted to pilfer a horse from a door-yard. He planned to load his knapsack upon it. He was escaping with his prize when a young girl rushed from the house and grabbed the animal's mane. There followed, a wrangle" (p. 12). In the Appleton text, a sentence was added at the close of the paragraph: "The young girl, with pink cheeks and shining eyes, stood like a dauntless statue." The addition was probably required to prevent any reader from imagining that the wrangle included physical contact between the soldier and the heroic girl. Then in the final chapter a one-sentence paragraph was tagged on to the end of the story: "Over the river a golden ray of sun came through the hosts of leaden rain clouds." This new image was almost certainly meant to offer the reader a gilt-edged assurance that Henry Fleming had indeed "emerged from his struggles" a changed man. As John T. Winterich remarked in 1951, this sentence "bears the unmistakable spoor of the editor" and "sounds like a concession to the send-the-audience-home feeling-good school." [11] Apparently, when this new ending was added, no thought was given to the fact that several times—in passages that were retained in the Appleton text—the "sky" was significantly characterized as utterly indifferent to the men and the battle.

It is difficult if not impossible to regard these cuts as Crane's final polishings of the story, or careful redraftings to perfect his original intention or embody a new one. Instead, the excisions were perfunctorily made by a process of cutting out large or small pieces and splicing loose ends together with almost no attempt at re-phrasing places where the deletions left the text obscure or incomplete. Realistic details that risked an affront to genteel taste were removed, and the pseudo-intellectual fanfare of Henry's desperate rebellions against nature or illusory embracing of it were cut in the attempt to recast him as a youth who finds courage and self-possession, instead of one who, if he changes at all, becomes at the end even more egotistical and obtuse than he is at the beginning.[12]

II

Accounting for the Cuts

A basic difficulty has existed for scholars wanting to account for the differences between the manuscript and the Appleton edition of *The Red Badge of Courage*: the manuscript text has become available in published form only little by little and in a manner that has hindered anyone from reading the story as Crane originally wrote it. In 1951 most of what was cut in the second-stage deletions was bracketed in the text proper of an edition edited by John T. Winterich for the Folio Society, but no mention of the much more sweeping first-stage deletions was made. After this, in *Stephen Crane: An Omnibus* (1952), R. W. Stallman included much more of the deleted material, bracketing the second-stage cuts in the text as Winterich had done, and footnoting passages that were marked out in the manuscript as part of the first-stage deletions.[13] But the *Omnibus* did not include the text of any of the four surviving pages from the deleted chapter twelve, although in a footnote the text of three early draft pages from this chapter was set out as a way of suggesting its probable content. Stallman mentioned the two pages from this chapter at the Houghton Library (one of these is a false start of page 98, not a final manuscript page), but apparently he had not discovered their whereabouts in time to include them in the *Omnibus*. In a 1955 bibliographical note Stallman printed and compared the text of the first page of chapter twelve in the manuscript (page 98 in the Berg Collection at the New York Public Library) and the text of the false start of that page in the Houghton.[14] And in the Signet paperback edition of *Red Badge* (1960) Stallman printed passages marked out in the manuscript, this time in an appendix, including all four of the pages known to survive from chapter twelve in addition to the draft pages from this chapter and the false start of page 98. Repeating the format of the Folio Society edition and the *Omnibus*, Stallman bracketed second-stage deletions in the text of the Signet edition. Then in 1972 Fredson Bowers edited a facsimile edition of the *Red Badge* manuscript which makes available by photographic reproduction the text of the bound pages in the Barrett Library, followed by the four surviving pages of chapter twelve, other pages which contain false starts, and the early draft pages.

Editions of *Red Badge* that have appeared since the Folio Society edition have, in most cases, not printed any of the passages that were marked out in the manuscript or the deleted pages of chapter twelve; but some have copied Winterich's bracketing format for including second-stage cuts; and others have set out some of the second-stage deletions in an appendix. By printing only the second-stage deletions or, in the case of Stallman's *Omnibus* and the Signet edition, by printing the first-stage deletions in footnotes or an appendix to the story, editors have, unconsciously and by implication, promulgated the notion that the later cuts have a greater degree of authority and critical relevance to *Red Badge*. But this notion is based on the distinction that arises only from the appearance of the manuscript which contains some passages marked out in pencil during the first-stage deletions, but which contains, intact, the material later cut from the Appleton typescript or proofs during the second-stage deletions. The fact is that Crane *finished* the story as he wanted it before *any* of the cuts was made. The excisions—both first-stage and second-stage— were made at a distant remove in time and intention from the story Crane completed in the manuscript and have no relation to the process by which that story came about. Even in the photographic *Facsimile* the pages of chapter twelve are reproduced separately—after all the pages of the bound manuscript appear in sequence—so that their integral place in Crane's original novel is tacitly abjured. No previous edition of *Red Badge*, then, has ever respected what Crane wrote.

Knowing that Crane allowed the novel to be published in its Appleton form, and having no evidence that he ever disavowed the Appleton text in any way, many critics and scholars have assumed that Crane made the cuts as part of the process of bringing the story to the form he desired.[15] But a few others have not been satisfied with simply calling the cuts authorial improvements. John T. Winterich, the first editor to include any of the excised material in an edition of *Red Badge*, saw immediately that the cuts did not have the appearance of authorial revision (although he did not consider the deletions a loss to the story): "One can only say that portions of the handwritten draft failed to survive into the printed text. Crane may have killed these passages in his final revision of the typescript. His editor may have killed them. More likely still, the slaughter was conspiratorial, with Crane and his editor each having a hand in it."[16] And in the *Omnibus*, R. W. Stallman judged some of the cuts, specifically the deletion of chapter twelve, as improvements, but his more general assessment came closer to describing the true effect:

Many of the passages that Crane expunged from the typescript or canceled in the manuscripts during the process of revision contribute additional symbolic overtones, reinforce the dominant patterns of imagery and meaning; they help toward illuminating what the book is really all about. Their omission is therefore a distinct loss not only to the imaginative scheme of relationships but also to the directional line of the author's concealed intention. A few of these expunged passages are furthermore a loss to the picturesqueness of the style.[17]

Several years later in his biography of Crane, having meanwhile edited the letters from Crane to Ripley Hitchcock and published a study of important variants between the privately printed *Maggie* and the expurgated Appleton edition, Stallman was willing to submit, without elaboration, that Crane "resented Hitchcock's tampering with *Maggie*, as he had done before with *The Red Badge*." [18]

Neither Winterich's early intuition of editorial intervention or Stallman's praise for the value of the excised passages prompted a textual scrutiny that took what Crane had in his manuscript as a completed version of the story. Subsequent editors either agreed or disagreed as to the suitability of printing some of the deleted material in an edition, but all held (and often militantly so) that Crane wanted the text cut, and that the Appleton edition represented his final intention concerning *Red Badge*.[19]

In 1968 Donald B. Gibson saw a distinction "between the novel Crane actually wrote and the one he *wished* to present to the public. Clearly they are not the same." But thinking that "we will never know exactly why Crane chose to make public the one novel but not the other," Gibson did not pursue the topic.[20] Joseph Katz stated in 1969 that to include the deleted material in an edition "is to ask a reader to absorb a work that was never meant to exist." But Katz later qualified this pronouncement (although only concerning the second-stage deletions), saying, "of course some of the passages left uncanceled in the manuscript may not have appeared in the first edition through the tampering of an editor, not because of Crane's shifts in thinking about what he had written." [21] Then in 1976 in a review of both the *Facsimile* of the manuscript and the University of Virginia edition of *Red Badge* Hershel Parker asked, "Did Crane yield halfheartedly first to one advisor then another, gradually losing his sense of the work as an aesthetic unity and relinquishing his practical control of it in order to get it into print, however maimed?" [22] Parker submitted that a text of *Red Badge* which would truly serve critics could be satisfactorily reconstructed from surviving manuscript and rough draft pages. He observed that "the Appleton text . . . reached its final form as the result of omissions so hasty and ill-conceived that several passages still depend for their meaning upon passages which were excised." After examining the evidence of the texts and Crane's letters to Ripley Hitchcock, Parker, like Stallman, saw that the Appleton deletions were the result of "various outside pressures," not aesthetic revisions. Stallman and Parker went so far as to relate *Red Badge* and *Maggie*, because Hitchcock was in charge of the publication of both works, and because the Appleton editions of both works are clearly products of a process of reducing by excision what Crane originally wrote. But there still remained the task of bringing together the available biographical details surrounding the publication of *Red Badge*.

No evidence whatsoever exists to suggest that Crane conceived the cuts made in *Red Badge* of his own volition. But there is much evidence to the contrary. Close to a year and a half intervened between the time he completed the manuscript, probably early in 1894, and the time the Appleton revisions were made in the summer of 1895. It was time enough for a writer to want to take a second look at an old mansucript, but Crane was notoriously not a reviser; he endured a number of problems with publishers during this period, and he would have wanted to see the story in print as soon as possible.

His first collection of poems, published as *The Black Riders and Other Lines,* was accepted by Copeland and Day of Boston sometime in August or September of 1894. But the acceptance was accompanied by a demand that certain poems be excluded. And Crane wrote a sharp letter of protest on 9 September, outlining what he valued most in what they deemed objectionable:

> I should absolutely refuse to have my poems printed without many of those which you just as absolutely mark "No." It seems to me that you cut all the ethical sense out of the book. All the anarchy, perhaps. It is the anarchy which I particularly insist upon. From the poems which you keep you could produce what might be termed a "nice little volume of verse by Stephen Crane," but for me there would be no satisfaction. The ones which refer to God, I believe you condemn altogether. I am obliged to have them in when my book is printed.[23]

It is understandable that Crane wanted to be sincere in his first book to have a house imprint, but in spite of the staunchness in his protest he must have found that the publisher could be equally firm, for he compromised concerning the selection for *Black Riders,* apparently conceding the final say to the editors.[24]

Copeland and Day was not the only publisher who disappointed

Crane at this time. *Red Badge* was tied up by S. S. McClure for several months, much to the author's chagrin. On 15 November 1894, after the story had been accepted by Bacheller & Johnson for newspaper serialization, he wrote to Hamlin Garland: "I have just crawled out of the fifty-third ditch into which I have been cast and I now feel that I can write you a letter that wont make you ill. McClure was a Beast about the war-novel and that has been the thing that put me in one of the ditches. He kept it for six months until I was near mad. Oh, yes, he was going to use it, but—Finally I took it to Bacheller's." [25] In this same letter he informed Garland that he had "just completed a New York book," which must have been *George's Mother*. Crane could be relieved if not happy about the newspaper appearance of *Red Badge*, even though this was yet another instance of having what he had written issued without any of the original "ethical sense." But as things stood in December of 1894, he had three complete novels with no publisher for any of them. There can be little doubt that he was more than anxious for a change in his fortunes as an author.

Just after the serialized *Red Badge* appeared (9 December 1894) in the New York *Press*, Crane took some stories to the Appleton offices, and when Hitchcock asked if he had something that was long enough to make a book,[26] he sent clippings of the serialization to the editor with a laconic disclaimer: "This is the war story in it's syndicate form—that is to say, much smaller and to my mind much worse than its original form." [27] Ironically, this is the only surviving mention by Crane of the "original form" of *Red Badge*—made in a letter to the editor who was to cause that form to be much altered before the book was published. Crane probably sent the clippings to Hitchcock with the understanding that, if the editor liked the serialized version of *Red Badge* well enough, he would read the full manuscript. Soon afterwards Crane did leave the manuscript at Appleton, then departed on an extended correspondence trip for Bacheller & Johnson in the South and West. In February Hitchcock wrote him, accepting *Red Badge*, and on 25 February mailed the manuscript to Crane in New Orleans for revision.[28] Crane returned it in early March, remarking that he had "made a great number of small corrections." [29] After this, Crane's itinerary took him to Mexico. He returned to New York in May, and signed the Appleton contract for *Red Badge* on 17 June.[30] A single letter to Hitchcock during the summer shows him approving the title-page proof in August.[31] The book was issued in early October.

In his preface to a 1900 memorial printing of *Red Badge* Hitchcock twice recalled the "delay in the proof reading" of the novel so that "the book was not issued until the autumn of 1895."[32] Although he claimed that the postponement was due to "Mr. Crane's absence in the South and West," it would have taken very little time to proofread, in any normal sense of the word, a small book like *Red Badge*. As it happened, the "proofreading" required the entire summer. From a letter that Hitchcock sent Crane in January 1896, accepting *The Third Violet*,[33] it seems that "proofreading" was a term the editor used to cover all operations he found necessary between the time a book was accepted and the time the final type was set—including the negotiating and carrying out of his own suggestions for revision. The stages in the revision of *Red Badge* and especially the selectivity of the second-stage deletions, would have required more than one conference between the author and editor. Crane would hardly have made the extensive cuts in the story while he was in New Orleans and then returned the manuscript to Hitchcock, referring to what he had done as "small corrections." This evidence, although not conclusive by itself, suggests very strongly that the delays Hitchcock recollected in 1900 owed, in part, to his editorial call for alterations and to Crane's making the cuts—a process that Hitchcock had postponed until Crane returned from his correspondence trip and he could talk to the author in person.

While the story of the Appleton *Red Badge* from acceptance to first printing is revealed only superficially by surviving documents, a picture of the working relationship between Crane and Hitchcock can be shown from letters that concern two of Crane's other Appleton books, *The Third Violet* and *Maggie*. On 6 January 1896, three months after the Appleton *Red Badge* was issued, Hitchcock accepted *The Third Violet*. But in his letter he worried that the main characters were "slangy in their conversation," and he thought the heroine might be "a little more distinct." He also mentioned that he wanted to see Crane in person to "talk over the story." His tone was deferential, but Crane knew the meeting was not to be denied; a few days after receiving Hitchcock's letter he wrote to Nellie Crouse: "I have a new novel coming out in the spring and I am . . . obliged to confer with the Appleton's about that."[34]

In order to allow "plenty of time for the proof reading" Hitchcock set March or April as the projected month for publication of *The Third Violet*. But publication was put aside for over a year. Apparently in search of a more likely sequel to the successful *Red Badge* the editor set Crane to work revising *Maggie*, which Crane had paid to have printed privately almost three years before in 1893. Many extant letters document the process of revisions. In February Crane wrote to the editor: "I am working at

Maggie. She will be down to you in a few days. I have dispensed with a goodly number of damns";[35] and later that month: "I will send you *Maggie* by detail. I have carefully plugged at the words which hurt";[36] and in still another letter: "I send you under two covers six edited chapters of Maggie to see if they suit." [37] In addition to the revision of specific words mentioned by Crane in his letters, a long passage describing a "huge fat man"—the most repulsive of the men Maggie solicits in chapter seventeen—was deleted for the Appleton edition. The differences between the 1893 version of *Maggie* and the Appleton text taken together with Crane's letters to Hitchcock show that the editor was directly responsible for Crane's making extensive revisions in the Bowery story before it became an Appleton book. And they show that Crane, even with the new leverage of the success of *Red Badge*, was revising to suit the editor's stipulations, probably somewhat surprised at being able to look forward to publication of a story which he told Nellie Crouse was "the worst—or the most unconventional" of himself.[38]

Hitchcock, it seems, was a skillful entrepreneur, more ready than other editors of his time to accept stories that were troublesome or that other houses had rejected and then make them publishable by calling for alterations. In early 1898 while he was still with Appleton he accepted Edward Noyes Westcott's *David Harum* after it had already been turned down by several editors. He later recalled to a friend that "the manuscript was nearly a foot high when it came to me." [39] From Westcott's letter of reply to Hitchcock's acceptance it is clear that the editor had suggested the excision of some thirty thousand words in addition to a reordering of sections of the story.[40] Westcott died shortly after the novel had found its publisher, and the changes made in the manuscript of *David Harum* could not have been authorial, but they were extensive, and it is certain that Hitchcock engineered them, perhaps in collaboration with Westcott's close friend Forbes Heermans.[41] The result was that *David Harum* became a household word in America and was an astonishing success for decades as a novel, play, and film. In the early 1900s Hitchcock, then with Harper's, encouraged Theodore Dreiser on different occasions and accepted *Jennie Gerhardt* in April 1911, but then "displeased Dreiser" by insisting on "cuts and revisions so extensive that Dreiser was charged $600 against royalties for Harper's editorial work." [42]

Three consistencies, then, bear on explaining the cuts in *Red Badge* as editorially imposed. In the late nineteenth century controversy over realism versus romance was often in the foreground of literary discussion. The most powerful editors of the time were attuned to if not representative of "the inconsistent, yet potent force known as middle-class morality."[43] Authors, especially "realists," could be condemned for creating characters such as Huckleberry Finn who were not models of proper behavior, or for offering social portraits that were "too honest" like Crane's *Maggie*, or for writing anything that verged on blasphemy such as the poems rejected by the editors of Copeland and Day for inclusion in Crane's *Black Riders*. In the manuscript of *Red Badge* Henry Fleming denounces God, country, military officers, and all humanity and then becomes a battle hero while remaining blindly selfish and self-deluded. All of this happens without explicit authorial condemnation or any conventional "poetic" justice. It seems hardly out of key with the literary climate of the time that such a characterization would be seen by an editor as unconventionally risky. Also, there is consistency in Hitchcock's calling for cuts in Crane's *Maggie*, in Westcott's *David Harum*, and in Dreiser's *Jennie Gerhardt*. Lastly, there is consistency in Hitchcock's requesting Crane to make changes in other novels, *The Third Violet* and *Maggie*, just after *Red Badge* was published. If these related consistencies regarding the tastes of the period, Hitchcock's known editorial practices with other authors, and his specific dealings with Crane did not exist, the cuts in *Red Badge* would be mysterious indeed.

When Crane first sent clippings of *Red Badge* to Hitchcock, his hopes for seeing one of his novels issued by a major house were undoubtedly high. After *Maggie* had been rejected by such powerful New York editors as Richard Watson Gilder and Hitchcock himself,[44] and after his experiences with Copeland and Day, Crane would have understandably become cynical about the exigencies of publication enforced by the moralistic literary climate of his time. He was impoverished and anxious for publication. Despite serious disappointments he continued to write by virtue of fierce resolution and the encouragement of William Dean Howells and Hamlin Garland. When he took *Red Badge* to Appleton, Crane knew that no major house would issue a book it felt was "unsafe"—a book that chanced adverse reviews because it contained passages that could be considered distasteful or immoral or in any way seemed too unconventionally risky. When Hitchcock called for revisions of *Red Badge* more than a year after the story had been completed and months after it had been drastically condensed for newspaper serialization, Crane probably felt that acquiescence to the editor's suggestions was the only way he was likely to see the novel printed in anything that approached its "original form."

III

The Appleton Final Chapter and the
Manuscript Final Chapter

The basic interpretive disagreements about *The Red Badge of Courage* in modern criticism arise mainly over the final chapter which Crane originally intended as a quiet but sharply ironic coda demonstrating Henry Fleming's continuing proclivity for youthful egotism and self-delusion. Since in the Appleton edition the final chapter was left especially confusing and incoherent by the second-stage deletions, it is natural that critics have found that chapter difficult or impossible to explicate. A recent essay (1974) by Robert Rechnitz opens with the observation that "Studies of *The Red Badge of Courage* continue to question whether the intention of the novel's final paragraphs is literal or ironic";[45] Rechnitz himself concludes that "it is impossible to take the final four paragraphs as either intentionally straightforward or ironic in tone"; and he agrees with Richard Chase that, ultimately, "these paragraphs reflect Crane's embarrassment 'about the necessity of pointing a moral.'"[46] Rechnitz is correct in observing that the final paragraphs of the Appleton text are obscure. But Chase's hypothesis proceeds from the assumption that the Appleton version of the final chapter represents Crane's intentions for ending the novel. Even if Crane was "embarrassed" about moralizing, this would have no bearing on the textual problems in the final chapter, for they exist solely because of the excisions. To agree with Chase and others who have said that Crane failed as an artist, that he could not write a satisfactory final chapter to *Red Badge*, is to deny the existence of the chapter he *did* write, the one which ends *Red Badge* in the manuscript.

In fact, the final chapter of the Appleton edition was so altered that it was left problematic in much more than the last four paragraphs, and much more than the "tone" was rendered ambiguous. By offering in this section a demonstration of why the Appleton text does *not* make sense, followed by an interpretive reading of the same chapter as it stands in the manuscript, I hope to show how different these two versions of the ending are; and as a by-product of this demonstration, make clear why critics have had such difficulty in explicating the story.

Crane's irony is often brought into final focus in a distinct kind of narrative ending that he used in works both before and after *Red Badge*: a concluding scene in which one of the characters falsely interprets the main events of the story or is seen to be unable to interpret them at all. The irony of these scenes of interpretation or impasse must be discerned almost entirely by the reader, as Crane offers few if any clues. "I try to give to readers a slice out of life," he once remarked, "and if there is any moral or lesson in it I do not point it out. I let the reader find it for himself." [47] In the final section of "The Blue Hotel" the Easterner, thinking back on the Swede's death months after it occurs, offers the cowboy a "fog of mysterious theory" to explain the cause of that death. But he betrays the real reason for his lingering concern over the incident when he reveals that he had known the hotelkeeper's son Johnny was cheating in the game of high five. We are able to infer, then, that the Easterner's uneasiness about not having courage enough to speak up is the real "interpretation" he feels. Something of this sort occurs in the final chapter of *Maggie*. Maggie's mother responds to the pleas of her neighbors to forgive her now deceased daughter for becoming "ruined" and descending to prostitution, crying, "Oh yes, I'll fergive her! I'll fergive her!" But nothing in the story even hints that she has compassion enough to forgive anyone for anything. Crane seems to be saying, instead, that her own part in Maggie's downfall is beyond all but the most transcendent forgiveness: she has committed the unpardonable sin against the human heart. The endings of *George's Mother* and "The Monster" find the main characters literally thoughtless. George is silent in the room as his mother dies, but from a nearby apartment is heard the voice of a neighbor scolding her son, implying George's guilty sense of having played a part in his own mother's death. In the final scene of "The Monster" Dr. Trescott can do little more than count the fifteen empty teacups that represent the community's ostracism of his family, the ambiguous price of his attempts to act altruistically toward the burned black man who has indeed become a monster for all concerned. The pattern common to these scenes is the appearance of the story's most culpable character shown in the final moments to be utterly blind to the degree and nature of his moral failing or psychological weakness. Depending on the measure of their blindness and the circumstances involved, Crane probably felt and intended to evoke varying degrees of sympathy for these characters. But what is more important, he wanted the reader to experience the complex mixture of moral and psychological uncertainty the characters feel. With no intrusive authorial commentary or any dispensations of poetic justice, the reader must engage his own discernment and find his own grounds for judgment.

Crane's original design in the final chapter of *Red Badge* was to have Henry Fleming recall from the first day of battle those experiences about which he is still ashamed, and then have him contrive justifications and excuses to resolve his shame. The experiences in question are his flight from battle (which lost most of its sting after his success on the second day), his denunciations of the cosmos, and his desertion of the tattered soldier. But in the Appleton edition Henry could not reflect on his rebellions against the heavens because they had already been deleted in the manuscript. Nor could he offer his highly questionable "plan for the utilization of a sin" to justify his desertion of the tattered soldier if he was to be pushed toward the character of a morally changed hero. In the Appleton final chapter Henry's guilt over these experiences is still evoked, but only shreds of the original justifications appear. With these justifications deleted along with other material, the chapter is erratic and confusing and terminates on an inapproprirate note, the bright promise of "Over the river a golden ray of sun came through the hosts of leaden rain clouds." In short, the ambiguity in the final Appleton paragraphs that Rechnitz and others have noted exists for one reason: *because things are missing.**

About midway in the Appleton final chapter Henry has his first guilty thoughts: "Nevertheless, the ghost of his flight from the first engagement appeared to him and danced. There were small shoutings in his brain about these matters" (p. 229). The Appleton text reads "these matters," but there is only one "matter" present, because the appropriate revision was not made at the time of the excision of the other matter which appeared after "danced" ("Echoes of his terrible combat with the arrayed forces of the universe came to his ears"). In the Appleton edition Henry has a passing response to "these matters": "For a moment he blushed, and the light of his soul flickered with shame"; but it is passing indeed, for the next paragraphs which contained Henry's "explanation" and "apology" for his rebellions were cut. The following paragraph in the Appleton text opens with Henry's immediate conjuring of a different problem from the previous day: "A specter of reproach came to him. There loomed the dogging memory of the tattered soldier" (p. 230). Henry's thoughts about his desertion of the tattered soldier continue, interrupted at one point by a snatch of dialogue from the soldiers near him, until the matter is closed by a sentence that begins the fifth-to-last paragraph: "Yet gradually he mustered force to put the sin at a dis-

---

* In the following three paragraphs which discuss the Appleton final chapter, page notations that appear parenthetically in the text are keyed to a first printing of *The Red Badge of Courage* (New York: D. Appleton & Co., 1895).

tance" (pp. 231–32). But the reader never learns about the nature of Henry's "force" or what kind of "distance" is involved, because—except for this sentence—the Appleton edition deleted all of a two-paragraph description of how Henry transforms his "sin" into a usable voice in his moral conscience. The sentence beginning "Yet gradually" originally served to introduce this description; in the Appleton text, however, the sentence was spliced onto the paragraph that *followed* Henry's rationalizing process. A short phrase—"And at last"—was added at the beginning of the next sentence to imply the duration of the excised process of distancing and ease the transition to Henry's final thoughts on his rebellions: "Yet gradually he mustered force to put the sin at a distance. And at last his eyes seemed to open to some new ways. He found that he could look back upon the brass and bombast of his earlier gospels and see them truly. He was gleeful when he discovered that he now despised them" (p. 232). Henry may well be both gleeful and despising here all at once, but careful readers of the Appleton text can only be confused, wondering if they have not forgotten something, namely the "earlier gospels." None of their brass and bombast was any longer in the story.

Having the apparent notion that either glee or despisal or both taken together are convictive, the narrator seems to proceed positively and unhesitatingly in the next Appleton paragraph: "With this conviction came a store of assurance. He felt a quiet manhood, nonassertive but of sturdy and strong blood. He knew that he would no more quail before his guides wherever they should point. He had been to touch the great death, and found that, after all, it was but the great death. He was a man" (p. 232). The reader, however, has reason to be less than convinced by Henry's "store of assurance," for there is no "conviction" left: deletion of the two paragraphs which originally preceded its mention having removed the "conviction" on which Henry's assurance is founded—his sense that he is "tiny but not inconsequent to the sun." The reader of the Appleton text is also left to wonder who Henry's "guides" might be in this paragraph, since they were lost as a consequence of the excisions.

The next, third-to-last, paragraph in the Appleton edition begins, as it does in the manuscript, in high Biblical style: "So it came to pass that as he trudged from the place of blood and wrath his soul changed" (p. 232). Then there is a paraphrase of Henry's thoughts which includes a Biblical allusion: "He came from hot plowshares to prospects of clover tranquilly, and it was as if hot plowshares were not. Scars faded as flowers." The ironic tone of this allusion to Isaiah 2:4 ("They shall beat their swords into ploughshares") is clear in the manuscript when preceding it in one of the deleted passages appears the sentence, "It had been necessary for him to swallow swords that he might have a better throat for grapes"—a highly ironic echo of Revelation 19:15.[48] But without this foregoing irony, Henry's transposition from hot ploughshares to clover seems intended literally and in concert with "his soul changed." And the two final Appleton paragraphs seem to support the idea that Henry has changed as he turns "with a lover's thirst to images of tranquil skies, fresh meadows, cool brooks—an existence of soft and eternal peace"; finally, nature herself smiles overhead, dramatically parting the clouds at just the right moment.

The heavy-handed cutting that went into the preparation of *Red Badge* for Appleton publication concerned itself only with the removal of certain pieces of the story, not at all with recasting what remained into an intelligible form. As a consequence, the final and, in some ways, most important chapter was rendered incoherent; and critics like Rechnitz and Chase have been left with the job of explicating an impossible text.

In the final chapter as it appears in the manuscript Henry moves through a series of moods: self-congratulation, lingering shame, whimsical ratiocination, guilty fear, utter self-delusion, and finally dreamy tranquility. As already mentioned, several parallels exist between this chapter and chapter sixteen in the manuscript; but in the final chapter, Henry seems more subtly self-deluded, having moved further into the empty regress of his vanity. He awakens from his battle-sleep to "study his deeds—his failures and his achievements," and by exonerating himself of the former and exulting in the latter he can conclude that he is "not inconsequent of the sun." Henry's most delusive thought follows from this, that death is "for others," but equally crucial to his final portrayal is Crane's use of Wilson's response to the report of Jimmie Rogers's death which closes a sequence of incidents that begins in chapter fifteen.

As if Crane were inviting us to think that the youth will learn by the example of his friend, it is Henry who in chapter fifteen notes the "remarkable change" in Wilson: "He seemed no more to be continually regarding the proportions of his personal prowess. . . . There was about him now a fine reliance. He showed a quiet belief in his purposes and his abilities" (pp. 67–68). Shortly after this recognition, Wilson, in his new character, interferes when three soldiers of his company, including one Jimmie Rogers, seem about to fight among themselves. Wilson prevents the fight, but reports an unexpected consequence to Henry: " 'Jimmie Rogers ses I'll have t' fight him after th' battle t'-day,' announced

the friend as he again seated himself. 'He ses he don't allow no
interferin' in his business. I hate t' see th' boys fightin' 'mong
themselves'" (p. 69). Rogers is next mentioned at the opening
of chapter nineteen, after the first fighting of the day has taken
place; this time he is badly wounded, "thrashing about in the
grass, twisting his shuddering body into many strange postures"
(p. 81). Again in his new character Wilson volunteers help: "The
youth's friend had a geographical illusion concerning a stream
and he obtained permission to go for some water. Immediately,
canteens were showered upon him. 'Fill mine, will yeh?' 'Bring
me some, too.' 'And me, too.' He departed, ladened. The youth
went with his friend, feeling a desire to throw his heated body
into the stream and, soaking there, drink quarts" (p. 82). No
water is found, but we can see that Wilson is thinking and acting with compassion; the other soldiers only want their canteens
filled, and Henry is dreaming of a soak in the cool water.

These two brief mentions of Rogers are designed to build toward
a climactic scene in the final chapter in which his death comes
as an unexpected report. (Since the culminating scene did not appear in the Appleton text, the other mentions were left dan-
gling.) [49] Coming to the final chapter, the reader has good reason
to think that Henry and Wilson are equals by virtue of their similar heroism in the regimental charge. But as they walk along together after the battle, Wilson is thinking of Jimmie Rogers while
Henry has begun to "study his deeds." And when Rogers's death
is told, their responses are much different.

> His friend, too, seemed engaged with some retrospection for
> he suddenly gestured and said: "Good Lord!"
> "What?" asked the youth.
> "Good Lord!" repeated his friend. "Yeh know Jimmie Rogers?
> Well, he—gosh, when he was hurt I started t' git some water
> fer 'im an', thunder, I aint seen 'im from that time 'til this. I
> clean forgot what I—say, has anybody seen Jimmie Rogers?"
> "Seen 'im? No! He's dead," they told him.
> His friend swore.
> But the youth, regarding his procession of memory, felt glee-
> ful and unregretting, for, in it, his public deeds were paraded
> in great and shining prominence. Those performances which
> had been witnessed by his fellows marched now in wide purple
> and gold, hiding various deflections. They went gaily, with
> music. It was pleasure to watch these things. He spent delight-
> ful minutes viewing the gilded images of memory. (p. 106)

Crane makes an obtrusive show of Henry's self-absorption with all
the narrative irony balanced neatly on the "But" which follows
"His friend swore." Unlike Wilson, Henry has not exchanged his

youthful egotism for a mature humility and regard for his fellow man. This is the second of the moments in *Red Badge* in which Wilson is informed that another soldier has been killed; the first is when he learns of Jim Conklin's death from Henry in chapter fifteen and is regretful. In both cases there is the added poignancy that these soldiers have been Wilson's antagonists, although under different circumstances—Conklin before Wilson's change in character when he is still an argumentative "loud soldier" and Rogers after Wilson has changed and attempts to be a peacemaker among the men.

Crane seems to have contrived Henry's thoughts in the next paragraph just as ironically in relation to another earlier scene: "He said to himself again the sentence of the insane lieutenant: 'If I had ten thousand wild-cats like you, I could tear th' stomach outa this war in less'n a week.' It was a little coronation" (p. 106). The lieutenant makes this remark in chapter eighteen after Henry has continued to fire at the battlefield without noticing that the enemy has retreated and his fellows have stopped firing. Much more of a "coronation" for Henry to recall would be the statement of the colonel reported in chapter twenty-two that Henry and Wilson "deserve t' be major-generals" for their part in the charge. But in his vanity Henry imagines a scene in which only he has been congratulated.

Henry's train of egotistical reflection halts when he remembers "his flight from the first engagement" and "his terrible combat with the arrayed forces of the universe." It remains, at this point, to be seen whether his proclivity for self-justification has abated. Obviously it has not, for his explanation and apology for his flight and rebellions are that

> those tempestuous moments were of the wild mistakes and ravings of a novice who did not comprehend. . . . It had been necessary for him to swallow swords that he might have a better throat for grapes. Fate had in truth, been kind to him; she had stabbed him with benign purpose and diligently cudgeled him for his own sake . . . now that he stood safe, with no lack of blood, it was suddenly clear to him that he had been wrong not to kiss the knife and bow to the cudgel. (pp. 106–107)

This is not far from the reflective conclusion that Henry arrives at in chapter sixteen when he feels certain his cowardice will not be discovered: "in all his red speeches he had been ridiculously mistaken. Nature was a fine thing moving with a magnificent justice" (p. 72). Crane never intended that Henry's concept of the heavens be of serious philosophical importance; the importance lies in his characterization of Henry as repeatedly projecting his feelings to a vision of his "place" in the universe relative to a deterministic and judicial supernatural power.

As soon as Henry is able to explain away his rebellions, "the dogging memory of the tattered soldier" looms before him. Henry's cowardice is of much less concern now that he has fought well on the second day of battle, but his betrayal of the tattered soldier haunts him as a sin more serious than his violation of conventional codes of heroism. His guilt is severe enough to make him withdraw into silence as he thinks, for a moment, that his error may "stand before him all of his life." But he improvises an ingenious escape:

> Yet gradually he mustered force to put the sin at a distance. And then he regarded it with what he thought to be great calmness. At last, he concluded that he saw in it quaint uses. He exclaimed that its importance in the aftertime would be great to him if it even succeeded in hindering the workings of his egotism. It would make a sobering balance. It would become a good part of him. He would have upon him often the consciousness of a great mistake. And he would be taught to deal gently and with care. He would be a man. (p. 108)

Henry has the correct formula for manhood here, as that formula has been defined by Jim Conklin, by the cheery-voiced stranger who returns Henry to his regiment in chapter thirteen, and by the changed Wilson. But the narrator's ironic labeling of Henry's scheme as a "plan for the utilization of a sin" which Henry must combine with "his successes, or public deeds" before he is fully content, suggests that Crane was showing, in Henry, the same psychological irony described by one of Pascal's *Pensées*: "When someone realizes that he has said or done something silly, he always thinks it will be the last time. Far from concluding that he will do many more silly things, he concludes that this one will prevent him from doing so." [50] That is, we are being given a highly ironic indication that "the workings of his egotism" are not lessened and that, unlike Wilson, Henry has not been changed by experience.

After his plan for the utilization of a sin restores Henry's composure to some extent, he once again becomes an amateur theologian with a generous new conception of the cosmos and his own modest but not unremarked place in it:

> He was emerged from his struggles, with a large sympathy for the machinery of the universe. With his new eyes, he could see that the secret and open blows which were being dealt about the world with such heavenly lavishness were in truth bless-

ings. It was a deity laying about him with the bludgeon of correction.

His loud mouth against these things had been lost as the storm ceased. He would no more stand upon places high and false, and denounce the distant planets. He beheld that he was tiny but not inconsequent to the sun. In the space-wide whirl of events no grain like him would be lost. (p. 108)

These two paragraphs are those which contain the conviction that brings Henry's "store of assurance" in the next paragraph. Here, as in chapter sixteen, when he is self-satisfied Henry concludes, in a vain fantasy, that he is noticed by the heavens; in the earlier "rebellious" passages when he feels guilty he concludes, with the same vanity inverted, that a universal law, blind to his individual situation, is entirely responsible.

His conviction concerning his place in the universe leads in the following paragraph to the notion that "He had been to touch the great death and found that, after all, it was but the great death and was for others." As Mordecai Marcus has observed, the last four words of this sentence—which were deleted in the Appleton text—reveal "a Henry who completely misses the most important thing he could have learned." [51]

The chapter ends quietly. Henry is self-satisfied and thinks, just as he did in the opening of chapter six after he stood and fought in his first engagement, that war is somehow behind him: "He had rid himself of the red sickness of battle" (p. 109). And so he turns "with a lover's thirst, to images of tranquil skies, fresh meadows, cool brooks; an existence of soft and eternal peace." None of which, from a literal point of view, he will find on the next day; none of which, from Crane's point of view, he has earned on this day.

IV

The *Red Badge of Courage* Nobody Knows

"It is a very comfortable and manful occupation to trample upon one's own egotism," Stephen Crane wrote to Nellie Crouse shortly after *The Red Badge of Courage* had been published. In the same letter he confessed, "When I reached twenty-one years and first really scanned my personal egotism I was fairly dazzled by the size of it. The Matterhorn could be no more than a ten-pin to it." [52] Henry Fleming's youthful egotism, in so far as it precludes compassion and retreats quickly when faced with the disfavor of others, is primarily what makes *Red Badge* a novel about a *young* man. But Crane's idea of "youth" in the story connotes more generally a psychological and philosophical immaturity or ignorance, not necessarily related to being young in years. Henry remains a "youth" to the end, because he never comes to accept his place in the universe by perceiving the relative insignificance and precariousness of his own, or any, life in the inexorable *now* of time and chance. Instead, he periodically imagines that he enjoys a private relationship with the heavens and thinks of himself with cosmic vanity: as if he were considering a universal state of affairs. Henry's egotism, to draw on Crane's own comparison, is not only larger than the Matterhorn but larger, in effect, than the indifference Crane believed existed between nature and mankind.

Crane was unmistakably an ironist. Irony was, for him, not simply a literary technique but a deep-seated attitude toward reality. He imagined the all-encompassing irony of an amoral distance between mankind and the universe; he saw earth-bound ironics in the myriad hierarchies and machinery of society; and he was fascinated by the ironic tendency of men to offer self-serving interpretations of complex events.

Red Badge can be seen as a structure of three broad ironies. First, Henry Fleming ascribes his actions in battle, whether cowardly or heroic, to the guidance of a cosmic agency, while in many passages throughout the story nature is described as indifferent to the war:

> As he gazed around him, the youth felt a flash of astonishment at the blue pure sky and the sun-gleamings on the trees and fields. It was surprising that nature had gone tranquilly on with her golden processes in the midst of so much devilment. (pp. 29–30)

Second, although Henry Fleming is constantly terrified of being discovered and condemned as a coward by his comrades, what he receives from others—both his two friends, Conklin and Wilson, and two strangers, the tattered soldier and the cheery man—is compassion and kindness. Third, Henry's hope of ascending to manhood through heroism in battle is treated ironically in that Henry does become a hero but does so without gaining a mature understanding of life or a change in his character that would be commensurate with such understanding.

Crane viewed reality ironically, but not pessimistically. From his best fiction a central ethical idea can be inferred: a code of compassion and duty toward others, "a comprehension of the man at one's shoulder" he once called it.[53] This code can also be seen to be embodied in a passage from another of his letters to Nellie

Crouse in which he offered an enigmatic view of wisdom and human kindness:

> For my own part, I am minded to die in my thirty-fifth year. I think that is all I care to stand. I don't like to make wise remarks on the aspect of life but I will say that it doesn't strike me as particularly worth the trouble. The final wall of the wise man's thought however is Human Kindness of course. If the road of disappointment, grief, pessimism, is followed far enough, it will arrive there. Pessimism itself is only a little, little way, and moreover it is ridiculously cheap. The cynical mind is an uneducated thing.[54]

This melancholy passage implies Crane's belief that in a universe indifferent to men, acts of kindness ultimately define humanity. Kindness is wisdom in action, proceeding, in part, from an intuitive understanding of the nature of reality in the largest possible sense. In acts of kindness, then, one becomes fully human.

In *Red Badge* as Crane completed it in manuscript, the ironies overlap to provide the context in which Henry Fleming never comes to comprehend the man at his shoulder. But with the deletion of Henry's monologues and his excuse for deserting the tattered soldier, his "fraternizing with nature" was no longer the focus of his characterization. And when the last reference to Jimmie Rogers was cut, Wilson's function as a foil to Henry's intransigence was likewise lost. Finally, the various connections between Conklin's death, Henry's desertion of the tattered soldier, and his self-rationalizing were obscured when his conclusion that death is "for others" was removed from the final chapter. The reading of the story that follows here intends to show that *Red Badge* as completed in the manuscript is a successfully unified narrative, and that the intellectual point and emotional substance of that narrative was almost entirely removed by the Appleton deletions.

The beginning of *Red Badge* is archetypal: a young man sets off to war not knowing what will happen to him in battle or how he will react, and of course he finds things other than he expected. We learn in chapter one that Henry is from the country, and he later tells the cheery man that his regiment is the 304th New York. He has been brought up on a farm in a Christian family and his father has apparently died: his mother gives him a Bible as he leaves and reminds him that his father "never drunk a drop 'a licker in his life an' seldom swore a cross oath." He has had some high school education at the "seminary" where he says farewells, and we learn in chapter three that he puts a measure of stock in himself as a "fine mind." As soon as he is alone after running from the first battle and thereafter, he attempts to recover a sense of personal dignity by philosophical rationalizations. His thoughts, which are often couched in figurative speech that includes strikingly diverse images set side by side ("stone idols and greased pigs"), are a compound of fallacious generalizations about nature and the human race, self-justifications based on nineteenth-century theories of natural selection and social progress, vague allusions to martial tradition from both classical and current literature, and vestiges of many Biblical passages.[55] In the final chapter, for example, he thinks of himself in terms reminiscent of God's response to the creation: "He saw that he was good." No other Crane character, either before or after *Red Badge*, has so lively a talent for elaborate excuse-making.

The action of *Red Badge* falls into two major sequences. The first sequence—Henry's wandering behind the battle lines in chapters six through thirteen—contains the events that are most likely to have the effect of diminishing his youthful egotism. The second sequence—Henry's successful soldiering with the regiment in chapters seventeen through twenty-four—dramatizes ironies of battle heroism and builds toward Henry's reflections in the final chapter. In what may be taken as transitional scenes between these sequences, Henry is "wounded," the cheery man appears to guide him to camp, and we find that Wilson has undergone a change in character. The close of the novel is Henry's misdirected interpretation of his accumulated experiences, and the reader must judge these final reflections from what is learned about Henry in earlier scenes.

While Henry is separated from his regiment in chapters six through thirteen, his moral courage, not his physical courage, is tested. After overhearing at the close of chapter six that the regiment has successfully held its position without him, he wanders throughout the next seven chapters in the vicinity of the battle— a decidedly moral landscape—thinking that he is more sinned against than sinning, questioning and denouncing the gods, encountering the grotesque and pitiable sights of other unfortunates, until he is safely returned to his fellows, those he fears will most reject him. In his experiences behind the lines Henry sees how nature and fate have dealt with other soldiers: the veil is pulled away from the realities of life that war exposes overwhelmingly. War casualties have an implicit universal significance, and a full apprehension of that significance should lead Henry to compassion and humility, superseding his anxiety over his temporary loss of nerve in battle. But fearing the potential scorn of his fellows, Henry takes all that he sees—the dead man in the forest, the procession of the wounded, the death of Jim Conklin, and the helpless tattered soldier—as if it were commissioned by the powers of fate to mock his earlier cowardice and probe his conscience. He angrily rebels against those gods he conceives to be responsible, believing that he has been singled out for his experiences, and that in being able to perceive the injustice of circumstance, he somehow deserves fairer treatment.

The various scenes in chapters seven through ten lie at the story's symbolic center and excite Henry's most energetic rationalizing. In these scenes the grim underside of life's cyclical processes and the indifference of fate to human virtue are dramatized unforgettably. In chapter seven when Henry throws a pine cone at a squirrel and it runs away he concludes that "Nature had given him a sign" to explain his own flight from battle. He discards this notion that nature is "of his mind," however, when he discovers a dead Union soldier in a green "chapel" of arching boughs and is "for moments turned to stone." At last he runs, "pursued by a sight of the black ants swarming greedily upon the grey face and venturing horribly near to the eyes" (p. 37). It is an image that suggests the indifference of natural process to human dignity, but Henry interprets the scene as an indication of universal malice: "all life existing upon death, eating ravenously, stuffing itself with the hopes of the dead." Here and afterward, because he judges nature according to his own needs, nature will always appear to be either entirely for or entirely against him.

Fascinated by the sounds of war he hears at a guilty distance, in the next chapter Henry is drawn toward the battle: "he must go close and see it produce corpses." He comes upon a grotesque procession of wounded men, including one who has a shoeful of blood and hops "like a school-boy in a game"; he hears another, who is marching "with an air imitative of some sublime drum-major," "his features . . . an unholy mixture of merriment and agony," sing a sardonic nursery tune of resignation and death:

> "Sing a song 'a vic'try
> A pocketful 'a bullets
> Five an' twenty dead men
> Baked in a—pie." (p. 40)

This procession dramatizes the democracy of battle for the men, a "pitiless monotony of conflicts" that does not proceed according to the notions of romance, or glory, or "civilized" fighting that Henry had when he left home. Instead of feeling compassion for these wounded, however, Henry thinks of his own plight as a guilty outcast, and wishes that "he, too, had a wound, a little red badge of courage."

Jim Conklin's death and Henry's desertion of the tattered soldier are foreshadowed as Henry walks along with the procession. He notices a man who has "the grey seal of death already upon his face" and whose eyes are "burning with the power of a stare into the unknown." The tattered soldier then attaches himself to Henry until, in a foreshadowing of the desertion in chapter ten, Henry slips away from him, unnerved by his question, "Where yeh hit, ol' boy?" In the next chapter, while he is wishing for a red badge of courage, Henry discovers, to his horror, the identity of the soldier whose face is sealed by death and whose eyes are still fixed in a stare into the unknown:

> "Gawd! Jim Conklin!"
> The tall soldier made a little common-place smile. "Hello, Henry," he said.
> The youth swayed on his legs and glared strangely. He stuttered and stammered. "Oh, Jim—oh, Jim—oh, Jim—"
> The tall soldier held out his gory hand. There was a curious, red and black combination of new blood and old blood upon it. "Where yeh been, Henry?" he asked. He continued in a monotonous voice. "I thought mebbe yeh got keeled over. There's been thunder t' pay t' day. I was worryin' about it a good deal." (pp. 42–43)

Conklin's concern for Henry links him to the tattered soldier, the cheery man, and Wilson, each of whom express a similar concern for him. After Henry promises Conklin he will stay with him, he and the tattered soldier who has reappeared see Conklin make a crazed run into the fields and then die grotesquely: "For a moment, the tremor of his legs caused him to dance a sort of hideous horn-pipe. His arms beat wildly about his head in expression of imp-like enthusiasm" (p. 45). In this *danse macabre,* Conklin's death acquires a symbolic dimension of the "great death": the fate men share distinct from the vicissitudes of their separate lives—exactly the death that Henry, in the final chapter, will conclude is "for others" only.

Conklin's death is the culmination of a series of incidents that begin in chapter three when Henry looks keenly at a dead soldier with "the impulse of the living to try to read in dead eyes the answer to the Question." Then in chapter seven he is surprised by the dead man seated against a tree in the woods and feels a "subtle suggestion to touch the corpse." Watching his childhood friend die, Henry is made a witness to the knife-edge that balances human life and to the "unknown" that his dying friend's eyes have penetrated beyond that edge. Before the battle, Conklin is portrayed as a "tall soldier" with both courage and self-possession, a natural infantryman who accepts "new environment and circumstance with great coolness" and who walks along with "the stride of a hunter, objecting to neither gait nor distance." But Conklin is mortally wounded in his first engagement. Henry can learn from this death that fate is ultimately indifferent to individual virtues. He should be humbled by what he sees, and afterward be ready to take nothing for granted about his own destiny. But his immediate reaction is angrily rhetorical; he shakes his fist at the battlefield and seems "about to deliver a phillipic," but no words come except "Hell—". His frustrated anger covers his inability or refusal to identify himself with the most intense moment of truth in the story.

The tattered soldier, present at the scene of Conklin's death, is one of Crane's most effective characterizations: a yokel whose abject humility contrasts with Henry's intellectualizing and egocentrism. The tattered soldier can be seen as "the thing itself," a man alone, completely at the mercy of his basic needs. His whole life seems defined in the few speeches Crane gives him—his admiration for the army, his distracted wish for pea soup, his mention of being father to a "swad a' chil'ren," and his account of a friend Tom Jamison whom he pathetically confuses with Henry when the youth deserts him. Like Henry, the tattered soldier has run from the battle front (after being shot); and like Jim Conklin, who is also badly wounded, he has a genuine concern for Henry's wellbeing. He serves at Conklin's death to share Henry's horror and grief, giving substance to the youth's experience. His innocent solicitude, however, proves most threatening to Henry's shame.

The tattered soldier's appeals to Henry are made from the position of a stranger with no claim to Henry's friendship such as Conklin has, and Henry apparently feels little or no responsibility for him. There is no doubt that Henry realizes how badly the tattered soldier is wounded, for he abandons him even while seeing "that he, too, like that other one was beginning to act dumb and animal-like" (p. 48). In deserting the tattered soldier Henry belies the sincerity of emotion he seemed to feel at Conklin's death as well as his promise to remain with his dying friend. It is central to the story that Henry's *fear of social condemnation proves stronger than any basic impulse to compassion for others*, even after he has had the very experiences most likely to inspire such compassion.

When Henry looks back to see the tattered soldier "wandering about helplessly in the fields," he laments only for himself: "The simple questions of the tattered man . . . asserted a society that probes pitilessly at secrets until all is apparent." Characteristically, his frustration provokes a misplaced anger against nature and a scorn of mankind:

Nature was miraculously skilful in concocting excuses, he thought, with heavy, theatrical contempt. It could deck a hideous creature in enticing apparel.

When he saw how she, as a woman beckons, had cozened him out of his home and hoodwinked him into wielding a rifle, he went into a rage.

He turned in tupenny fury upon the high, tranquil sky. He would like to have splashed it with a derisive paint.

And he was bitter that among all men, he should be the only one sufficiently wise to understand these things. (p. 49)

Henry's anger is indeed a "tupenny" fury because it is pessimistic and cynical, involving a convenient separation of himself from the rest of men. Here, as elsewhere in *Red Badge*, the heavens he addresses, of which the sky is always the symbol, are omnipotent and beyond appeal. When he is guilty and fearful, he rebels against an ultimate cause; when he is self-satisfied and feels secure, he is much at home with the same distant agency: the justice of the world hangs balanced or imbalanced depending upon his emotional caprice. In the scenes just past, Henry has dissociated himself from the concrete and particular: namely, the wounds of other soldiers, the death of Jim Conklin, and the plight of the tattered soldier. In his rebellion against nature, he covers his uncertainty and guilt with a diatribe on death in the abstract and universal. Not identifying with the other soldiers around him or admitting to his own errors, he ironically finds respite in angry generalizations about the motives of "all men" and the errors of nature.

Chapter eleven finds Henry still alone after deserting the tattered soldier. The energy of his anger against nature has subsided temporarily—to return in chapter twelve—and he broods on the distance he feels between himself and the other soldiers, convinced that he will never be equal to them. He then considers ways that he might redeem himself. His first idea is to return to the battle, and he sees himself, in imagination, "a blue desperate figure leading lurid charges with one knee forward and a broken blade high." But this plan is deterred by various objections. His thoughts then change direction, and he wishes that the Union forces be defeated in order that "there would be a roundabout vindication of himself. . . . A serious prophet, upon predicting a flood, should be the first man to climb a tree" (pp. 52–53). But, reflecting on this wish, he denounces himself as "the most unutterably selfish man in existence." Henry's thoughts in this chapter primarily expose his acute self-consciousness concerning the opinions of others. At the close of the chapter, he can only presuppose what his conscience tells him is inevitable: his return to camp, the contempt of his comrades, and his appearance in the eyes of all to be a "slang-phrase."

Chapter twelve—the original chapter twelve—contains the longest and most complex of Henry's rebellions. His philosophical scheming is pushed to its most imaginative extreme. Like the rebellious passages that close chapters seven and ten, it begins at a moment when he is cornered by fear of social condemnation— in this case, the embarrassment of rejoining his regiment that he imagines in the previous chapter. At the outset of the chapter, he is still convinced of his uniqueness among men, but he has changed his mind about the heavens to the extent of thinking that there is "no malice in the vast breasts of his space-filling foes" (p. 54). Mulling, then, over traditional codes of conduct, he conceives the possibility of becoming a reformer working to prevent mankind from carrying on their lives according to a "universal adoration of the past," especially where standards of courage are concerned:

> He thought for a time of piercing orations starting multitudes and of books wrung from his heart. In the gloom of his misery, his eyesight proclaimed that mankind were bowing to wrong and ridiculous idols. He said that if some all-powerful joker should take them away in the night, and leave only manufactured shadows falling upon the bended heads, mankind would go on counting the hollow beads of their progress until the shriveling of the fingers. He was a-blaze with desire to change. He saw himself, a sun-lit figure upon a peak, pointing with true and unchangeable gesture. "There!" And all men could see and no man would falter. (p.55)

Henry's plan to become the world's savior is the pivot of his selfrighteousness: he can imagine changing all of society, but not changing himself. Predictably, however, his mood turns around and he abandons "the world to its devices," giving up his dreams of world-reconstruction and sinking into despair with the conviction that he measures "with his falling heart, tossed in like a pebble by his surpreme and awful foe, the most profound depths of pain" (p. 56).

He then arrives at his most irrational plan in which he regresses somewhat comically:

> Admitting that he was powerless and at the will of law, he yet planned to escape; menaced by fatality he schemed to avoid it. He thought of various places in the world where he imagined that he would be safe. He remembered hiding once in an empty flour-barrel that sat in his mother's pantry. His playmates, hunting the bandit-chief, had thundered on the barrel with their fierce sticks but he had lain snug and undetected. They had

searched the house. He now created in thought a secure spot where an all-powerful eye would fail to perceive him; where an all-powerful stick would fail to bruise his life. (p. 57)

Although he recognizes that the arrayed forces of the universe are omniscient and omnipotent, Henry still hopes to avoid them. He thinks that there is "in him a creed of freedom which no contemplation of inexorable law could destroy." But it is just such thinking that will prevent him from living at ease among others. In chapter twelve Henry is probably as far from identifying with humanity and from envisioning his true place in the universe as he becomes in the story. His idea of a creed of freedom that is special to him alone marks the extent of his youthful self-absorption. He recollects his flour-barrel escape with the same smug content he apparently felt while hiding from his playmates. Thus far in the novel, he has ventured further and further from seeing who he really is to imagining himself a privileged being in an abstract "scheme of things," precisely the illusion that prevents him from any comprehension of the actual man at his shoulder.

The cheery-voiced stranger who appears only in the next chapter, after Henry has been "wounded" by another Union soldier, disrupts the mood of Henry's despair and isolation. Like Henry, this stranger has been separated from his regiment in the confusion of battle, and, like Henry, only hours before he has seen a friend die whom he "thought th' world an' all of." But, unlike Henry, he has the strength of his cheerful attitude and is resolutely able to "beat ways and means out of sullen things" to help the hurt and exhausted youth find his camp. In the dramatic structure of *Red Badge* the force of the single scene in which the cheery man appears derives mainly from how his attitude and the aid he readily gives Henry contrast with Henry's own fearful, disoriented desertion of the tattered soldier under similar circumstances. Moreover, coming immediately after Henry's cynical and despairing diatribe in chapter twelve (the original chapter twelve) this stranger's demeanor suggests Crane's code of kindness that emphasizes the magnanimity of not succumbing amid adversity to cynicism. The cheery man serves as a moral touchstone in the story. He has the cardinal virtues: self-possession, optimism, and a mature courage for selfless action. At the end of the chapter, Crane makes a point of Henry's not seeing the cheery man's face, although the reader cannot yet fully appreciate the fact's significance. The point is that Henry takes no step, then or later, toward becoming like him.

At the moment of his return to camp, Henry is passed from the cheery man, a stranger, to his friend Wilson who welcomes him back "with husky emotion in his voice," then offers him his own coffee and bedding. Returned to his regiment, Henry is once again a member of the army—no longer a wandering individual, but a soldier defined by duty, in the company of others who share that duty. Something of this sort occurs in both *Maggie* and *George's Mother*, written just before and just after *Red Badge*. In these stories the main characters first appear isolated by psychological and moral confusion. They then join groups in which they are, ironically, even more isolated. Maggie Johnson becomes one with the "painted legions" of the city's prostitutes after being rejected by her boyfriend and turned out of her house. George Kelcey joins a crowd of Bowery toughs after losing his job and being intimidated by his mother's disappointment. Like Henry Fleming, these youthful characters are first established as neither sufficiently perceptive nor sufficiently resolute to maintain their balance in a morally complex situation. Then, in the latter part of the stories, they are caught up in or swept along by identification with a group, which for them means a diminishing of moral conflict, an adoption of posed self-assurance, and a consequent loss of personal identity.

In *Red Badge* the two main sequences of action—Henry's experiences while he is alone behind the lines and his success as a soldier after he is returned to the regiment—provide the basis for the final ironies toward which the story moves. In the latter part of the novel Henry becomes superficially what he hopes to be from the beginning, a hero with a measure of recognition and glory and self-satisfaction; but as the final chapter shows, he does so without achieving compassion for others or any self-knowledge from which he can evaluate his earlier failings in a mature light.

Wilson functions importantly in the latter chapters as Henry's foil, the index of his failure to change. Less memorably characterized than Jim Conklin, the tattered soldier, or the cheery man, he is closer to Henry's youthful, unformed character than any of the other soldiers in the story. Wilson apparently acts the part of a "loud soldier" in the opening scenes only to cover or forestall his own doubts about going into battle. Then before the first engagement he predicts that he is going to be killed, and, ignorant of Henry's own fears, he gives Henry a packet of letters with a "quavering sob of pity for himself." After this, he does not reappear until Henry is returned to camp by the cheery man.

Henry humbly accepts Wilson's kindnesses on the night he returns, but awakens the next day, irritable and complaining, bragging about the fighting he had "seen over on th' right" during the previous day's battle. On the same morning he notices that a profound change has taken place in Wilson:

He seemed no more to be continually regarding the proportions of his personal prowess. He was not furious at small words that pricked his conceits. He was, no more, a loud young soldier. There was about him now a fine reliance. He showed a quiet belief in his purposes and his abilities. And this inward confidence evidently enabled him to be indifferent to little words of other men aimed at him. (pp. 67–68)

The circumstances of Wilson's change are left a mystery. But in the course of his first day of fighting, he has seen behind the mask of appearances to a core of truth where the judgments of men are inconsequential, and only their recognition of and compassion for one another remain in the shared lot of experience. With the advent of his new understanding, Wilson's youthful personality of a blustering "loud soldier" has vanished, and he can openly admit to Henry, "I believe I was a pretty big fool in those days."

Although Henry is aware of the change that has occurred in Wilson, he neither identifies with nor attempts to measure himself against it. Furthermore, despite Wilson's solicitude and warmth, Henry, still fearful of discovery, cannot accept his friendship; instead, he comes close to perpetrating a bit of calculated meanness toward him though Wilson is unaware of it. The scene takes place in chapter sixteen when Henry is hesitant about returning Wilson's letters, preferring to retain the packet as "a small weapon with which he could prostrate his comrade at the first signs of a cross-examination." This plan does temporarily restore Henry's self-confidence, and he relaxes into delusions about the recent past: "indeed, when he remembered his fortunes of yesterday, and looked at them from a distance he began to see something fine there. He had license to be pompous and veteran-like" (p. 71). Later, when Wilson asks for the letters, Henry is so thoroughly obtuse that he takes credit for the *kindness* of remaining silent in the face of his friend's embarrassment, although the reason for his silence is that he finds himself unable to think of anything cutting to say:

> He had been slow in the act of producing the packet because during it he had been trying to invent a remarkable comment upon the affair. He could conjure nothing of sufficient point. He was compelled to allow his friend to escape unmolested with his packet. And for this he took unto himself considerable credit. It was a generous thing. (p. 73)

At the close of this chapter, Wilson has the letters, and Henry is dreaming on—this time of "his mother and the young lady at the seminary" listening to his stories of "brave deeds on the field of battle."

While establishing Henry's heroism as a soldier in the closing chapters, Crane is also concerned with showing the ambiguous nature of psychological states that motivate brave deeds in battle.

Fundamental to the novel is a distinction between physical courage and that genuine regard for others which constitutes ultimate moral courage. Crane's showing the motives for battle valor to be ambiguous—in the face of the high position such heroism holds among the standards of manhood that Henry hopes to fulfill—gives much of the special quality to *Red Badge* as a war story. First in the early and then in the closing chapters, Henry and the other soldiers fight in a state of "battle-sleep," a condition in which the ego is obliterated and the individual is "not a man but a member" who is "welded into a common personality" and "dominated by a single desire" (p. 26). At one point Crane calls this state a "temporary but sublime absence of selfishness." Cowardice, then— as in the case of Henry's flight on the first day—is a kind of magnified self-concern that occurs when the imagination takes over, when normal consciousness is displaced by panic, when the odds appear disproportionately overwhelming. Crane develops the nature of Henry's battle-sleep with such comments as, "His mind took a mechanical but firm impression, so that, afterward, everything was pictured and explained to him, save why he himself was there" (p. 86). And in chapter seventeen Henry is shown to be so wildly absorbed in fighting that he continues to shoot even after his comrades have ceased and the enemy has visibly retired.

Besides this psychological state of battle-sleep, Crane introduced other ironies specific and integral to Henry's success as a soldier. After seeing the wounded Jimmie Rogers in chapter nineteen, Henry and Wilson go in search of water; they overhear a staff-general report to the division commander that their regiment fights "like a lot 'a mule-drivers." This same general then volunteers Henry's regiment for a charge, and there is the commander's grim augury: "I don't believe many of your mule-drivers will get back" (p. 83). Strangely, the prediction does not cause either Wilson or Henry apprehensions serious enough to keep them from performing heroically. On the second day of battle, Henry has become angered at the enemy, and he is further incensed by the general's insult and takes this anger into battle, which keeps his attention on the immediate realities of the fighting at hand. Another explanation for his success appears in a passage in chapter eighteen: "He had not deemed it possible that his army could that day succeed and, from this, he felt the ability to fight harder" (p. 79). Finally, the success of Henry and Wilson during the battle is not offered as an implicit ideal of behavior. Crane was careful about providing a tag to the last battle that prepares for the irony of the final chapter. The concluding skirmish in chapter twenty-four turns around the "grim and obdurate" group of Confederate soldiers who appear more witless than heroic when questioned as prisoners, and who obstinately stay and fight even when their fellows are running away and death or capture is inevitable—plainly, bravery can be irrational and foolhardy; action and character are not to be taken as synonymous or even synchronous.

Stephen Crane was sensitive to the pathos of all moments in which men, alone, doubt the outcome of their lives, and by these doubts feel separated from the society of others. *The Red Badge of Courage* is the story of an episode in the life of Henry Fleming that dramatizes such doubts, and uses them as the stepping-off point for Henry's several misconceptions about himself and reality. The process of Henry's failure to gain any real understanding of himself or compassion for others is the story of the novel. Implicit in this story is Crane's feeling that full humanity involves an intuitive sympathy with other human beings that asserts itself against the moral indifference of the universe and cuts across the equally indifferent human ego; a sympathy founded on an ultimate awareness of the mixture of frailty and strength particular to each person.

The crucial dialectic of the novel, then, is between ignorance and knowledge. Henry does not come to learn that all men share a place in the universe, nor does he find compassion in battle. But the mystery of both physical and moral heroism resides, finally, in each man's thoughts and feelings pressing along separate paths in the continuum of war, perhaps breaching final walls to understanding and action, perhaps not. Conklin is a man before he goes to battle; Wilson becomes one; Henry does not change. From the first, we sense the advancing edge of Henry's expectations for himself; but as the story proceeds, in the no man's land between his wavering self-image and his intermittent scorn and eagerness for bravery, there is no footing for a real change to prevail, never an awakening in him to what manhood is, only the error of his delusive explanations.

NOTES

1. I am grateful for the help of Hershel Parker who provided the impetus for this essay by suggesting in the fall of 1975 that I reconstruct the manuscript of *The Red Badge of Courage*, then read what Crane had written. "*The Red Badge of Courage* Nobody Knows" first appeared in *Studies in the Novel*, 10 (1978), 9–47. It is printed here in a revised and expanded form. Parenthetical references to *Red Badge* that appear throughout the essay are keyed to page and line of the present edition, with the exception of the opening of section III where pages of the Appleton first printing are quoted.

2. These first close readings appeared in *The Explicator:* R. B. Sewall, "Crane's *The Red Badge of Courage*," *Explicator*, 3 (May 1945), item 55; Winifred Lynskey, "Crane's *The Red Badge of Courage*," *Explicator*, 8 (Dec. 1949), item 18. As R. W. Stallman has observed in *Stephen Crane: A Critical Bibliography* (Ames: Iowa State Univ. Press, 1972), p. 365: "With Sewall's article and Lynskey's rejoinder the critical warfare about *The Red Badge of Courage* begins." Sewall and Lynskey were divided about whether Henry Fleming comes to a "moral victory" or an "undeserved reward" in the final chapter.

3. The source for Hitchcock's early rejection of *Maggie* is a memoir by Willis Fletcher Johnson, "The Launching of Stephen Crane," *Literary Digest International Book Review*, 4 (April 1926), 288–90. Donald Pizer, in his introduction to a facsimile of the privately printed *Maggie* (San Francisco: Chandler, 1968), p. xiv, has rightly pointed out that some of Johnson's dating is awry and that he borrows from Thomas Beer's biography of Crane rather than writing wholly from personal recollection. But the recollections, although they contain errors, are clearly an attempt to get the true story on record, and Johnson and Hitchcock had indeed been colleagues on the New York *Tribune*. There is more corroborative support for Johnson's assertion in that when Hitchcock suggested a revised version of *Maggie* for Appleton publication, he did not have a copy of the *Maggie* which Crane had privately printed in 1893; therefore he must have made his recommendation based on an earlier reading of the story. (See Crane to Hitchcock, 4–6 Feb. 1896 in *Stephen Crane: Letters*, ed. R. W. Stallman and Lillian Gilkes [New York: New York Univ. Press, 1960], p. 112.) Lastly, Crane apparently did not offer either *Maggie* or his other Bowery novel, *George's Mother*, to Hitchcock after the success of the Appleton *Red Badge*, which is more understandable if the editor had already turned down *Maggie*.

4. My thanks to Michael J. Plunkett, assistant curator of manuscripts, and the staff at the University of Virginia Library for very encouraging help while I was examining the manuscript and other Crane materials in the summer of 1976; to Kenneth A. Lohf, librarian for rare books and manuscripts, at the Butler Library at Columbia for allowing me access to the original manuscript pages; to Heddy A. Richter at the University of Southern California Library; and to the librarians at the Houghton Library and the New York Public Library. Fredson Bowers has edited *The Red Badge of Courage: A Facsimile Edition of the Manuscript*, 2 vols. (Washington, D.C.: NCR/Microcard, 1972 and 1973), which makes available by photographic reproduction all of the manuscript pages.

5. The newspaper version is available in facsimile: *"The Red Badge of Courage" by Stephen Crane: A Facsimile Reproduction of the New York "Press" Appearance of December 9, 1894*, introd. Joseph Katz (Gainesville, Florida: Scholars' Facsimiles & Reprints, 1967). Also see the bibliographical description of the six newspaper appearances in *The Red Badge of Courage*, ed. Fredson Bowers, introd. J. C. Levenson (Charlottesville. Univ. Press of Virginia, 1975), pp. 249–52.

6. The excerpt was titled "In the Heat of the Battle," *Current Literature,* 18 (Aug. 1895), 142–43.

7. Both R. W. Stallman in *Stephen Crane: Letters* p. 51, n. 49, and William L. Howarth in *"The Red Badge of Courage* Manuscript: New Evidence for a Critical Edition," *Studies in Bibliography,* 18 (1965), 245, agree that Crane left the manuscript which survives in the Clifton Waller Barrett Library at the University of Virginia with Ripley Hitchcock at the Appleton offices in January, 1895 before he departed on a correspondence trip for the next five months; and that whatever changes he made in *Red Badge* before an Appleton typescript was made, he made in this manuscript. In February Hitchcock sent the story to Crane for revision while the author was in New Orleans. Crane returned it in early March, remarking that he had "made a great number of small corrections" (Crane to Hitchcock, 8 March 1895, *Letters,* p. 53). In his letters to Hitchcock at this time, Crane explicitly mentions "the Mss," "the manuscript," and "the Ms"; and Hitchcock's note at the top of one of these letters reads "Ms sent by express Feb. 25." Fredson Bowers, however, has conjectured an elaborate theory about typescripts and their carbon copies (none of which survives) that presupposes the long cuts in the manuscript were made before Crane took *Red Badge* to the Bacheller & Johnson syndicate in 1894, that he made his revisions for Appleton in a carbon copy of the typescript that was made for the syndicate typesetting, and that Appleton set from this marked up carbon copy.

Bowers's hypothesizing begins in his introduction to the *Facsimile* of the manuscript (pp. 47–51), but it is more explicitly spelled out in the University of Virginia edition of *Red Badge:* "A typescript for the book made independently of the typescript for Bacheller, both stemming from the Barrett MS, is an impossible hypothesis: both the newspaper version and the book repeat common departures from the MS that can be identified as typist's errors" (p. 207). The upshot is that Bowers calls the most reasonable assumption—that Appleton had their own typescript made of *Red Badge*—an "impossible hypothesis"; but he reaches this conclusion on meagre evidence that indicates no such thing.

Bowers's list of "common departures"—where the newspaper text agrees with the Appleton text, but the manuscript is different—other than those he himself ascribes to "fortuitous agreement," number only three. (There are well over one hundred instances where the Appleton edition and the manuscript agree and the newspaper version departs markedly.) Bowers concludes his setting out of this evidence with an even more implausible assertion that reverses his own line of argument by claiming that since the newspaper text and the Appleton edition *differ* in one instance *this time* it is because both the syndicate compositors and the Appleton compositors were reacting to the same "typist's errors" which appeared in the Bacheller typescript, but not in the manuscript. Such confusing and inadequate evidence inhibits serious reply by requiring that it deal polemically with minutiae. Here I will briefly present facts (some of which Bowers overlooks) that very strongly tend to date the excisions made in the manuscript as occurring after the syndicate version was set, which means they were part of the preparation of the story for Appleton publication.

The variant readings between the newspaper version of *Red Badge* and the Appleton edition show that Crane was in the middle of making at least one kind of consistent revision when the newspaper text was set— that of changing the names, Fleming, Wilson, and Conklin, to "the youth," "the loud soldier" or "his friend," and "the tall soldier." In the newspaper version these often appear simply as "he" or "him" and in one instance as "the tall private" and "the loud young one" (referring to Conklin and Wilson); but in the Appleton edition they appear consistently as "the youth," "the loud soldier," and "the tall soldier." The point is that when the syndicate text was set, Crane was apparently still hesitant about these changes, but while he was preparing the story for Appleton he knew exactly what he wanted, and in almost every case in the manuscript the final readings are corrected to exactly the way they appear in the Appleton edition. (See 3.28–29, 4.28, and 10.24–25 in the "Historical Collation" of the Virginia *Red Badge* where the variant readings are given.) This evidence indicates that these changes were made *after* the newspaper serialization, and that Crane was, indeed, revising the manuscript for Appleton publication.

In addition to this evidence, a crucial textual document was overlooked by Bowers when he conjectured regarding the typescripts of *Red Badge*. This is the prepublication excerpt from chapter IV which was printed in *Current Literature.* Apparently, in the summer of 1895 Crane took the four pages now missing from chapter IV in the manuscript to the editor of this journal for the typesetting of the excerpt. This shows that Crane did have the manuscript in New York in the summer of 1895 when the cuts in *Red Badge* were almost certainly made. (Bowers thinks the four pages were removed as part of an authorial revision.) See Henry Binder, "Unwinding the Riddle of Four Pages Missing from the *Red Badge of Courage* Manuscript," *Papers of the Bibliographical Society of America,* 72 (1978), 100–106.

The greatest problem with Bowers's hypothesis is that if what he says were true then the first-stage deletions and the second-stage deletions were made months apart. But this is difficult to imagine since much of what was cut in the second-stage deletions referred to the monologues cut in the first-stage deletions and also removed shorter monologues that were much of a piece with the passages cut in the manuscript. Bowers does see that the second-stage cuts were made for Appleton, and he does recognize that these cuts contained "the introspective examination of the youth's states of mind" (Virginia edition, p. 229), but he apparently thinks that Crane made the second-stage cuts in chapters sixteen and twenty-five in New Orleans in February-March 1895 while on his correspondence trip. Bowers never refers to these cuts explicitly, but only mentions the removal of "about 1,250 words" that "had an important effect on the shape of the latter part of the book" (Virginia edition, p. 229). Effect they had indeed; but it is impossible to think that Crane drastically and illogically changed a novel that had just been accepted and then referred to the changes as "small corrections" when he mailed the manuscript back to the publisher! The basic mistake of Bowers's hypothesis is that it concerns itself with and relies on documents that do not survive—and in the case of the "carbon" of the Bacheller typescript, a document that may never have existed—instead of relying on the documents that do survive, the draft and the final manuscript of *Red Badge* and Crane's letters.

8. No previous mention of these poets appears on any surviving manuscript or early draft page; they may well have been mentioned on one of the pages lost when chapter ten was cut. (See Textual Note at 72.7.)

9. In the passage deleted at the close of chapter fifteen Henry probably recalled his desertion of the tattered soldier for the first time. (See Textual Note at 70.27.)

10. There was also one bit of recasting in chapter ten that occurred at some point between the completion of the manuscript and the printing of the Appleton edition. In the manuscript, just before he deserts the tattered soldier, Henry wonders, "Was his companion ever to play such an intolerable part? Was he ever going to up-raise the ghost of shame on the stick of his curiosity?" (p. 47). In the Appleton edition, these sentences were changed to read, "His companions seemed ever to play intolerable parts. They were ever upraising the ghost of shame on the stick of their curiosity."

11. *The Red Badge of Courage*, ed. John T. Winterich (London: The Folio Society, 1951), p. 25.

12. Although my argument is that what Appleton printed was a watered-down story, *Red Badge* as published retained enough of the essential Crane to evoke several comments from contemporaries concerning its innovativeness and liberating influence. A reviewer for the *National Observer*, 15 (11 Jan. 1896), 272, wrote, "Some of Mr. Crane's descriptions both of scenery and mental phases are very happy, and in the death of 'the tall soldier' he is really powerful. Many readers will not like the book the less for its entire lack of feminine interest and character. We are beginning to hope from a like lack in several other works of fiction we have met lately that ladies are really getting a little less fashionable at last." And Robert Bridges, writing in *Life*, 27 (5 March 1896), 176–77, commented that, "the 'women problem' has become a pale and unsubstantial phantom in fiction; and one may be glad that it has been shelved even if it took a baptism of blood to do it. Americans can rejoice that while England sent us in the pestilence of the new-woman novel and play, we have furnished England with the most potent antidote for the poison yet found in Stephen Crane's surprisingly vivid story *The Red Badge of Courage*." After *Red Badge* had become successful, Elbert Hubbard claimed that if Crane "never produces another thing, he has done enough to save the fag-end of the century from literary disgrace," *Roycroft Quarterly*, 1 (May 1896), 26. In a letter to Max J. Herzberg, 19 October 1921, Ellis Parker Butler recalled: "It was not until Stephen Crane, standing on the bank, tossed the 'Red Badge' into the stream that any real writers dared start across from the safe old-style literature toward the realistic goal on the other side of the stream. The 'Red Badge' was undoubtedly the first permanent stepping stone from the real literature of our early days to the real literature of tomorrow. Its instant popularity made it 'safe'—in the sense of approval by the reading public—and the reading public began to

believe that other realistic fiction might be 'safe.' Having put a foot on the 'Red Badge' and found it bore a man's weight we were encouraged to take another step and try another stepping stone." (This typed letter is bound in *Stephen Crane—A Chorus of Tributes* in the Stephen Crane Collection in the Clifton Waller Barrett Library at the University of Virginia Library.)

13. *Stephen Crane: An Omnibus*, ed. R. W. Stallman (New York: Alfred A. Knopf, 1952).

14. R. W. Stallman, " 'The Red Badge of Courage': A Collation of Two Pages of Manuscript Expunged from Chapter XII," *Papers of the Bibliographical Society of America*, 49 (1955), 273–77.

15. The conclusions drawn by these critics and scholars are generally formulated in an impressionistic sentence or two without evidence and simply extend their own critical judgments on the Appleton *Red Badge*. These conclusions fall into four categories, either holding that Crane wanted to have less "irony" in the story, that he wanted a quicker narrative "pace" or a more "condensed" narrative, that he changed his thinking about the story (at some unspecified time) and decided to remove some ideas or "themes" he had begun with, or that he decided to change Henry Fleming as a character. For arguments on removal of irony see Stanley B. Greenfield, "The Unmistakable Stephen Crane," *PMLA*, 73 (1958), 571; and Mordecai Marcus, "The Unity of *The Red Badge of Courage*," in *The Red Badge of Courage, Text and Criticism*, ed. Richard Lettis et al. (New York: Harcourt, Brace & World, 1960), p. 195: "It is obvious that Crane has vastly improved his conclusion by his excisions. Without these excisions the final chapter would be quite ambiguous and would suggest that Crane regarded Henry ironically to the very end." For arguments based on "pace" or a happy condensing of the story see Winterich, Folio Society edition, p. 25; Thomas A. Gullason, *The Complete Novels of Stephen Crane* (Garden City, N.Y.: Doubleday, 1967), p. 801; Bowers, "The Text: History and Analysis," in the Virginia *Red Badge*, p. 229; and Richard Chase, "A Note on the Text" in *The Red Badge of Courage* (Boston: Houghton Mifflin, 1960), p. xxi: "I have thought it best not to restore what Crane himself wanted left out (not of great bulk, in any case), because, as it seems to me, every passage he expunged, without exception, is inferior to the whole, being either inept, sententious, thematically misleading, or merely superfluous (in a story which the author himself was correct in thinking a little too long for its subject)." For arguments concerning theme or philosophy see Olov W. Fryckstedt, "Henry Fleming's Tupenny Fury: Cosmic Pessimism in Stephen Crane's *The Red Badge of Courage*," *Studia Neophilologica*, 33 (1961), 277; Edwin H. Cady, *Stephen Crane* (New York: Twayne, 1962), p. 126; Levenson, Introduction to the Virginia *Red Badge*, pp. lv–lvi; and James B. Colvert, "Stephen Crane's Magic Mountain," in *Stephen Crane: A Collection of Critical Essays*, ed. Maurice Bassan (Englewood Cliffs, N.J.: Prentice-Hall, 1967,) pp. 97–98: "In effect, Crane was attempting to eliminate the emphasis on Henry's struggle against a hostile Nature and the issue of the hero's sentimental misreading of Nature's meaning. . . .

In short, the moral issue which Crane raises in his treatment of Nature in the novel is abandoned—or rather Crane attempts to abandon it." Finally, for arguments that Crane wanted to change Henry Fleming (and, indeed, Henry's characterization was changed when the cuts were made) see William L. Howarth, "*The Red Badge of Courage* Manuscript: New Evidence for a Critical Edition," *Studies in Bibliography* 18 (1965), 241; Pizer, *The Red Badge of Courage*, A Norton Critical Edition, 2nd ed. (New York: W. W. Norton, 1976), p. 112; and Frederick C. Crews, "A Note on the Text," in *The Red Badge of Courage* (Indianapolis: Bobbs-Merrill, 1964), pp. xxx–xxxi: "The omitted passages consist of minor variations of phrasing, prolix extensions of dialogue, and ponderously ironical commentary on the progress of Henry Fleming's soul. These latter passages are suggestive, to be sure, but they reveal a heavy-handed, sarcastic treatment of Henry that Crane had the good sense to modify."

16. Folio Society edition, p. 23.

17. *Omnibus*, p. 217.

18. R. W. Stallman, *Stephen Crane, A Biography* (New York: Braziller, 1968), p. 199.

19. The question raised for many critics and scholars is, What is to be used as evidence for determining an author's final intention? The most ready answer in the case of *Red Badge* is to accept the Appleton text as Crane's intention, because it is the version that was printed. But the unsatisfactory state of that text requires explanation. The simplest explanation, which is supported by all the factual evidence that has come to light, is that Crane's intention for the story he completed in manuscript was one thing; but his intention in making the cuts before Appleton publication was quite another, being neither an extension of his original intention, nor a matter of aesthetic revision.

20. Donald B. Gibson, *The Fiction of Stephen Crane* (Carbondale and Edwardsville: Southern Illinois Univ. Press, 1968), p. 68.

21. Joseph Katz, "Editor's Note" to *The Portable Stephen Crane* (New York: Viking Press, 1969), p. xxii; Katz, "Practical Editions: *The Red Badge of Courage*," *Proof*, 2 (1972), 306.

22. Hershel Parker, rev. of *The Red Badge of Courage: A Facsimile Edition of the Manuscript*, ed. Bowers and *The Red Badge of Courage: An Episode of the American Civil War*, ed. Bowers, introd. Levenson, *Nineteenth-Century Fiction*, 30 (1976), 562.

23. Crane to Copeland and Day, 9 Sept. 1894, *Letters*, pp. 39–40.

24. I am indebted to Joseph Katz's telling of the story of the negotiations between Crane and Copeland and Day in his introduction to *The Complete Poems of Stephen Crane* (Ithaca: Cornell Univ. Press, 1972). Other details are added to this story by Bowers in *Poems and Literary Remains*, ed. Bowers, introd. Colvert (Charlottesville: Univ. Press of Virginia, 1975), pp. 193–201.

25. Crane to Hamlin Garland, 15 Nov. 1894, *Letters*, p. 41.

26. This account of Crane's visit to the Appleton offices is given by Ripley

Hitchcock in his preface to *The Red Badge of Courage* (New York: D. Appleton & Co., 1900), pp. v–vi.

27. Crane to Hitchcock, 18 Dec. 1894, *Letters*, p. 46.

28. See Crane to Hitchcock, 12 Feb. 1895, *Letters*, p. 51; and Crane to Hitchcock, 20 Feb. 1895, *Letters*, p. 53.

29. Crane to Hitchcock, 8 March 1895, *Letters*, p. 53.

30. The Appleton contract for *Red Badge* is reproduced in the *Stephen Crane Newsletter*, 2 (Summer 1968), 5–10.

31. Crane to Hitchcock, 26 Aug. 1895, *Letters*, p. 62.

32. Hitchcock, pp. vi, ix.

33. This typed letter signed by Hitchcock is the only known letter of acceptance for any of Crane's Appleton books. The letter is tipped in a first edition of *The Third Violet* in the Dartmouth College Library and is reproduced here by courtesy of the library. Walter W. Wright, chief of Special Collections at Dartmouth, gave me very welcome assistance. The letter is described in Herbert Faulkner West, *A Stephen Crane Collection* (Hanover, N.H.: Dartmouth College Library, 1948), p. 8. It is on the stationery of D. Appleton & Co., 75 Fifth Avenue, New York:

January 6th, 1896

Stephen Crane, Esq.,
  Hartwood, N. Y.

Dear Mr. Crane:

We shall be happy to publish "The Third Violet" and I enclose agreements for your signature. I hardly know yet how we shall issue the book. It is rather short for the Town and Country Library and rather long for the 75 cent series. Perhaps we shall publish it at $1, but I can determine that better after obtaining an exact estimate of length from the printer.

I wish you were here in the city for I should like to talk over the story with you. I should make any suggestions with the greatest diffidence, for your pictures of summer life and contrasting types and your glimpses of studio life are so singularly vivid and clear. I have found myself wishing that Hawker and Hollended [sic] were a trifle less slangy in their conversation, and that the young lady who plays the part of the heroine was a little more distinct. You will pardon these comments I am sure, for I think you know my appreciation of your work and the value that I set upon the original flavor of your writing. Sometime, perhaps, we can talk the matter over. It will probably not be desirable to publish before March or April so that there will be plenty of time for the proof reading. I will let you know as soon as the style of the book is settled.

Very sincerely yours,

Ripley Hitchcock [signed]

34. Crane to Nellie Crouse, 12 Jan. 1896, *Letters*, p. 100.

35. Crane to Hitchcock, 4–6? Feb. 1896, *Letters*, p. 112.

36. Crane to Hitchcock, 10 Feb. 1896, *Letters*, p. 113.

37. Crane to Hitchcock, 15 Feb. 1896, *Letters*, p. 117.

38. Crane to Nellie Crouse, 5 Feb. 1896, *Letters*, p. 112.

39. William W. Ellsworth, *A Golden Age of Authors* (Boston: Houghton Mifflin, 1919), pp. 185–86.

40. Edward Noyes Westcott to Ripley Hitchcock, 19 January 1898. This letter is in the Butler Library at Columbia University.

41. I am indebted to Ann Hrycyk in the Reference Department at the Onondaga Public Library, Syracuse, New York, for a description of the *David Harum* typescripts which are in the library's holdings. In the Hitchcock papers which are at the Butler Library at Columbia, several mentions are made by Hitchcock's second wife of his explicit part in the revision of *David Harum*.

42. W. A. Swanberg, *Dreiser* (New York: Charles Scribner's Sons, 1965), p. 144.

43. Arthur H. Quinn, "The Establishment of a National Literature," in *The Literature of the American People* (New York: Appleton-Century-Crofts, 1951), p. 738.

44. See Thomas Beer, *Stephen Crane, A Study in American Letters* (New York: Alfred A. Knopf, 1923), pp. 83–86, for the account of Crane's taking the manuscript of *Maggie* with a note of introduction from his brother, Townley, to Gilder at the offices of *The Century* in March of 1892, and Gilder's rejection of the story because it was "too honest" in an interview with Crane on the following day.

45. Robert Rechnitz, "Depersonalization and the Dream in *The Red Badge of Courage*," *Studies in the Novel*, 6 (1974), 76, 86.

46. Chase's comments appear in his introduction to the Riverside edition of *Red Badge*, p. xiii. Others who have felt that *Red Badge* demonstrates a failure on Crane's part to handle his material are Colvert, "Stephen Crane's Magic Mountain"; Levenson in the Virginia *Red Badge*, pp. lv–lxxvi; and Stallman, *Bibliography*, pp. 533–34.

47. This quote is from a letter that appeared in *DeMorest's Family Magazine*, 32 (May 1896), 399–400. The letter is reproduced in full in *The Portable Stephen Crane*, ed. Joseph Katz (New York: Viking, 1969), pp. 534–535.

48. The passage echoed is: "And out of his mouth goeth a sharp sword, that with it he should smite the nations: and he shall rule them with a rod of iron: and he treadeth the winepress of the fierceness and wrath of Almighty God."

49. To my knowledge, the only critic who has ever mentioned Jimmie Rogers is Wayne Charles Miller, *An Armed America, Its Face in Fiction: A History of the American Military Novel* (New York: New York Univ. Press, 1970), p. 79. Reading the Appleton text, it is impossible for Miller to know Crane's intention concerning Rogers; nevertheless, he rightly senses Rogers's importance: "Finally, at the very moment that Henry

awakes to find himself a knight, Crane undercuts the idea of any heroics by presenting the thrashing, screaming, and dying Jimmie Rogers."

50. Pascal, *Pensées*, trans. A. J. Krailsheimer (London: Penguin, 1966), p. 358.

51. Marcus, p. 194.

52. Crane to Nellie Crouse, 6 Jan. 1896, *Letters*, p. 98.

53. Crane to Willis Brooks Hawkins, about 5 Nov. 1895, *Letters*, pp. 69–70. The passage reads: "We in the east are overcome a good deal by a detestable superficial culture which I think is the real barbarism. Culture in it's true sense, I take it, is a comprehension of the man at one's shoulder. It has nothing to do with an adoration for effete jugs and old kettles. This latter is merely an amusement and we live for amusement in the east."

54. Crane to Nellie Crouse, 12 Jan. 1896, *Letters*, p. 99.

55. Compare Crane's description of the hotelkeeper's language in "The Blue Hotel": "Scully's speech was always a combination of Irish brogue and idiom, Western twang and idiom, and scraps of curiously formal diction taken from the story-books and newspapers."

Statement of Editorial Policy

The text of *The Red Badge of Courage* prepared for this edition has been edited in accordance with the rationale of copy-text formulated by W. W. Greg in 1950.[1] Greg's rationale for scrupulous consideration of all forms of a work to be edited provides the most conservative procedural principles for an editor wishing to respect an author's intentions. According to Greg, the earliest finished version of a work—the author's manuscript if available—is adopted as a copy-text. The copy-text is followed except where the author later changed it or where obvious errors occur. Changes that the author made in successive typescripts, proofs, galleys, impressions, and editions are emended into the copy-text. The editor must, however, be cognizant that unauthoritative variants are often introduced into later states of a text by persons other than the author, sometimes inadvertently, sometimes intentionally, sometimes with the explicit or implicit consent of the author for aesthetic improvement or necessary correction, but sometimes not. Greg's rationale is a classically simple theory applicable even in the case of an editorial problem as complex as that of *Red Badge*.

In editing *Red Badge* for the present volume I have focused primarily on the substantial differences between Crane's final manuscript and the first book-length edition published by D. Appleton & Co. in 1895. The differences exist because just prior to publication of the first edition the story, as Crane had completed it in manuscript, was shortened by two series of cuts; the first series was made in the manuscript and the second in the Appleton typescript or proofs. Owing to the size of the cuts and the problem of why they were made, Crane's aesthetic, psychological, and moral intentions are brought in question.

Taking the manuscript of *Red Badge* as copy-text, an editor is left to explain the sizable cuts made for the Appleton edition before he accepts or rejects them, one by one, as authoritative changes. The argument that lies behind this edition, presented in "The *Red Badge of Courage* Nobody Knows," is that there is a sufficient concurrence of evidence—textual, biographical, historical, and aesthetic—to show that though the deletions were made by Crane he made them not on his own, to improve the story he had already completed, but to comply with the request of his editor

159

at Appleton. On the assumption that the cuts are unauthoritative—that is, not what Crane himself wanted for literary reasons—I have edited the novel from Crane's manuscript to recover as fully as possible the story as he originally completed it.

The basic editorial policy for this edition has been to follow the manuscript in all details; when the text of the manuscript is problematic (for example, when words are missing), readings have been adopted from the early draft, the prepublication excerpt, or the Appleton edition.[2] In three instances where pages were removed from the manuscript and are presumed lost, sources other than the manuscript have been used as copy-text. For the latter half of chapter four, the prepublication excerpt becomes copy-text; and at the close of chapter ten and for two paragraphs in chapter twelve the early draft is used (see Textual Notes at 23.21, 49.9, and 55.30).[3]

Specific textual problems are discussed in the notes following this statement, but four decisions adhered to in the preparation of the text can be outlined here. The first concerns several instances of minor variation in wording between the manuscript and the Appleton edition. For example, "The while" was change to "Meanwhile" (2.16), "As he heard them" was changed to "As he listened" (32.45), and "whiskers jest that color" was changed to "whiskers jest like that" (61.15–16). Of these variations in wording some instances are identical or similar to changes that Crane's editor made or required Crane to make in other works published by Appleton; some of the changes are most likely Crane's own revisions; and many are so neutral that one can only guess as to their origin. In accord with the basic conservative policy adopted for this edition, I have followed the manuscript in all these cases.

The second decision concerns the treatment of Crane's punctuation, grammatical usages, and spelling. Except in cases where a simple emendation prevents needless ambiguity, Crane's manuscript punctuation has been carefully preserved (as called for by Greg's theory). The same is true of grammatical usage, though I have changed "bore" to "borne" once, "were" to "was" once, and "was" to "were" three times (these changes were also made in the Appleton edition). Crane's misspellings have been corrected throughout; however, all spellings that can be distinguished as acceptable for his time (such as "woful" instead of "woeful") have been retained. Contractions such as "aint" and "can't" appear in the manuscript sometimes with and sometimes without an apostrophe. Crane was inconsistent about using the apostrophe, and either form would have been acceptable at the time he was writing, and so these contractions have been allowed to stand as written. In general, I have made no attempt to regularize or modernize what Crane wrote, or to follow the Appleton edition in matters of punctuation, usage, or spelling, since the numerous changes made for the Appleton text were almost surely editorial and impose a textbook consistency that is not preferable to Crane's intuition.

In the matter of aberrant spellings that Crane used to represent the sound of vernacular speech, a more difficult question arises. Apparently at the suggestion of an early reader of the manuscript, he made some effort to normalize these forms.[4] The changes he made amounted to little more than simple spelling revisions ("yeh" to "you," "fer" to "for," "allus" to "always," "t'" to "to," and so on). These alterations were made desultorily and sporadically in the manuscript and were not completed in the Appleton edition. It seems that Crane realized at some point the task was ill-advised and served no good purpose, and so he abandoned it. As a result, some speeches appear in the Appleton text with the revised spelling, but most do not. For example, "Where yeh goin', Jim? What yeh thinkin' about?" sounds fine as originally written. These lines were among those revised inconsistently in the manuscript and appear in the Appleton edition as "Where yeh goin', Jim? What you thinking about?" Even if the revisions had been completed as begun, to revise the dialectal spellings without a concurrent revision of diction and syntax would have created awkwardly spurious forms of speech (see, however, notes at 8.16 and 20.25). For the present text, I have adopted a policy of reversion to the original spellings in the manuscript, thus restoring the original consistency of the speeches and Crane's intention to place his characters in the stream of vernacular fiction popular in America during his time.

A fourth policy concerns another change that Crane began to make in manuscript before the novel was accepted by Appleton: the alteration of proper names to descriptive phrases. For example, Henry Fleming became simply "the youth," Jim Conklin became "the tall soldier," Simpson became "the corporal," and Wilson became "the loud soldier" or "the youth's friend." Crane completed these changes for the Appleton edition and I have adopted them for the present text on the grounds that Crane apparently made the changes on his own along with corresponding adjustments to fit them to the story (see note at 68.1–2), and that these changes are an improvement that does not run against his original conception.

The Textual Notes that follow this statement of policy primarily offer discussions of the six gaps left in the final manuscript as a result of pages being lost when the Appleton deletions were made. The notes analyze available evidence regarding the amount and probable content of the text that is lost. Other notes concern interpretive issues raised by study of the manuscript.

1. "The Rationale of Copy-Text," *Studies in Bibliography,* 3 (1950–51), 19–36.

2. The main documents in the textual history of *Red Badge* are listed in the first paragraph of section I of "The *Red Badge of Courage* Nobody Knows." The notes to that paragraph contain citations of the *Facsimile* edition of the manuscript (which reproduces the pages of both the final manuscript and the early draft), a facsimile of one of the newspaper printings, the prepublication excerpt, and the University Press of Virginia edition of the novel which contains an "Historical Collation" listing the variants between the manuscript, the newspaper printings, the Appleton edition, and the first English edition published by William Heinemann.

3. Not all the pages of the early draft have survived. Only for the ending of chapter ten and for two paragraphs in chapter twelve does text of the draft exist that can be used to restore passages lost from the final manuscript.

4. Fredson Bowers conjectures that the reader who suggested the changes in dialect was Hamlin Garland; see the manuscript *Facsimile,* I, 9–10. In the Virginia edition of *Red Badge,* Bowers's treatment of Crane's inconsistent revision of dialect spellings differs from mine; see pp. 194–198 and 230–234 in that edition.

Textual Notes

The following notes and the parenthetical citations that appear in the course of the individual discussions are keyed to page and line of this edition. Page numbers of the *Red Badge of Courage* manuscript are cited by Crane's original pagination; photographic reproduction of the manuscript pages is available in Fredson Bowers, ed., *The Red Badge of Courage: A Facsimile Edition of the Manuscript* (Washington, D.C.: NCR/Microcard, 1972 and 1973).

Title Two titles, the final title and an earlier title, appear on the first page of the manuscript. The earlier title—*Private Fleming / His various battles.*—is deleted in pencil. The final title was first used for the newspaper serialization of the story which appeared in December 1894. The change may have been occasioned sometime before this, however, by Crane's decision to alter proper names to descriptive phrases, since one result of that alteration is that the name Fleming appears very seldom in the text.

8.16, 31.5, 77.11, 77.13 Apparently while in the course of revising dialectal speeches in the manuscript, Crane deleted "here" four times where he had used "this here" or "these here" as colloquial idiom. On the assumption that these deletions are of a piece with his inconsistent and unfinished normalization of dialect, I have let them stand. (See Statement of Editorial Policy.)

12.6–7, 13.5–7, 22.23–27 At eight places in the manuscript—scattered among chapters two, three, and four—bits of the soldiers' dialogue were marked with a query or an "X" for revision or deletion by a hand that is apparently not Crane's. Of these marked places, at the three noted here Crane made deletions in pen or pencil. The markings occur at places where the soldiers' banter is tuned in an ironically mocking or humorous key, but there is no apparent reason why a reader of the story would have thought these particular bits of dialogue should be altered or excised. In the first two instances noted here, the excised dialogue adds information that is pertinent to the coherence of the narrative. These bits of dialogue have been restored for the present text, since there is some question as to who marked them for revision and why.

163

19.15, 89.41, 91.42–43, 92.10, 94.4, 97.10 In the course of changing proper names to descriptive phrases in the manuscript Crane also changed mentions of Lieutenant Hasbrouck from "the young lieutenant" or "the youthful lieutenant" to simply "the lieutenant." At the six places noted here, he did not make the change. These six instances, which apparently represent simple oversights, have been emended to read "the lieutenant" in accordance with the other changes. (See note at 68.1–2.)

20.25 Apparently while in the course of revising dialectal speeches in the manuscript, Crane deleted "fool" here, reducing Conklin's expletive from "damn'-fool-cuss" to "damn'-cuss." Since it is likely that this change was part of Crane's inconsistent and unfinished normalization of dialect, and no evidence exists on which to base an alternative explanation, I have let the expletive stand as originally written. (See Statement of Editorial Policy.)

23.21 The ellipsis at this point represents text that appeared on p. 41, the first of the four concluding pages of chapter four in the manuscript, pp. 41–44, which are now missing and presumed lost. Except for a portion of what appeared at the top of p. 41, the text of these pages is readily recoverable, since it survives both in a prepublication excerpt and in the Appleton edition. The text at the top of p. 41 apparently consisted of the last of the exchange of rumors by the soldiers, logically continuing up to "The din in front swelled to a tremendous chorus. The youth and his fellows were frozen to silence" (23.22–23) which appeared at mid-page on p. 41. Since Henry Fleming ("the youth") does not speak any of the rumors on the surviving pages of chapter four (through p. 40), apparently he joined the soldiers' banter at some point on p. 41 in the portion of text that is now missing.

The loss of the rumors that appeared on p. 41 is the outcome of two separate events. The first occurred in the summer of 1895 after Appleton had made a typescript. Crane apparently took pp. 41–44 of the manuscript to the editor of a New York journal *Current Literature* for the typesetting of a prepublication excerpt. The passage that *Current Literature* excerpted began on p. 41 with "The din in front" and continued to the end of chapter four. After type was set for the excerpt, the four manuscript pages were probably discarded.

The second event, a separate one, apart from Crane's removing pp. 41–44 for the prepublication excerpt, is that Appleton did not print a large portion of the rumors beginning with "Hear what th' ol' colonel ses, boys" on p. 40 (23.3) and continuing through "The din in front" on p. 41. And so neither *Current Literature* nor Appleton used the text that appeared at the top of p. 41—but for different reasons. *Current Literature* wanted only the self-contained battle scene that began after the rumors were concluded. The motive for the Appleton excision is uncertain. The result of these separate events is that the text which appeared at the top of p. 41 was not set in type and is now lost. Since the prepublication excerpt is closest to the manuscript, being apparently set from the four holograph pages with no intervening typescript, it has been adopted as copy-text for the latter half of chapter four. (See Henry Binder,

"Unwinding the Riddle of Four Pages Missing from the *Red Badge of Courage* Manuscript," *Papers of the Bibliographical Society of America*, 72 (1978), 100–06.)

38.6 The ellipsis at this point represents text that appeared on the final page of chapter seven in the manuscript, p. 66, which is now missing and presumed lost. The ending of this chapter was deleted in the manuscript beginning on p. 65 with "Again the youth was in despair" (37.42). This ending consisted of Henry Fleming's first rebellion against nature. Other such rebellions, which were also deleted in the manuscript, appear at the close of chapter ten and throughout chapter twelve. With the excision made here, chapter seven ends at mid-page in the manuscript, the lower portion of p. 65 being deleted in pencil. From Crane's page-by-page word counts that appear on the versos of some manuscript leaves, Fredson Bowers has computed that approximately eighty words appeared on p. 66, and it is possible that only that much text is lost. (See the Virginia edition, p. 241.)

47.45 These two sentences appear in a slightly revised form in the Appleton edition: "His companions seemed ever to play intolerable parts. They were ever upraising the ghost of shame on the stick of their curiosity." Crane performed no other specific recasting—as opposed to cutting— of a character's thoughts between the manuscript and the Appleton edition. In light of the policy of this edition to follow the manuscript in all details, these sentences are allowed to stand as they appear in the manuscript.

49.9 The ellipsis at this point represents text that appeared on the four concluding pages of chapter ten in the manuscript, pp. 86–89, which are now missing and presumed lost. The text printed after the ellipsis is the ending of the chapter as it appeared in Crane's early draft.

Pages 86–89 were removed when the ending of chapter ten, consisting of Henry Fleming's second rebellion against nature, was deleted beginning on p. 85 with "Promptly, then, his old rebellious feelings returned" (48.43). With the excision, chapter ten ends at mid-page in the manuscript, the lower portion of p. 85 being deleted in pencil.

The text deleted on p. 85 appears in the present edition up to "He kept an eye on his bath-tub, his fire-engine, his life-boat, and compelled" (49.9)—the final words on that page. The beginning of Henry's rebellion as it appears in the draft is very close to what appears, deleted in pencil, on p. 85 and is set out here for comparison.

> Promptly, his old rebellious feelings returned. He thought the powers of fate had combined to heap misfortune upon him. He was a victim.
> He rebelled against the source of things, according to his law that the most powerful should receive the most blame.
> War, he said bitterly to the sky, was a make-shift created because ordinary processes didn't furnish deaths enough. To seduce her victims

The remainder of the rebellion as it appears in the draft follows the ellipsis in the present text.

Apparently, Crane made a substantial expansion of Henry's thoughts in this chapter ending between draft and manuscript. In the draft, the rebellion runs about a page and a half. In the manuscript, it extends for three and a half to four and a half pages. (See, however, the analysis of Crane's word counts in the Virginia edition, p. 241.) It is unlikely that Crane would have altered the essential tenor of Henry's rebellion here, and the draft version of the chapter ending can probably be taken as equivalent to the essential mood and direction of Henry's thoughts as they appeared in the manuscript. It seems very likely that a good portion of the expansion Crane made was the addition of some paragraphs in which Henry commiserates with the "poets of black landscapes" that he recalls in chapter sixteen (see note at 72.7).

55.30, 56.3 The ellipses at these two points represent text that appeared on the third page of chapter twelve in the manuscript, p. 100, which is now missing and presumed lost. The two paragraphs that appear between the ellipses in the present text are recovered from Crane's early draft.

Pages 98–103 were removed from the manuscript when the entire chapter twelve, which comprised Henry Fleming's third and longest rebellion against nature, was deleted. Crane apparently kept at least four of these six pages in his possession after removing the chapter from the manuscript. If he kept p. 100 (or p. 103) they have not turned up.

Chapter twelve ran to six pages in both draft and manuscript. A comparison of the three draft pages that survive indicates that Crane revised and expanded only slightly between the two versions. The draft paragraphs used here, then, can be taken as closely equivalent text for most of what appeared on p. 100.

57.18 The ellipsis at this point represents text that appeared on the final page of chapter twelve in the manuscript, p. 103, which is now missing and presumed lost. There is no indication of how much text appeared on that page; a full page would have contained some 250–325 words. (See note at 55.30.)

68.1–2 Before Crane began changing proper names to descriptive phrases in the manuscript, this sentence read "He was not a youth." As William L. Howarth recognized in making a study of the manuscript ("*The Red Badge of Courage* Manuscript: New Evidence for a Critical Edition," *Studies in Bibliography*, 18 (1965), 239–40), after Crane began changing the names he also took steps to make Henry Fleming the only "youth" in the story. Howarth's explanation and comment is worth quoting: "On the battle-field that is the world of *The Red Badge*, a man's character is measured by his ability to profit from experience. Wilson moves toward a maturity that Fleming will never grasp, and Crane chose to indicate his hero's pathetic inadequacy by labeling him the only 'youth' in a company of men. After Fleming's recognition of Wilson's accomplishment, Crane bestowed upon the latter a distinctive new title: 'the youth's friend' or 'comrade'—never again was he to be known as 'loud' or 'young.' " Howarth also pointed out that Crane set himself to changing any descriptions of Lieutenant Hasbrouck as "the young lieutenant" or "the youthful lieutenant" to "the lieutenant" (see note at 19.15).

70.27 The ellipsis at this point represents text that appeared on the final page of chapter fifteen in the manuscript, p. 126, which is now missing and presumed lost. The ending of this chapter was deleted in the manuscript beginning on p. 125 with "He went into a brown mood" (70.5). With the excision, chapter fifteen ends at mid-page in the manuscript, the lower portion of p. 125 being deleted in pencil.

There is no precise indication of how much text appeared on p. 126, but some conjecture can be made regarding the content. The deleted chapter ending consisted of Henry Fleming's reflection on the events of the previous day. Almost certainly his next thought following "His pride had almost recovered its balance and was about" is a guilty recollection of his desertion of the tattered soldier. In the story, Henry commits three acts that cause him to be ashamed: his flight from battle, his rebellions against nature, and his desertion of the tattered soldier. At the outset of Henry's reflections in the passage deleted here, he recalls the first two of these acts. What logically remains, then, to thwart the "almost recovered" balance of his pride is his betrayal of the tattered soldier. Furthermore, it is reasonable that Henry would recall the desertion in this chapter, otherwise no mention of it occurs until the final chapter where his thoughts again touch on the same three acts and clearly establish his desertion of the tattered soldier as the most serious of his errors.

72.7 The poets referred to here occupy Henry's thoughts for three paragraphs and are clearly *recalled* by Henry from an earlier mood of despair; however, no earlier mention of these poets appears on any of the extant pages of the manuscript or early draft. In this chapter the three paragraphs concerning the poets make up a manifestly self-contained phase in Crane's elaboration of Henry's new optimistic mood—a refutation of the poets of "black landscapes." It seems likely, therefore, that Henry's earlier thoughts about these poets appeared in a similarly self-contained passage that served to elaborate a despairing mood.

The probable conclusion is that the earlier mention of the poets appeared on pages of the manuscript lost when Henry's rebellions against nature were deleted from chapters seven, ten, or twelve; and it is not difficult to establish chapter ten as the most likely among these. At the close of chapter seven, Henry has his flight from battle and the apparition of the dead soldier in the forest to dismay him, but he has not yet witnessed the procession of the wounded in chapter eight or the death of Jim Conklin in chapter ten which are surely the blackest "landscapes" in the story. Furthermore, it seems that the ending of chapter seven was not long enough for a mention of the poets to have appeared there in any detail. If the poets were part of Henry's thoughts in chapter twelve, they could have appeared only on the final page of that chapter. But this would be an unlikely turn for his thinking to take after he has just been concocting on the bottom of the preceding page a scheme to avoid his own fate. The rebellious passage that closes chapter ten, however, would have allowed ample space for Henry to commiserate with poets. And just such a self-contained elaboration of Henry's rebellion would seem a very plausible part of the expansion that Crane made in revising the ending of chaper ten from draft to manuscript (see note at 49.9).

84.4 In the course of revising proper names to descriptive phrases in the manuscript, Crane changed "Wilson" to "the youth" for this speech and "Fleming" to "his friend" for the next, thus committing an apparent error. Wilson would logically have first reply to the soldiers' accusation that he is lying; and since he gives the initial report concerning the impending charge, it makes little sense for him to have the *next* speech as if Henry were the one who had brought the news. For the present edition, the original speakers have been restored and indicated by the descriptive phrases Crane used consistently elsewhere in the novel.

109.4 The world of "oaths and walking-sticks" is the world of vehement commitment to soldiering epitomized by Lieutenant Hasbrouck. This reference was obscured, perhaps inadvertently, when Crane changed a description of the lieutenant's sword as his "walking-stick" in chapter twenty-one (91.33) to his "cane." (This was first noticed by R. W. Stallman in *Stephen Crane: An Omnibus* [New York: Alfred A. Knopf, 1952], pp. 222, 346.)

List of Editorial Emendations

The copy-text for *The Red Badge of Courage* printed in this edition is mainly Stephen Crane's handwritten final manuscript. Most of the pages of that manuscript are in the Clifton Waller Barrett Library at the University of Virginia Library. Of the six pages of chapter twelve that were removed from the manuscript one page is in the Berg Collection at the New York Public Library; one page is in the Houghton Library at Harvard; and two pages are in the Butler Library at Columbia; the other two pages have not turned up. Copy-text for the latter part of chapter four (23.22–25.16) is the prepublication excerpt that appeared in *Current Literature* in August 1895. Copy-text for the ending of chapter ten (49.9–49.37) is a portion of p. 75 and p. 76 of Crane's early draft; copy-text for two paragraphs in chapter twelve (55.31–56.3) is a portion of p. 86 of the early draft; the draft appears on the versos of some of the manuscript leaves in the Barrett Library.

The following list, keyed to page and line of the present text, is a table of all emendations that I have made in the copy-text sources. The emended reading appears first, followed by a slash, followed by the copy-text reading. When the early draft (ED) or the Appleton first printing (A) is the significant source of an emendation, it is cited parenthetically, as are Textual Notes that contain discussion relevant to specific emendations. All other emendations—many of which agree with the Appleton edition—are my own.

To avoid burdening the list with instances of the same correction, words that Crane misspelled consistently throughout the manuscript are itemized first as follows:

appalling / apalling	its / it's
borne / born	lying / lieing
breathing / breatheing	perceive / percieve (all forms)
command / cammand (all forms)	receive / recieve (all forms)
conceive / concieve (all forms)	sandwich / sandwhich
dilapidated / delapidated	seize / sieze (all forms)
familiar / familar	solemn / solomn (all forms)
gaping / gapeing	wa'n't / w'a'nt (all forms)
grimy / grimey	writhing / writheing

1.22 blue-clothed / blue clothed (ED, A)
1.30 trousers' / trouser's
2.31 attacks, / attack (A)
2.32 wished to / wished (A)
2.34 across / acros (A)
2.37 wall / walls (ED)
3.32 had had / had, had
3.35 ethical / ethicical
4.25 a-thinkin' / a-thinkin
4.29 "I've / I've
4.32 so's / s'os
4.33 "An' / An'
4.42 "Young / Young
5.5 "Yeh / Yeh
5.8 "I / I
5.25 borne / bore (A)
5.36 privileges / priveleges
6.30 The youth / Fleming (A)
6.33 The youth / Fleming (A)
6.38 him / Fleming (A)
7.3 the youth / Fleming (A)
7.5 veterans' / veteran's
7.21 sufficient / sufficent
7.31 what's / whats
8.16 this here story'll / this story'll (See note.)
8.17 did." / did.
9.34 unsatisfactory / unsatisfoctory
10.1 known / know (A)
10.15 confidant / confidante (A)
10.21 development / developement
10.23 unseen, / unseen
11.7 The youth / Fleming (A)
11.42 bodies of marching / bodies marching (A)
12.6–7 We're . . . behint 'em." (See note.)
12.14 youth / youth.
12.18 often, / often
12.28 behind / behint
13.5 gin' / 'gin'
13.5–7 "Gin' . . . thunder." (See note at 12.6–7.)
13.18 intercourse / intercouse
14.15 fightin' / fightin
14.22 ¶ (A)
14.45 loud / blatant (A)
15.10 resemblance / resemblace
15.21 thoughts / thought (A)
16.6 clothing / clotheing
16.24 were / was (A)
16.35 rhythmically / rythmically
16.39 men / man (A)
17.6 tread / tred
17.28 exceeded / acceded
17.37 receding / recedeing
18.44 The youth / Fleming (A)
19.15 the lieutenant / the youthful lieutenant (See note.)
19.17 young man / Fleming (A)
20.3 became another / became a another
20.25 damn'-fool-cuss / damn'-cuss (See note.)
20.27 do some / do a some
20.36 communing / cummuning
21.18 increased / encreased
22.23–27 "Th' boys . . . "Well—" (See note at 12.6–7.)

22.29 Hannises' / Hannises
22.30 Hannises' / Hannises
23.18 an' / an
23.28 storm-banshee / storm banshee (ED)
23.29 exploding redly, / exploding, redly (ED)
24.20 Saunders's / Saunders 's (A)
24.21 shrank / sank (A)
25.24 feign / fiegn
25.24 despise / dispise
26.18 school-mistress / shool-mistress
26.19 repetition / repition
27.36 querulous / querelous
28.4 magician's / magacian's
28.7 were / was (A)
28.29 he had been / he been (A)
28.44 silent / silence
30.9 mopped / moped
30.27 the youth / Fleming (A)
30.42 countenances / coutenances
31.5 this here second / this second (See note at 8.16.)
31.7 Smithers / Smither's (A)
31.9 ¶
32.1 suddenly dropped it and / suddenly and (ED)
32.43 went across/ went a across
33.3 groveled / grovelled
33.8 disputing / disputeing
33.15 The youth / Fleming (A)
34.37 paean / peaen
35.2 imbecile / embecile
36.1 sees / see
36.3 thick / thicks
36.19 rhythmical / rythmical
37.33 bonds / bounds (A)
37.39 squawk / sqawk
38.25 foreign / foriegn
39.6 was / were (A)
39.42 school-boy / school boy (ED)
39.45 ¶
40.4 vic'try / vic'try"
40.5 A . . . bullets / "A . . . bullets"
40.6 Five . . . men / "Five . . . men"
40.7 Baked / "Baked
40.36 officers / officiers
41.7 The / the
41.12 sufficient / sufficent
41.19 the youth / Fleming (A)
41.33 'but / but
41.36 "Well / Well
42.33 the youth / Fleming (A)
42.36 Henry / Flem (A)
42.41 Henry / Flem (A)
43.4 b'jiminy / b'jiming
43.8 soldier / soldier.
43.9 guardian / gaurdian
43.17 Henry / Flem (A)
43.23 Henry / Flem (A)
43.29 Henry / Flem (A)
43.32 Henry / Flem (A)
43.35 loyalty/ loyality
44.9 soldier / youth (A)
45.11 increased / encreased
45.44 philippic / phillipic

46.32	stayin' / stayin
47.13	"Yeh / Yeh
48.6	who had been / who been (A)
48.10	The youth / Fleming (A)
48.11	looking / looked (A)
48.29	¶
49.13	she saw the / she the
49.14	things did / things and did
49.23	collections / collection
49.31	woman / women
50.11	symmetrical / symetrical
50.38	than / that
51.28	rear-ward / rear-word
51.32	explanation / explantion
52.36	compunctions / cumpunctions
52.44	the youth / Fleming (A)
53.5	the youth / Fleming (A)
53.17	villain / villian
54.3–4	Where's Henry Fleming / Where's Fleming (A)
55.1	privilege / previlege
56.39	exceed / accede
57.26	tree-tops / tree-top (A)
58.13	The youth / Fleming (A)
58.30	the youth's / Fleming's (A)
59.38	blue / blue, (A)
60.26	¶
60.29	whether / wether
60.40	lift / left (A)
61.35	the youth / Fleming (A)
61.39	The youth / Fleming (A)
61.43	the youth / The youth
62.7	and / and, (A)
62.29–30	the loud soldier / Wilson (A)
62.30	the youth's / Fleming's (A)
62.31	Henry / Flem (A)
62.33	well, ol' / well, Flem, ol' (A)
62.33	the other / Wilson (A)
62.36	The youth / Fleming (A)
62.39–40	the loud soldier / Wilson (A)
63.3	His friend / Wilson (A)
63.7	talkin' / talkin
63.9	Henry / Flem (A)
63.14	the youth / Fleming (A)
63.16	his friend / Wilson (A)
63.18–19	the youth's / Fleming's (A)
63.21	The youth / Fleming (A)
63.23	the corporal /Simpson (A)
63.23	the youth's / Fleming's (A)
63.24	Henry / Flem (A)
63.25	the loud private / Wilson (A)
63.26	a / 'a (A)
63.30	The youth's / Fleming's (A)
63.30	his friend's / Wilson's (A)
63.31–32	the corporal's / Simpson's (A)
63.32	submitted / submitting (A)
63.35	The corporal / Simpson (A)
63.35	Henry / Flem (A)
63.37	The youth / Fleming (A)
63.37	the corporal / Simpson (A)
63.42	contact with the / contact the (A)
64.34	snoring / snoring, (A)
65.9	soldier, / soldier
65.10	Henry / Fleming (A)
65.12	amateur / ameteur
65.23	tying / tieing
65.28	aching / acheing
65.28	cloth / clothe
65.32	Henry / Flem (A)
65.37	rest." / rest.
66.35–36	thick-spread / thick spread (A)
66.36	pallid / palli
66.40	squawking / sqawking
67.1	his friend / Wilson (A)
67.16	The youth / Fleming (A)
67.20	Henry / Flem (A)
67.31	an' / an
68.1	conceits / conciets
68.2	soldier. / soldier
68.13	peak / peek
68.17	Henry / Flem (A)
68.29	Henry / Flem (A)
69.30	He / He's
69.40	Henry / Fleming (A)
70.2	fightin' / fightin
72.2	developing / developeing
72.34	He had been / He been (A)
73.22	he had been / he been (A)
74.29	Rappahannock / Rappahanock
74.36	omens / omems
75.16	a / a'
76.2	losin' / lossin'
76.3	a / 'a
76.23	the youth's / Fleming's (A)
76.38	crackle / crackl
77.11	these here woods / these woods (See note at 8.16.)
77.13	these here cussed / these cussed (See note at 8.16.)
77.25	wastin' / wastin
77.31	resumed his dignified / resumed his his dignified
77.37	the youth's / Fleming's (A)
78.3	there was a / there a (A)
78.16	uninitiated / unitiated
79.16–17	and his fellows / and fellows (A)
80.36	Henry / Flem (A)
81.14	tree, / tree',
81.15	Th' / 'Th'
81.17	an / an'
81.19	an / an'
82.1	shrieked / shreiked
82.32	the youth / Fleming (A)
82.39	sliding / slideing
83.18	a / 'a
83.39	yeh t' git / yeh git
84.4	the youth's friend / the youth (See note.)
84.6	the youth / his friend (See note at 84.4.)
84.7	talkin' / talkin
84.11	The youth's friend / Wilson
84.24	shepherds / sheperds
85.11	goal / gaol (A)
85.29	light-footed, / light-footed (A)
86.5	impression / impressions (A)
86.16	the youth / Fleming (A)
86.43	He / His
87.15	regiment, / regiment (A)
87.44	on'y / o'ny

88.23	valueless / valuless
88.44	ludicrous / ludicruos
89.24	fell / felt
89.27	time / time,
89.41	The lieutenant / The youthful lieutenant (See note at 19.15.)
90.6	and rage was / and was (A)
90.7	upon the officer / upon officer (A)
90.8	and his / and as his
90.14	riveted / rivetted
91.14	allusions / illusions
91.20	preceding / precedeing
91.23	Henry / Flem (A)
91.40	it / them (A)
91.42–43	the lieutenant / the youthful lieutenant (See note at 19.15.)
92.6–7	plentifully / prentifully
92.10	the lieutenant / the youthful lieutenant (See note at 19.15.)
92.23–24	The youth / Fleming (A)
93.18	Some who had / Some who who had
93.19	grimmest / grimest
94.4	the lieutenant / the youthful lieutenant (See note at 19.15.)
94.11	incredibly / incrediby
94.18–19	perspiration / perpiration
94.29	exertions / erertions
94.34	wrenched / wrenched, (A)
95.20	whether / wether
95.32	The youth / Fleming (A)
96.2	behind / b'ehind
96.38	th' / th
96.38	th' / th
97.2	major-generals.' " / major-generals.'
97.10	the lieutenant / the youthful lieutenant (See note at 19.15.)
97.30	most / most,
98.7–8	The youth / Fleming (A)
98.16	new / nw
98.24–25	The youth's / Fleming's (A)
98.32	the youth / Fleming (A)
98.44	The youth / Fleming (A)
99.25	small / small,
99.32	ceased their / their ceased
99.33	was an instant / was instant (A)
100.19	the youth's / Fleming's (A)
101.35	He himself / He, himself
102.23	were / was (A)
103.37	privilege / privelege
104.6	to be in / to in (A)
104.8	The youth / Fleming (A)
104.14	sufficiently / sufficently
104.16	A few / a few
104.25	The youth / Fleming (A)
105.13	parallel / paralell
105.21	the youth's friend / Wilson
105.27–28	trampled / trammeled (A)
106.41	portentous / portentious
107.10	the youth / Fleming
107.14	Conklin / the tall soldier (A)
107.16	him / Fleming (A)
107.20	Henry / Flem (A)
108.2	fool." / fool.

END-OF-LINE HYPHENATION

The following list itemizes end-of-line hyphenations in the copy-text sources which I have kept as hyphenated compounds in the present text based upon Crane's identical or similar usages in the manuscript.

6.27	sun-tanned
7.1	hell's-fire
7.28	broken-bladed
9.16	a-fightin'
9.31	new-born
13.16	Camp-fires
13.24	tree-top
14.1	peek-ed
15.36	camping-place
17.34	sun-struck
33.30	war-god
39.18	awe-struck
39.34	smoke-fringed
48.12	animal-like
49.3	make-shift
59.43	war-machines
61.7	sure-'nough
61.10	t'-night
61.13	a-draggin'
61.26	a-lookin'
73.4	terror-struck
79.14	knife-like
85.2	a-horseback
90.15	mule-driver
91.38	under-lip
96.31	jim-hickey
100.12	mule-driver
103.18	color-bearer
103.35–36	prisoners-of-war
105.39	counter-shot
108.42	hot-ploughshares

In order to facilitate accurate quotation, the following list itemizes end-of-line hyphenations in the present text which should be quoted as hyphenated compounds.

5.28	up-raised		64.31	brass-mounted
5.38	martial-spirit		64.39	Over-head
6.38	be-whiskered		66.35	thick-spread
8.12	out-an'-out		67.8	up-lifting
8.39	kit-an'-boodle		68.20	kit-an'-boodle
12.29	river-bank		71.20	good-humor
13.38	imp-like		74.19	dirt-hills
15.12	out-cast		79.15	death-struggle
21.29	spell-bound		79.41	rifle-barrel
27.18	world-sweeping		80.27	wild-cats
27.28	low-toned		90.9	mule-drivers
31.36	thick-spread		90.11	mule-drivers
37.1	silver-gleaming		91.3	panic-stricken
37.9	half-light		91.23	good-bye-John
39.45	drum-major		93.36	red-bearded
40.38	powder-stain		94.26	re-called
44.17	out-cry		98.12	church-like
46.8	jim-dandy		100.2	mud-diggers
47.21	a-shootin'		103.35	prisoners-of-war
57.9	bandit-chief		105.40	up-heavals
62.34	sure-enough		106.3	view-point
63.39	fire-light			
64.3	number-ten